GW00394040

Sherlock Holmes

The Strange Case of the Pale Boy
& other mysteries

Susan Knight

Edited by
David Marcum

Copyright 2023
Susan Knight

The right of Susan Knight to be identified as the author of this work has been asserted by her in accordance with the Copyright, Designs and Patents Act 1998.

All rights reserved. No reproduction, copy or transmission of this publication may be made without express prior written permission. No paragraph of this publication may be reproduced, copied or transmitted except with express prior written permission or in accordance with the provisions of the Copyright Act 1956 (as amended). Any person who commits any unauthorised act in relation to this publication may be liable to criminal prosecution and civil claims for damage.

All characters appearing in this work are fictitious or used fictitiously. Except for certain historical personages, any resemblance to real persons, living or dead, is purely coincidental. The opinions expressed herein are those of the authors and not of MX Publishing.

Hardcover ISBN 978-1-80424-280-3
Paperback ISBN 978-1-80424-281-0
ePub ISBN 978-1-80424-282-7
PDF ISBN 978-1-80424-283-4

Published by MX Publishing
335 Princess Park Manor, Royal Drive, London,
N11 3GX
www.mxpublishing.com

Cover design by Brian Belanger

For Kayla and Charlotte

Introduction

These stories first appeared in various volumes of *The MX Book of New Sherlock Holmes Stories* from 2019 to 2023, as follows: *The Case of the Short-sighted Clown* (Vol. XX), *Abracadaver* (Vol. XXII), *A Simple Matter* (Vol. XXIV), *The Strange Case of the Pale Boy* (Vol. XXVI), *The Mystery of Maple Tree Lodge* (Vol. XXX), *Dr Watson's Dilemma* (Vol. XXXI), *The Strange Case of the Man from Edinburgh* (Vol. XXXIII), *The Mystery of the Murderous Ghost* (Vol. XXXV), *The Adventure of the Death Stalker* (Vol. XXXVIII).

All royalties from the sales of these anthologies go to support a school for special needs students at Undershaw, former home of Sir Arthur Conan Doyle.

The editor, David Marcum, sometimes gives his writers a trigger or a task to fulfil. Thus, there may be a Christmas theme (as in my *Mystery of Maple Tree Lodge*). Or a development of one of the many 'untold cases' mentioned in the original stories, those Dr Watson has not yet written up. We, his modern-day interpreters, must then take on the challenge (*A Simple Matter*).

In several of my stories, Dr Watson mentions his wife, Mary, whom he met during Holmes's investigation into *The Sign of Four*. Sadly, according to Conan Doyle, she dies young, leaving Watson broken-hearted, but at least he is then able to move back into Baker Street, to continue helping Holmes with his investigations.

It has been both a privilege and fun to contribute to these collections, writing in the voice of Dr Watson and keeping as close as possible to the tone and style of the original canon. For me, Dr Watson has become as irresistible an alter ego as Mrs Hudson, the narrator of my novels.

Susan Knight

CONTENTS

The Case of the Short-Sighted Clown

Despite it being near midsummer, the morning was dull enough, and I had settled down in my slippers and smoking jacket to peruse the newspapers and generally not bestir myself. I skimmed past reports of the preparations for our dear Queen's Diamond Jubilee celebrations, loitered briefly over news of the publication of a novel entitled *Dracula* by one Bram Stoker that looked diverting enough if somewhat sensational, noted the continuing search for Lord Tonbridge in connection with the murder of his wife's personal maid, and observed with a degree of disappointment, being a Surrey supporter, that Lancashire was likely to win this year's County Cricket Championships.

One article, however, particularly caught my attention, and required a deeper study. It concerned horrifying news from Assam of an earthquake that had claimed fifteen-hundred dead. Following my military service in that part of the world, I have always taken a special interest in the Indian sub-continent. Indeed, I have friends and colleagues still living there and was now hoping that they had survived the disaster.

While I was scanning the news to find further details, Holmes, already dressed to go out, burst into the room. I read action on his face.

"Ah, Watson," he said. "You are here. Capital. I see there is nothing of great moment to detain you and would be delighted if you would join me on an expedition as soon as you can get dressed."

I groaned. Unless this was a case of overriding interest, I would much rather have stayed home with my newspapers. But Holmes persisted.

"We will be detained overnight, so bring the usual necessaries with you."

I groaned some more.

"An overnight expedition," I asked. "Where to?"

"To the seaside, my dear friend," he replied, eyes gleaming. "The seaside and the circus."

I was aghast.

"Seaside! Circus! Holmes, you cannot be serious."

"I assure you that I am most serious, Watson. I have always, you know, wished to revisit Sanger's Circus, after it so sadly moved out of London. You recall, do you not, the Amphitheatre that used to stand by Westminster Bridge. What a place that was! What shows they put on there!"

To say that I was taken aback is hardly to give justice to the amazement with which I received this speech. Never before, in all the years I had been acquainted with the great detective, had he expressed any notion so frivolous.

He continued, one might even say merrily, rubbing his hands, "Sanger's now has a permanent base in Ramsgate, and I find I have an overwhelming desire to witness again this company which, by-the-bye, is reputed to be much admired by none other than Queen Victoria herself."

I am afraid I was still gaping at my friend and could not bring myself to utter a word in reply.

"You look surprised, Watson, and yet is it not true that recently the two of us have exerted our mental and physical capabilities to the extreme, and dearly need a rest."

This was a reference to our trip to Cornwall two months earlier, when Holmes was supposed be recovering from a bout of nervous exhaustion. Instead, we found ourselves caught up in yet another fiendish crime, written up by me as "The Devil's Foot", resulting in a near-death experience for the both of us.

He now continued. "Are we not due some diversion? Are we not due some fun? And by the seaside too. A much more civilised seaside, I might add, than Mount's Bay."

My mouth dropped open still further. Fun at the seaside was the very last thing that I associated with my friend.

"Come, come," he went on, amused by my stupefaction. "Unless you pull yourself together, Watson, we shall miss the train, and that would be a great pity."

Thus it was that, very shortly after, we were in a cab making with all speed for Charing Cross Station. I could see that Holmes was absorbed in thought, a smile occasionally playing over his thin lips. He was to astonish me further that day – I knew it.

We arrived just in time for the train and found a carriage to ourselves. Soon we left the city behind and rumbled into the garden of England that is the county of Kent. The landscape before my eyes was of rolling fields dotted with farms and oast houses where, as I understand the procedure, hops for local ales are laid out to dry. The round brick structures, with their conical roofs and white chimneys, form a most attractive sight. I tried to call Holmes's attention to them but he seemed more interested in his pipe, and I soon gave up and returned to my newspaper and the deadly events in Assam.

On arrival at Ramsgate, we immediately took rooms in the Railway Hotel, a somewhat down-at-heel establishment but, as Holmes remarked, "Convenient for our purposes." We left our bags and walked the short distance to the centre of the town. I had never before had occasion to visit this once-fashionable resort and was struck immediately by the faded elegance of the Georgian buildings that lined its crescents, the pleasant walks beneath cliffs so white they might rival those of Dover, and a sandy beach which almost made me regret that I had omitted to pack my bathing attire.

However, it seemed that the fun we were to have in this place resided not in any of these delights, but in the Amphitheatre that housed Sanger's Circus – the next performance of which, as we ascertained, was to take place at six o'clock that evening. We purchased our tickets and then, not having eaten a morsel since Mrs. Hudson's admittedly substantial breakfast, found ourselves a tavern that served a decent mutton pie and local ale, and feasted most satisfactorily.

"I fear," Holmes remarked, spooning up his gravy with something resembling a relish unusual for him, occasioned perhaps by the fresh sea air, "that this new amphitheatre will bear a feeble enough resemblance to that splendid edifice in Lambeth. However, it will serve, Watson. It will serve."

Yes, but for what, I wondered. I had started harbouring dark suspicions regarding our presence in this town. Holmes had the look about him that I recognised so well – the look that signalled that the chase was on. But when I quizzed him, he simply repeated, "It will be fun, Watson. Just you wait and see."

Before six o'clock, we duly presented ourselves at the Amphitheatre and were shown to a box with crimson drapes. I had never visited the famed Lambeth establishment, and so was not disappointed by this one, while Holmes pronounced himself to be well-enough satisfied. We had a splendid view out over the stage and, although I am not a frequenter of such entertainments, the excitement of the crowd pouring into the galleries around us transferred itself to me and I soon found myself agog with anticipation. I looked across at Holmes, who seemed to share my emotions, his eyes shining, his long nose twitching, like a foxhound at the hunt.

What can I say of the ensuing performance? How we the audience all exclaimed at those sleek Arabian horses speeding around the ring, mounted by acrobats who leapt and somersaulted from one to the next in the most death-defying ways, or at the lady who posed as Britannia with at her feet a lion as tame-seeming as a puss cat, caressing his fur, letting him lick her hand (I have seen lions in the wild and know of what bloody ferocity they are capable – he could have bitten off her hand in a trice), or the wire walkers and trapeze artists flying above our heads in defiance of Mr. Newton's Law of Gravity. How we laughed at the knock-about clowns, with their red noses and grotesque make-up, trying in vain to best the white-face in his motley costume and pointed hat, their worst efforts rebounding back on them, constantly getting themselves drenched with water, kicked on the backside, or slapped about the head.

The next act thrilled me even beyond all the preceding. I have, of course, seen elephants in both Africa and Asia, and was not so amazed as my neighbours at the agility and intelligence of these magnificent beasts, even when they performed a charming little dance or lifted young ladies high in the air with their trunks. Yet even I could not suppress a gasp when one of the young ladies laid herself down under the raised foot of the biggest elephant of all. In a second she could have been crushed to death. I glanced around at Holmes to judge his reaction – but he was nowhere to be seen. How long he had been gone I could not even say, I had been staring so hard at the performers all the while.

Knowing my friend, I understood that he must have good reasons which would become apparent in the due course of time, and so I sat back again to enjoy the show. First came the jugglers, tossing a seemingly infinite number of balls into the air or spinning plates on slim poles held in their mouths. Then a fire eater and a sword swallower. As a medical man, I was particularly interested in the physical issues relating to the latter two acts. For the sword swallower, I reasoned that once past the pharynx and oesophageal sphincter, the rapier could be lowered straight down into the stomach, though progressing, it must be said, dangerously close to the aorta, the heart, and the lungs. And how to control the gag reflex? It was certainly an amazing feat.

As for the fire eater, whose act consisted in taking some inflammable spirit into his mouth and igniting it so that a massive flame spurted out, dragon-like, I was just trying to judge how this was possible without inflicting severe burns on the mouth and throat, recalling those natives I had observed in India who thought nothing of walking over red hot coals, when the clowns tumbled in again. There seemed to be more of them now, all vying to persecute the white-face, who, lordly as ever, frustrated their every attempt. They kept trying to whisk off his face a gigantic pair of green spectacles and sometimes even succeeded, leaving white-face to chase the thief around the ring, until he managed to grab the scamp by the scruff of his neck, kicking him on the backside so that he cannoned across the ring, and then with exaggerated dignity replacing the spectacles on his own nose. It was most comical. Next, one of the clowns urged another through mime to swallow a sword. We roared with laughter as the reluctant sword swallower kept hesitating, while the first flapped his arms like a chicken.

Then the horses returned, and the clowns tried most hilariously to emulate the leaps and bounds of the acrobats, their apparent clumsiness almost requiring even more skill than that of the tumblers themselves. Indeed, it appeared inevitable at any moment that one or other clown would be crushed beneath those racing hooves as they swung perilously under the belly of the beasts. One daredevil with a most villainous painted visage even managed to clamber on top of a horse's back and stood balancing there for some seconds, waving, it seemed, right at me, until he leapt off again and tumbled over the sawdust of the ring. How we cheered! How we applauded!

At last the show was over and still no sign of Holmes. I lingered in the hope of seeing him amidst the diminishing throng but without success. Wherever could he be? Then I had a sudden fearful thought.

What if his enemies had followed him here and abducted him under my very nose? Colonel Moran was capable of anything. I blamed myself. I should have kept watch instead of letting myself be distracted by the show. It was with trepidation, therefore, that I hurried back to the Railway Hotel.

There, to my great relief, tempered with no little annoyance, I found my friend comfortably reclining in the snug, calmly smoking his pipe, a mug of ale at his elbow.

"What kept you, Watson?" he enquired.

"Where were you?" I countered, not mentioning my worries concerning his safety, which no doubt he would have found foolish.

"My apologies. I bumped into an old acquaintance and quite lost track of time," he said. "I trust you enjoyed the rest of the show."

"Indeed, I did." I started to regale him with an account of the acts. "I cannot see," I said, "how the fire eater avoids getting terrible burns on his mouth."

"Come, come, you as a doctor should understand the basic science of the trick. When the man closes his mouth, the oxygen that stokes the fire is cut off and it goes out."

"Yes, but it is still very dangerous," I could not help but add. "I'm sure there must be some terrible accidents."

"No doubt, if the practitioner doesn't take the correct precautions. But tell me, did you not enjoy the clowns the most?"

"The clowns?" I replied. "Indeed they were very comical, but I think the elephants were the best."

"Pah, elephants!" Holmes exclaimed, and would have said more on the subject, had a noisy crowd not just then entered the public bar.

"Why," I said, glancing through the glass partition. "Aren't these circus folk?"

"I believe some of them are staying here," Holmes drawled.

7

My suspicions that this was not the simple excursion Holmes had claimed it to be were renewed and I peered more closely at my friend.

"Holmes," I said, "there is a rim of white on your face and something in your hair. Allow me."

I stepped forward and brushed at his head, picking up one or two of the flakes and examining them.

"Sawdust!" I exclaimed.

"Oh, Watson, I fear you have found me out. Now at last I may retire and leave the detecting to you."

"But I don't understand."

"You still do not see. Ah, my friend, my friend." He sighed, then, "Walter!" calling to the group in the bar. "Walter, a moment if you please."

An elderly man detached himself from his party and joined us in the snug. Holmes was smiling broadly, as was this new arrival.

"Watson, meet Walter, the old acquaintance of whom I was just now speaking."

"So did you enjoy yourself, Mr. Holmes?" the man asked. "Looked like it anyway. Like old times it were. If ever you wants a job…"

"Do not tempt me, Walter," Holmes laughed. "And pray, let me buy you a mug of the best Kentish ale. It is the least I can do."

"I won't say no to that, Mr. Holmes," replied the old man. "Indeed and I won't."

I looked from one to the other, totally mystified.

"Poor Watson," said Holmes. "Let me put you out of your misery. You see, one summer when I was a lad of fourteen, Walter and his troupe came to the town where I was holidaying with my parents and brother Mycroft. Every night I crept out in secret to mix with the circus folk."

"Indeed, Dr. Watson," the old man said, "we thought that when we left town, young master Sherlock would come along with us for certain."

Again I found myself gaping in astonishment. I suppose I had never thought of Holmes as a boy, or if I did, it would have been as a studious solitary lad, never one making merry with the circus.

"I sometimes regret, Walter," my friend went on, "that I did not do that very thing. How differently my life would have turned out."

"You had a natural talent, Mr. Holmes. Well, you proved that tonight, didn't you."

Suddenly I realised what had been right under my nose.

"That was *you* in the ring – the clown on horseback!" I exclaimed. "That was you, Holmes, was it not?" Now I understood the greasepaint on his face, the sawdust in his hair.

"Did you see me wave at you?" Holmes chuckled.

"You could have been killed."

"I admit, I am not as flexible as I was at age fourteen, and yet I acquitted myself not too badly, though I am perhaps a little bruised."

"So was it for that, so you could play stupid tricks, and worry me half to death, that you dragged me to Ramsgate?" I asked, my anger rising.

Holmes became suddenly serious,

"No, my dear friend, not for that. Not at all."

The door of the snug opened then and a young man entered, muffled as if against sharp mid-winter chills, when it was nearer mid-summer and still a balmy evening. The newcomer was wearing thick eyeglasses which flashed at the sight of us and he seemed about to withdraw again, when Walter called out to him, "Joey, don't go yet. Join us, please."

"Yes, Joey," said Holmes. "The ale is on me tonight. I insist on treating you."

The man hesitated, then shrugged and sat himself in a chair at a slight distance from the rest of us, away from the lamplight, while

Holmes signalled to the potboy to refill our mugs and bring a new one for our guest.

"You recognise Joey of course, Watson," said Holmes.

"Should I?" I replied, looking at the man. Did I imagine it or did he recoil from my gaze?

"Perhaps not without his white-face," Holmes smiled.

"Ah, the clown, the *auguste*," I said. The other seemed to relax. "It was a great show," I added.

He nodded in recognisance.

"A good name for a clown, Joey," Holmes went on. "After Joey Grimaldi, perhaps."

"Indeed." A low voice from our guest.

Walter meanwhile was casting searching glances from one man to the other. A strange tension had arisen. Something was up. I did not have to wait very long to learn what it was.

The potboy brought our mugs of ale and Holmes raised his to the newcomer.

"Your very good health, my Lord," he said.

The other started up, spilling his ale as he made for the door.

"Stop, sir, stop!" cried Holmes. "I mean you no harm! I am sorry to have frightened you."

What was this? I gazed in astonishment at the man, no white-face now needed, his face the colour of Ramsgate's chalk cliffs.

"Please to sit again, my Lord, and take my mug of ale. Your need is greater than mine."

That title again.

"I assure you that, without your whiskers, you are almost unrecognisable," Holmes went on. "Only for Walter's sharp eyes, and my own corroboration when I saw you back stage."

I tried to put whiskers on the shaved face. A sudden inspiration hit me.

"Lord Tonbridge!" I exclaimed.

"Hush, Watson," Holmes chided.

This was the man wanted for the murder of his wife's maid! I had seen his likeness in the paper that very morning.

"Walter sent me a telegram last night," Holmes continued. "He didn't wish to alert the police at once, to give you a chance to explain yourself."

"I am innocent," his Lordship whispered.

"And yet you have run away – gone into hiding."

"A foolish panic, I admit. But believe me I never harmed Marianna."

"It is said that you mistook the maid for your wife, whom you hate."

"I do not hate my wife."

"You were heard threatening her that afternoon."

Lord Tonbridge put his head in his hands in despair. "The evidence is against me, I know. But however far Lydia drove me, I would never have hurt her, never have killed her."

Holmes considered the man. "I am prepared to believe you," he said at last, "and I will try and help prove it. But in God's name, man, whyever take refuge in a circus, publicly on display to the whole world."

His Lordship explained that his first plan had been to flee to the Continent where he could have disappeared forever. But on arrival in the port of Dover, he had caught sight of a poster for Sanger's, with a grinning clown face on it.

"Since I was a boy," he said, "I have had a yen for the circus."

I glanced at Holmes, who was nodding with understanding.

"I thought it would be the perfect disguise," his Lordship went on. "As a clown in heavy make-up. And as you say, clean-shaven for the first time since I started to grow a beard. Who would recognise Lord Tonbridge, or even dream that the white-face could be he?" He turned to Walter. "And yet you recognised me."

Walter smiled. "I am like one of our elephants, your Lordship," he said. "I never forget. Not a face, anyway. Just like with Mr.

Holmes here, I remembered how you came to see the circus as a young lad. Night after night, you crept to the tent and asked me about the clowns, the animals. Of course, what you really wanted was to catch sight of young Rosa, our little trapeze artiste."

"Rosa, yes. I often wonder whatever happened to her." His Lordship's voice softened at the memory.

"She married Victor, the strong man, and had a litter of babies," Walter said. "I think they're up north, York way, these days."

"I'm glad she's happy," his Lordship remarked a little sadly.

"Anyway," Holmes interrupted, perhaps impatient with the notes of sentiment and nostalgia that had crept into the conversation, "we need a plan if we are to help you. I propose returning to London forthwith to interview all the witnesses, examine the murder scene, and see what emerges. I assume that her Ladyship is staying in the capital."

"Yes, she will be at our town house in Piccadilly. Lydia hates the countryside. But on what pretext will you visit her? My wife will hardly relish your presence if she knows that you are trying to clear my name."

Holmes gave him a sharp look. "Is that a fact? Interesting! Well, I will not tell her that, of course. Quite the opposite. She will think that I'm on her side. But first, please give me an account of the evening of the murder, as well as you can remember it."

"That's the problem, Mr. Holmes. I remember very little."

"Come, come, sir, that will not do. You remember little Rosa from fifteen years ago. You must remember what happened less than two weeks since."

"Well, now," his Lordship reflected. "I had been at my club, my usual refuge from the unpleasantness of the domestic scene. And had perhaps, as was my wont, partaken rather too lavishly of wine and brandy. To numb my senses, you understand."

My God, I thought – the poor gentleman, driven to drink.

"Hmm," said Holmes. "But I understand it was *before* you went out that you had been heard threatening Lady Tonbridge."

"She goaded me unmercifully, Mr. Holmes. I may have said some foolish things, but I almost feel that she put the words into my mouth. I remember at a certain moment she raised her voice and cried out, 'Don't strike me again, you brute!' when all I had done was to lay a hand upon her arm."

"I see. And it was for that reason you went to the club?"

"Indeed, the house has become intolerable to me." He paused. "No, I did not murder Marianna thinking it was my wife. I cannot imagine who might have done such a deed. I can only think it was an interloper come to rob us – it is well known that my wife has many valuable jewels. Perhaps the poor maid interrupted the thief and bore the fatal consequences." His Lordship peered hopefully at us through those thick glasses.

"Perhaps, perhaps," Holmes said. "And yet…"

"It was madness to run away, I know that now. Everyone thinks that it proves my guilt." Despair rang in his voice.

I decided to speak. "If you are innocent, Holmes will prove it."

"If?" the young man turned on me, suddenly imperious. "If? There are no 'if's' about it, Dr. Watson."

"Well, well," Holmes said, peaceably, "Let us try to collect some facts. You can start by telling me who was present in the house on the day in question?"

Tonbridge took off his glasses and squeezed his eyes shut, as if trying to reconstruct the scene in his head.

"Her Ladyship was there of course, and the servants… Well, our son James, but he is only four. His nanny, Rogers… Ah, I remember now. The lawyer, Mr. Shanks, was briefly at the house. Lydia had asked him to call. Something to do with a piece of property she inherited from her late godmother." He furrowed his brow in thought. "Miss Overton, the dressmaker came around as well, to fit yet another shockingly expensive robe for her Ladyship, which she will probably only ever wear the once. That was the reason for our row, in fact. The ruinously costly way of life that Lydia insists upon." He shook his head. "That is all, I think. Oh, Hobbes, the butler, informed me that the young man poor Marianna was seeing had been lurking in the kitchen at one time, against all the rules of the house."

Holmes sighed. "The young man's name?"

"I do not know it." Spoken with the dismissive arrogance of a man who hardly could be expected to be aware of the identity of one of his servant's followers.

"You are sure that is all, then?" There was a sardonic tone to Holmes's query.

"Yes – No, Lydia's brother had called in earlier, but like most of the others, I think he had left by the evening."

"Her brother?"

"Yes, Cedric. Cedric Crane. Her twin. He's an all-too-frequent visitor, I'm afraid."

"You don't like him?"

"Not at all. He's a wastrel and a parasite who can do no wrong in Lydia's eyes. Indeed, I had just announced a few days before that I would be stopping the allowance that Lydia insisted I bestow upon him. She was not at all pleased, but, Mr. Holmes, Cedric just fritters it all away – clothes, gaming, indulgences of all kinds. I told them for his own sake he should get himself some employment. Earn his keep."

Holmes considered this then asked, "No one else?"

"Not that I know of. At least, I don't think so – "

Holmes banged his hand on the table and we all jumped.

"Really, your Lordship. This will not do at all. Not at all. First you tell me no one was in the house, and now it seems a whole menagerie was present at one time or another."

"I apologise, Mr. Holmes. I do, indeed," replied the chastened gentleman. "I am most grateful for your interest and help. But at the

14

time of poor Marianna's murder… well, as I said, all of these visitors had left."

"So you know the time of her death, then?" Holmes fixed a piercing gaze on the young man.

"I… I assumed… I mean…"

"We make no assumptions. We only deal in hard facts." Then Holmes relented. "My dear fellow, you have gone through a great deal. I am sorry if I sound harsh. I assure you, Dr. Watson and I will do our very best to get to the bottom of the matter. But it is still not clear to me exactly why you should be suspected to the extent that you felt the need to take flight."

"Oh," replied his Lordship. "Well, because I found her."

"No more than that?"

Tonbridge looked discomforted. "It didn't look good, Mr. Holmes. As I told you, I had returned late from my club and went to my study, where I'm afraid that I partook of more brandy." He looked up as if expecting some rebuke. A weak man after all, I thought, easily put down. "I dozed off and… well… it would not be the first time that I have woken up in the study, sometimes spending the whole night upon the couch"

"Not this time."

"No, some noise disturbed me. I cannot say what it was. In my confused state, I simply wished to return to my bed. I left the study and almost stumbled over Marianna…" His voice broke at the memory. "It was quite dark, you know."

"The body was not there when you came back from the club."

"Oh no. That would be impossible. She was lying right by the door. I would swear on the Bible that she wasn't there earlier. I should have had to have step over her to gain access to the room, and I did not."

With great delicacy, Holmes raised his hands and joined the fingers of each, closing his eyes as if praying. He was clearly deep in thought, envisaging the scene.

15

"Was the body cold?" he asked at last.

"Good Lord, man, I didn't touch her! I could not. And how could she be cold? I wasn't asleep for more than an hour."

"What then?" asked Holmes. "You raised the alarm?"

"I didn't have time. The next thing that I knew, my wife was standing at the head of the stairs, staring down at me. Then she started screaming. Hobbes the butler arrived soon after, and the other servants. I cannot recall exactly. It is all such a horrible blur. I heard Lydia cry out, 'Murderer! He has killed her!' Mr. Holmes... the way they all looked at me..." The young gentleman broke down entirely.

"Calm yourself, sir," Holmes said sternly. "We need your clearest recollections. Tell me, were you wearing your eyeglasses at the time?"

"Of course, I am almost blind without them."

"And yet you performed perfectly well at the circus. I didn't see you wearing them then. Apart from the sham ones, of course."

"I can explain that," said Walter, who had been sitting quietly the while, as had I. "Surely you observed how the other clowns led him around and put him in the right place?"

"I did, but I thought it was part of the act."

"It is a strange thing, though," said Tonbridge, "and I have only just thought of it. Before I left for the club that night, I couldn't find my eyeglasses anywhere. They weren't where I thought that I'd left them, and I had to leave without them."

"And yet you found them on your return."

"No, indeed. They were still missing. Luckily, I keep a spare pair at the club."

"A-ha!" Holmes said smiling and rubbing his hands. "Excellent. Excellent."

We all regarded him in amazement. How was this important?

"Well, your Lordship," Holmes continued. "Watson and I will take our leave of you. I hope to be able to give you some good news very soon."

And with that, we bade a somewhat surprised Walter and Lord Tonbridge a very good night and adjourned to our respective bedrooms.

"It is indeed a most interesting case, Watson, though not so complex after all," said Holmes as we journeyed back to London the following morning, having first sent a wire to Lady Tonbridge requesting an interview. "Things are starting to fall into place. I merely need to confirm my suspicions."

"Do you?" I asked. "It seems a complete puzzle to me. I was racking my brains all night. Do you think – maybe a lovers' tiff that went wrong? Who knows what sort of a ruffian Marianna had taken up with? Or perhaps indeed, as his Lordship suggested, it was some thief who broke in after the jewels and was surprised by the maid. In fact," I warmed to the thought, "the lover and the thief could be one and the same person."

"The mysterious interloper. Ah yes, indeed. It might well be, although the supposed thief got nothing for his pains. No jewels were found to be missing. So what do you think? Perhaps his Lordship murdered her, after all. That swift flight would not seem to be the act of an innocent man. And you have of course noted that without his eyeglasses he can hardly see anything. In the dark, he might well have mistook the maid for the wife he pretends not to loathe."

"But he said he was wearing eyeglasses."

"Watson, Watson… Have you met a murderer yet who told you the truth?"

Was Holmes serious? His words troubled me and, as we sped towards London, I sat staring at my hands, hoping it was the lover or the interloper because I should not like his Lordship to be guilty after all.

"But Watson," Holmes interrupted my thoughts, "you are missing the oast houses. Are they not a most pleasing sight?"

With all haste that very afternoon – so not, as Holmes said, to give Lady Tonbridge time to refuse our request – we arrived at the town house in Piccadilly. A dignified elderly butler I took to be Hobbes showed us into a splendidly appointed room that looked out through golden drapes at the bustling thoroughfare. A pale Chinese carpet partly covered a polished wooden floor. Delicate furnishings reflected an excellent if expensive taste. In particular, a chaise longue in the rococo style caught my eye – surely an antique. The delicious perfume in the air could be traced to a lavish display of mixed flowers standing in a Murano red-glass vase on a side table.

Her Ladyship joined us soon and received us graciously enough.

Lady Lydia Tonbridge proved to be an imposing young woman in her middle-twenties. Tall, in a fine dress of pearl grey silk and sparkling with some of those notorious jewels, her almost-white blonde hair raised in a lavish chignon, she was at the same time painfully thin and pale, those diamonds adorning a neck that was bony and scrawny. As for her bosom, it barely existed – she could have passed for a boy. Were she my patient, I should have prescribed a hearty diet of roast beef, mutton stew with dumplings, and plenty of rice puddings.

"You sent word that you have news of my husband?" she said, regarding us with slate grey eyes. "I hope he isn't planning to return here soon and finish the job."

A coarse-enough expression, I thought.

"You are convinced then that he is guilty of the crime and that you were the intended victim?"

"What other explanation could there be? So where is he, Mr. Holmes?"

"I have it on good authority that he planned to flee to the Continent and may now be in France."

"Ah, I suspected as much. Good riddance to the coward. Although of course," she added in a cold tone, "it would be preferable if he had been captured by the police, brought to trial, and hanged."

Good Lord, what a woman! What a wife!

"It is kind of you, of course," she added, "to come in person to set my mind at rest, and yet it seems an unnecessary journey. A letter would have sufficed."

Holmes put on his most charming smile, a smile that I often thought could charm a snake. "I was hoping," he said silkily, "that I might prevail on your Ladyship to indulge myself and Dr. Watson in a project on which we are engaged."

Her Ladyship regarded us quizzically.

"You may know," Holmes continued, "that I have some small interest in crime."

She bowed in acknowledgement.

"It just so happens that Dr. Watson and I are writing a monograph on notorious murders of the decade – "

Are we, indeed? First that I heard of it.

" – and I would like to include an account of the murder of your maid. Sad to say, the public love to read about the nobility when they have been found to be up to no good."

"So true, Mr. Holmes. So true… Alas, poor Marianna." Her Ladyship pressed a lacy handkerchief to her eyes. "If only I had not given her my old dress and shawl, Ralph might not have mistook her. But then – Oh God! It could have been me! I could have been the one so cruelly strangled to death. Horrible! Horrible!" She sank, quite overcome, onto the chaise longue.

19

At that moment, the door swung open and an exceedingly thin and fair young man entered, followed by a small child and a motherly looking person whom I took to be the nanny.

"Oh, my deepest apologies, Lydia," he exclaimed, looking askance at us. "I didn't know that you had company." The young man was so identical to her Ladyship that I judged him to be the twin brother. "I was just bringing Lord Tonbridge to see his dear mamma. He wouldn't stay away."

Lord Tonbridge – and the child's father not yet dead! I couldn't help but notice the boy's reluctance to run to his dear mamma, and how he was watching us all with wide eyes, clutching on to his nanny's skirts betimes, as if hoping they would envelop him.

"Cedric," said Lady Tonbridge, quite recovered from her previous emotion, "this is Mr. Sherlock Holmes and Dr... er... er..."

"Dr. Watson!" The young man strode forward and clasped each of us by the hand. He looked effete, a dandy, dressed in a pale suit with a flowered silk waistcoat, his jacket sporting a carnation in its buttonhole in the style of the followers of poor Mr. Wilde. Yet his grip was strong. "My dear sirs, I am most honoured to make your acquaintance. Cedric Crane, younger brother by a whole ten minutes of my dearest Lydia." He smiled, though his eyes were as flinty as hers. "I have long followed Mr. Holmes's illustrious career through your most excellent accounts, Doctor."

He was perhaps a little too enthusiastic, and his hand a little too wet.

"But to what do we owe this most delightful visit?" he went on.

Lady Tonbridge explained.

"Lord Tonbridge in France," he exclaimed. "Then you have nothing more to fear, Lydia."

"Just so long as he stays there, of course," her Ladyship said drily.

20

"And now Mr. Holmes," Crane went on, "you wish to see the scene of the crime, to write about it. Capital! I shall show you myself."

"Thank you," said Holmes gravely. I was sure, knowing his methods, that he wouldn't wish to be encumbered by the presence of such an overbearing young man. But how politely was he to extricate himself?

We left her Ladyship with her son, Holmes bending first to sniff at the fragrant flowers, shaking his head in an uncharacteristic appreciation of the blooms. As we quitted the room, I heard Lady Tonbridge mutter, "Rogers, I am not able for this now. Please take James to the nursery or out to the park or somewhere – anywhere, out of my sight."

A loving mother, indeed!

Holmes examined the study and the hallway outside in minute detail, with Crane and myself looking on, though what could be found there so long after the event was quite beyond me.

"Marianna was lying where exactly?" Holmes asked.

"Oh well," Crane said. "By the door, I think. I cannot say exactly. I wasn't present, you know."

"Then you weren't staying here that night?"

"No. Why would I?"

"Well, being so close to your sister…"

"Would that I had been here, Mr. Holmes!" he burst out. "I might have prevented this foul deed."

"How could you have done that?"

"Well…"

"You weren't to know that it would happen, were you?"

"No, of course not. But Ralph – Lord Tonbridge – had threatened Lydia earlier that day. He had struck her, you know."

"All the more reason, I should have thought, to stay and keep watch."

"Well, I didn't." Crane sounded petulant.

Holmes then asked to speak to the butler.

"Hobbes?"

"I understand that the butler was one of the first on the scene – after your sister, of course, but I really don't wish to trouble her further."

"Ah yes, yes. Hobbes. I'll fetch him." And Crane wandered off down the hallway.

"Watson, rid me of this boy, please. I don't wish him present while I talk to the butler."

"How am I to do that?"

"You must think of something."

An instruction I did not relish. When Crane returned with the butler, all I could devise was a request that he take me below stairs to talk to the servants to see if they had any evidence to provide.

"To give a full picture to our readers, you know," I added lamely.

Crane gave me a sharp look, which I returned with a blank one. Let him think me a fool. At any rate, it worked for, without demur, he led me down to the kitchen where I kept him with me for as long as I could, asking stupid questions of the cook and scullery maid, who had seen and heard nothing at all.

Meanwhile, Holmes was free to speak to Hobbes, and later gave me an account of what transpired. It seemed that the butler had been roused from his slumbers by her Ladyship's scream. It being about two o'clock of the morning, it took him several minutes to reach the sorry scene.

"Were the lights on?" Holmes asked.

"No," Hobbes replied, "but her Ladyship was holding a candle, which provided sufficient illumination."

"It was lucky she was up and about at the relevant time."

The butler bowed his head but made no reply to that.

"So what exactly did you see?"

"Her Ladyship was at the top of the stairs, sir, while his Lordship, seeming frozen with shock, was standing over poor prostrate Marianna." Hobbes shook his head at the memory.

"Was his Lordship wearing his eye-glasses?"

"His eyeglasses, sir? I'm sure I could not say."

"And yet, I suppose you are used to seeing him with his eyeglasses." Hobbes nodded. "So it might have struck you particularly if he was *not* wearing them."

"Yes, sir. I suppose that is very possible."

Holmes then asked what the butler did next and learnt that he had examined the body, to make sure life had left the poor girl. Something, I recalled, that his Lordship had been too fastidious to do.

"Was she warm or cold?" Holmes queried.

"Oh sir, she was colder rather than warm," Hobbes replied. "And already going stiff, you know. I thought that very odd, sir, if the murder had only just taken place."

"So do you think his Lordship did it?"

Hobbes paused, shocked perhaps at the brutality of the question, and then replied, "To be honest, no, sir. It is not in master's character to be violent. I have known him since the man was a boy, and a gentler person you could not hope to meet."

"Yet he threatened her Ladyship earlier," Holmes persisted. "He struck her."

"So they say, sir. So they say." (He laid heavy emphasis on the word "they".)

"If not his Lordship, Hobbes, then who do you think might have done the deed?"

The butler replied that he couldn't imagine. Marianna was a sweet girl with no enemies.

"Her young man perhaps?"

Hobbes was aghast. "Robin? Never! He adored her. They had an understanding, sir."

23

"Do you think it could have been an interloper, then?"

Hobbes raised his eyes to Holmes' face and looked him straight in the eye. "It depends what you mean by that, sir."

"A thief."

"Thieves come in different shapes and sizes, sir."

"What do you mean by that, Hobbes?"

The butler just shook his head, faithful retainer that he was, and would say no more.

"If someone wanted to conceal a body for a short time, where could they hide it?"

The new question made Hobbes start.

"Somewhere near enough to the study?" Holmes persisted.

After some thought, Hobbes suggested a recess under the stairwell, ever plunged in dark shadow. He indicated the place to Holmes, who looked but indeed could see very little.

It was at that moment that, unable to stay Cedric Crane's impatience any longer, I came up from the kitchen, the young man striding ahead of me.

"A lamp, Hobbes, if you please," Holmes was saying.

"A lamp?" Crane asked.

"Mr. Holmes wishes to look more closely under the stairs," Hobbes explained and set off to fetch a light.

"Under the stairs. Good heavens, man, why?"

"I think the body was perhaps concealed there before it was moved."

"Moved?" Crane's tone was suddenly shrill. "How can that be? Why would Ralph have strangled the woman and then moved her to his study door."

"Why, indeed. To incriminate himself perhaps."

The young man gaped.

"Or perhaps he was planning to carry her out of the house, but was interrupted by her Ladyship."

"Yes, perhaps, so. Indeed."

"No," Holmes shook his head. "No, I do not think so." He smiled, fixing that snake-like gaze upon the young man.

Crane froze. Then exploded.

"This is quite absurd, Holmes. I refuse to take part in this farce. I know your methods, oh yes. I know what you are up to." Cedric Crane's pallid face was now turning red with rage. "Leave this house immediately. Go, I insist upon it."

"I am sorry. Is it your place to give orders here?"

"Lydia will back me up. Lydia! Lydia!" Crane raced off to fetch his sister.

Meanwhile, Hobbes returned with the lamp. Taking it from him, Holmes proceeded to the understairs. I followed him but as far as I could see, the lamp revealed nothing but dust.

Several servants, curious at the noise, including those with whom I had spoken in the kitchen, had come to see what was going on, withdrawing behind half-open doors when their angry mistress burst on to the scene.

"Mr. Holmes, what is this? Doctor… whoever you are. Whatever is going on? You presume too much on my good nature, sir."

"He says that Ralph moved the body" Crane babbled. "Have you ever heard anything so absurd? Ha ha ha!"

"No, no, no. Not Lord Tonbridge," said Holmes, emerging from the recess. "He moved no one. He did nothing. The one who moved her was the one who wanted it believed that his Lordship murdered the maid. The cold-hearted devil who murdered her himself."

"Who?" asked Hobbes. "Who did it? What did you find?"

Holmes opened his hand. A few crushed petals lay there. "Hobbes, is his Lordship in the habit of wearing a flower in his buttonhole?"

"No, sir. I have never seen him wear such a thing."

We all looked at Crane, at his carnation. And he, panic-stricken, stared back as us. Then turned on his sister.

"It was all *her* idea! Lydia's idea. I never wanted to go through with it. Never – "

She struck his face so hard that even I flinched. "Fool!" she screeched. "Can you not see it is a trick? I saw Holmes take that flower just now from the vase. After two weeks, petals would not be so fresh." And she struck him again.

"Indeed, your Ladyship," Holmes said, "and yet I think the point is proved."

A few days later we found ourselves in the same lovely room where Lady Tonbridge had first received us. This time we were sitting with her husband, who was dandling his little boy, James, on his knee. From time to time he kissed the boy's head. I suppose he had thought never to see his son again.

"The plan," Holmes explained, "went somewhat awry when you fled the scene so quickly. The pair had expected that you would be arrested, charged, and perhaps, as Lady Tonbridge herself hoped, hanged for murder."

Lestrade, who was now in charge of the case, had reported back to us that, while Lady Tonbridge maintained a cold silence, Cedric was leaking like a bucket, as the inspector so colourfully put it. The pair had carefully concocted evidence against Lord Tonbridge, using the servants to confirm bad blood between husband and wife, particularly in the light of the staged "attack" earlier in the day, when Lady Tonbridge had made sure that everyone would hear her cry out, "Do not strike me again, you brute!" Not realising that his Lordship had a replacement set at his club, as Cedric further revealed, they had stolen and disposed of his Lordship's eyeglasses. Without them, the claim he had mistaken his victim would prove much more persuasive.

"Fiendish, fiendish." Lord Tonbridge stroked his son's hair.

That day, too, it seemed that Marianna had been lured by Lady Tonbridge to dress up in her clothes. The poor girl, according to Hobbes, had been delighted with the cast-offs. She had announced how she could cut a fine dash when next out with her beau. Alas, the poor girl never had the opportunity, strangled by Cedric and unceremoniously dumped under the stairs for some hours – *rigor mortis* having already started to set in – until Tonbridge returned from his club. As was his Lordship's habit, he went straight to his study. The noise he subsequently heard there was perhaps the body being moved into position, or perhaps just a sound intended to arouse him from his slumbers, with her Ladyship already waiting at the top of the stairs for him to emerge.

"I do not understand," his Lordship said. "Did Lydia hate me so much that she was willing to sacrifice an innocent to get rid of me?"

"I doubt if Lady Tonbridge has passion in her for that much hate," Holmes said. "Indifference to the lives of others, certainly. Her passion was greed, pure and simple. You were curtailing her spending. You cut off the allowance to her beloved twin."

"Yet, she had wealth in her own right. The inheritance from her godmother."

"Ah yes," said Holmes, "I have spoken to Mr. Shanks, the lawyer, on that very subject and have discovered that the inheritance Lady Tonbridge was expecting turned out to be a paltry sum after all. With you out of the way and the next Lord Tonbridge," here he indicated the child, "many years from his majority, she and Cedric could get their hands on the family money and indulge their extravagancies to their hearts' content – until the money all ran out, of course."

Lord Tonbridge shook his head. "Money truly is the root of evil. Speaking of which," he added, smiling wanly as he took an envelope from his breast pocket, pressing it into Holmes's hand. "Please accept this, with my deepest gratitude."

Glancing at the contents, Holmes remarked. "Too much, my Lord. Far too much."

"It can never be too much," Tonbridge replied, again kissing the top of his son's head. "And yet, there is after all one thing I regret: Never again to don the motley or whiten my face. Never again to enjoy the comradeship of the circus."

"I am sure," Holmes smiled, "that Walter, who indulged me with a turn in the ring, would certainly not begrudge it you, your Lordship, once in a while."

We all laughed at that, but I noticed a somewhat wistful expression cross Holmes's face. Was he perhaps wondering what his life would have been if, as a boy that time, he really had run away with the circus?

Abracadaver

"There you are at last, Watson," said Sherlock Holmes, buttering a piece of toast. "I was thinking you must have slept in this morning, until I observed that your top coat was missing. And now I see from the mud on your boots that you have been walking in the Regent's Park."

In fact, I had just then returned from a morning stroll in that very place, having been awakened early by the unseasonal sunshine on that sharp November day. However, on this occasion, Holmes's perspicacity failed to astonish me, since as he knew well that I am often in the habit of enjoying the delights of the nearby park. Now quite invigorated, I was ready to partake of the devilled kidneys that Mrs. Hudson had provided for our breakfast.

I was so engrossed in filling my plate that it was only when I had taken my first mouthful that I noticed Holmes looking at me with a small smile on his face.

"You have a healthy appetite, my friend," he said. "I envy you."

Indeed, in my professional capacity as a doctor, I had frequently been concerned at my friend's haphazard eating habits. He often went without altogether and, when he did finally sit at table, he took little relish in his food, seeming always preoccupied with something else. At this moment, he was waving a letter in my face.

"I received this in the morning post," he said. "It is from Mrs. Cecil Forrester and I find it, I have to say, as eccentric as one might expect from that person."

Holmes had recently assisted the said lady, a widow of enormous girth in her middle years, in a little domestic unpleasantness, the exposure of her steward. This man had, as it turned out, been embezzling her funds little by little over time, hoping presumably by that means to avoid notice. This Arthur Alexander fellow, however, proved no match for Holmes, who soon got to the bottom of the business. It was a sad enough case all the same because the said steward, a well-built and charming young man to all outward appearances, had become a firm favourite with Mrs. Forrester, and might indeed have been a beneficiary of the lady's will, had insatiable greed not overcome him. Alexander had escaped prison only through the good offices of Mrs. Forrester, an outcome I personally regretted, feeling that a bout of hard labour might do the young man the world of good and bring him to his senses. Instead, the kind-hearted lady had provided him with the wherewithal to leave England for South Africa, to start a new life.

"What does she say?" I asked.

"See for yourself." He offered me the letter, inscribed on the elaborately crested notepaper of the family, Mrs. Forrester having been an Honourable before her marriage, a title she still used on occasion. The shaky handwriting was presumably that of the lady herself.

I read what she had written and started to laugh.

"She offers two tickets for the Egyptian Hall this very night!" I cried. "In grateful thanks. Is she quite serious?"

"Yes. I should have taken it for a joke, too, had I not been acquainted with Mrs. Forrester's whimsical character." And he picked up the said tickets from beside his plate.

"Will you go?"

Holmes languidly took another piece of toast and stared at it, as if it might provide the answer. He sighed.

"Do you really consider that I should relish the prospect of a night at England's 'Home of Mystery', as I believe the place likes to call itself?"

Indeed, the Hall, a striking edifice in the style of an ancient Egyptian palace, and once a private museum, had become the location for shows of magic and spiritualism.

"It might be fun," I said.

The look he gave me was, had I been some lowly insect, utterly crushing.

"I find," he said, yawning, "that I am far too preoccupied with my monograph on the refinement of porcelain during the Yuan Dynasty to think of 'fun'. However, it would seem a shame for the tickets to go to waste, and I suspect that you yourself would not be averse to a night out…" He paused and looked quizzically at me. I have to confess that my friend knows my little weaknesses. I do enjoy a good show.

"Well," I replied, "as you say, Holmes, in the light of the lady's generosity, we should not want the tickets to go to waste. Who knows? The Great Maskelyne might be on the bill."

"Good," he went on, "and I was thinking that it might be a kindly gesture to take Mrs. Hudson with you. She gets out so little and has been so very good to us." So patient with Holmes's many quirks and unreasonable demands, I thought. "Unless of course you have anyone else in mind."

"Not at all," I replied. "Assuming Mrs. Hudson is free, it would be my pleasure to escort her."

Thus it was that, later that evening, myself and our good landlady, all a-flutter, took a cab to Piccadilly, where the Hall was situated.

Mrs. Hudson regarded with admiration the exotic frontage, with its carved sphinxes and scarabs inset into square cut stone pillars. "I have passed by here on many occasions, Doctor," she said, "but I never thought of entering it. It is quite a thrill, I can tell you."

I was delighted for her and admitted that it was a thrill for me as well, even though I was disappointed to learn from the lavish programme that those famed masters of illusion, Maskelyne and

Cooke, would not be performing that night. It seemed that they were away on tour in the United States.

The interior of the place was even more splendid than the outside: that great hall, lavishly adorned with more Egyptian motifs illuminated by sparkling chandeliers, leading through to the theatre itself. Our seats were well placed near the stage, for which I thanked the thoughtfulness of Mrs. Forrester.

Unfortunately, Mrs. Hudson, being of short stature, found that her view of the stage was effectively blocked by the head of the tall person in front of her. She would have to bob and bend continually to see around him. To change places with me would have proved of no avail either, since the person before me was as lofty as his neighbour.

It was at this point that the gentleman to Mrs. Hudson's left, on overhearing our dilemma, most courteously proposed that, since there was no giant in front of him, she take his seat, he being a man of at least equal height with Sherlock Holmes himself. I could see that our landlady was torn – it provided a much better prospect, and yet to change places would have put this unknown gentleman between herself and myself. A solution was finally found with him taking my place – a remove which, in the event, proved fateful.

I managed to exchange a few polite words with the kind gentleman before the start of the show. He informed me that he was a Mr. Hartley Jameson and that he was visiting London on business from Birmingham, where he owned an engineering company. He took Mrs. Hudson for my mother, which I think rather displeased that lady. In mitigation, I whispered to her that Mr. Jameson was evidently a very short-sighted gentleman, in dire need of a new pair of spectacles.

Soon enough the lights went down in the auditorium and a Mr. Charles Mellon, as described in the programme, started to play a suitably eerie overture on the pianoforte, a piece I recognised as the *Danse Macabre* by M. Saint-Saens.

"Ooh, Doctor Watson," Mrs. Hudson whispered, "it quite sends shivers down my spine."

I had to agree and must add that, in retrospect, the piece proved only too horribly appropriate.

Mr. Mellon finished with a flourish, we applauded heartily, and the heavy red velvet curtains swept back from the stage to reveal a scene more Far Eastern than Egyptian, with a painted backdrop depicting a waterfall plunging down a mountainside to a pagoda similar to the one in the Gardens at Kew. A small round man stepped forward. This was our *compere* for the evening, a Mr. Harold Quincy, who in addition proved to be a fine tenor when he regaled us, accompanied by Mr. Mellon, with renditions of *Come into the Garden, Maud* and *The Lost Chord.*

He then introduced the first act as Chinese Plate dancers come all the way from Peking, which explained the design on the backdrop. Mr. Mellon obliged with suitably exotic-sounding music. (I believe it was from a comic opera I once had the pleasure of attending – namely *The Mikado* by Messrs Gilbert and Sullivan, and thus Japanese in inspiration. But let us not quibble.) Six young ladies with Oriental features, in Chinese straw hats, tight-fitting embroidered blouses, and what I believe these days are called "bloomers", emerged from the wings, each clutching several long bamboo rods on which they had set plates a-spinning. They danced gracefully and performed other breath-taking acts of acrobatics while continuing to spin the plates. Such consummate skill. Clearly the plates could not be stuck to the poles, and yet we had to marvel that the performers managed not to drop a single one.

Mrs. Hudson whispered to me as we applauded that she was glad Phoebe wasn't present to see the show since she might be inclined to try the trick for herself – Phoebe being our clumsy young scullery maid, renowned for the amount of ware she somehow managed to break.

The next act was a gentleman named Felix Grau, a facial artist with an amazing mobility of expression, able to mimic with the aid of wigs and lights the features of several great personages of our time. I laughed particularly at his William Gladstone, our Prime Minister, stern-faced and side whiskered. Mr. Grau captured him to the life.

The act that had replaced Maskelyne and Cooke's celebrated illusions then followed. This was a magician of whom I had never heard, perhaps because he came, as the *compere* informed us, all the way from Paris. Monsieur Fantôme was his name, and he was accompanied by a pretty assistant, all dizzy curls and rosebud lips, somewhat scantily clad in the way of the French. Fantôme introduced this young person to us in his strong accent as Veronique.

He performed several tricks which I felt were appreciated more by Mrs. Hudson than by myself, since they were from the familiar run-of-the mill repertoire of linking rings, colour-changing scarves, and the production of a rabbit from a previously empty hat. Holmes, I felt, could have explained the deceptions in an instant. However, they were well received by the crowd.

Next, an upright cabinet was wheeled on to the stage. When M. Fantôme opened the door, we could see that there was room for a person to stand inside and he invited Veronique to do so. She feigned reluctance, perhaps because M. Fantôme was at the same time holding a fearsome looking sword that he had taken from a side table where several more of the same were lying. She tested the blade and apparently found it sharp, because she shook her curls vigorously and said, *"Non, non, non."*

For a moment, M. Fantôme looked nonplussed at her refusal, but then called upon the audience to persuade her. With one voice we exhorted her to "Go in!" and finally, she was prevailed upon to do so. M. Fantôme then shut the door upon her, locking it with a big key. Brandishing his sword, he thrust it with some force through a slit in the side of the cabinet. We gasped as it came through the opposite side and Mrs. Hudson clutched my arm in fear. The magician continued with the other swords until the cabinet quite bristled: surely anyone within must have been impaled. Mrs. Hudson squeezed my arm tighter.

M. Fantôme then called to Veronique, but there was no reply. Looking worried and shaking his head, he removed the swords, one by one, calling out each time to no avail. At least no blood was visible on the blades and Mrs. Hudson relaxed her grip somewhat.

With a flourish and the word "Abracadabra!" the magician swung the cabinet door open. Out stepped Veronique, none the worse for her ordeal. We cheered and applauded wildly.

M. Fantôme then addressed the audience again, challenging some brave Englishman – quipping "if any such there be" – to enter *La Boîte de la Mort*, The Cabinet of Death. At the same time, Veronique descended from the stage and cast her eyes over us. Several gallant gentlemen raised their hands, offering their services. It seemed, however, she had fixed upon my neighbour, Mr. Hartley Jameson, who, I believed, had not been one of those to volunteer. Nevertheless, he took her hand and followed her willingly enough, smiling back at me as he climbed up on to the stage, to the cheers of the audience.

Still smiling – And how can I ever forget that smile? – he entered the cabinet and the door was closed upon him. As before M. Fantôme plunged the swords, each one now offered to him by Veronique, through the cabinet wall. One, two, three, four . . . They all emerged from the other side.

"Are you well, Monsieur?" the magician asked each time, to which our erstwhile neighbour replied that he was.

And then the fifth sword. As Fantôme drove it in, there came a frightful cry such as I have never heard before and hope never to again, a scream of more utter agony and terror than I ever heard in all my time serving in Afghanistan.

At first the audience thought that it was part of the trick, that Mr. Hartley Jameson was a stooge acting out a previously agreed role, but then came the blood, the blood flowing out from under the cabinet door . . . Some people still laughed, but then fell silent. This was no trick. This was real.

M. Fantôme stood frozen. After a pause, amid a shocked silence, the curtains swung across the stage, blocking our view. Almost immediately, Quincy, the *compere*, came forward and announced, "Ladies and gentlemen, there has been a most unfortunate accident. I wonder if there is a doctor present here."

I had already leapt to my feet and made my hurried way on to the stage. The sight that greeted me there was truly dreadful. The cabinet door stood open revealing its grisly contents: The body of Mr. Hartley Jameson hanging impaled upon a sword while blood still flowed from a wound in his abdomen.

Examining him, I shook my head. There was no sign of life. M. Fantôme, standing at my side, moved to pull away the sword, but I halted him, merely pushing the door closed again, to hide the horrid sight.

"The police will wish to see this as it is," I said.

"The show cannot go on then?" asked the *compere*.

"Of course not!" I was shocked that he would even think it might. "But no one should leave the Hall until the police arrive."

Shaking his head, Quincy stepped out in front of the curtains to make the announcement to the horrified audience, requesting them to stay calm and to remain in their seats for the time being.

"How could this have happened?" I asked the magician.

"I know it not," Fantôme replied. He explained how the other swords had been trick ones, with retractable blades and a mechanism that sent their apparent tips out through the opposite side of the box. "But someone must have placed a real sword among the others. *O, Dieu, quelle horreur!*" He clutched his head. "But where is Veronique! Perhaps she knows more."

We looked around to find that young person huddled on the floor, sobbing and being comforted by one of the Chinese dancers

"*Mais c'est ma faute!*" she muttered. "It is my fault." And she collapsed into a further wail of weeping.

I was on the point of crossing over to tend to her when someone new rushed through the curtains on to the stage. To my enormous astonishment, it was none other than Sherlock Holmes, his face haggard with concern.

"My dear Watson!" he exclaimed, observing the blood on my hands. "You are injured but alive. Thank God for that."

I have to say I was rather surprised at his passion and soon reassured him that I was not injured in the least, the blood being that of Mr. Hartley Jameson. I opened the cabinet door to show him the poor man.

"Most astonishing," he said, viewing the scene with his customary marked attention

"But why," I asked, "did you think that I was the victim? And whatever brought you here in the first place?"

"To answer your second question first," he replied, "I decided this morning that it would be a courtesy to write to Mrs. Forrester, thanking her for the tickets. Imagine my surprise and shock when she replied by the evening post that she knew nothing of the matter." He looked at me with a frown.

"She didn't send them?" I said. "But who then?"

"That, my friend, is the question. I realised immediately that something was seriously amiss, and with all haste came here to try and prevent a catastrophe. When I asked Mrs. Hudson where you were, she told me that something frightful had happened and pointed to the curtains. My dear fellow," and I cannot help but think I detected some strong emotion in his usually measured tones, "I feared the worst."

"Well, you can see that I am unhurt, but that the poor fellow there has suffered a fatal accident."

"An accident!" replied Holmes. "I think not. This is no accident."

"What then? Surely not murder?"

"Oh, indubitably. But why *this* man? What has he done to deserve such a fate?"

"It has surely to be random," I said, explaining what little I knew about Mr. Hartley Jameson.

"You mean, he was sitting beside you?" Holmes asked, with a fresh gleam in his eye. "That is most significant."

"In fact, he was sitting in my seat." I then recounted how we had exchanged places so that Mrs. Hudson might see the stage.

"A-ha!" Holmes exclaimed. "Well, it seems you have had the most lucky escape, but at a terrible cost to this fellow."

"You think that I was the intended victim? But how can that be?"

"You, or perhaps me, since the tickets were intended for the two of us."

"Good Lord!" I cried, looking at him in horror.

"Who picked out Mr. Jameson to come on stage?"

I indicated the magician's assistant, Veronique. Holmes went over to her and spoke in low tones. She looked up at him with a tear-stained face, and replied at length and with emotion. Then he came back to me.

"What did she say?"

"It is most interesting. She claims that some fellow gave her a golden sovereign to pick out the man in Row B, Seat 15."

"Did she not think it strange?"

"I think she considered it well-paid for a moment's work. The man told her he wished to have a laugh at the expense of his friend."

"Some laugh!" I commented. "Was she able to give a description of the fellow?"

"In some detail. He was of tall stature, having a face adorned with thick black whiskers, and wearing a hat pulled down over his eyes."

"A disguise, then?"

"Possibly."

I considered the matter. "So whoever sent us the tickets, this stranger presumably, thought that either you or I would be in that very seat. Poor Mr. Jameson. If only he had not been so quick to be polite."

"You and Mrs. Hudson may be grateful that he was."

I could not deny the fact as it related to myself, but added, "Oh, Mrs. Hudson was at no risk. Fantôme specified a man. An Englishman, actually."

"An Englishman?"

"A brave Englishman. I think it was supposed to be a French joke."

"Ah."

We were interrupted then by the arrival of the police, in the familiar wiry form of Inspector Lestrade, along with a couple of uniformed constables, as well as Armitage, a doctor often employed by Scotland Yard.

"No need to say anything just now about our suspicions," warned Holmes. "I first wish to look further into the matter myself."

Lestrade was evidently most surprised to see us but, on hearing of the circumstances – we did not mention how we had obtained the tickets – was inclined to put it down to a lucky coincidence. I told him what I knew, and what I had observed, no more and no less.

"It would seem," Lestrade remarked, "to be a tragic and most unfortunate accident, although," and here he looked around, lowering his voice, "I shall be investigating that Frenchie, just in case."

Holmes and I left him to his work and at last rejoined poor Mrs. Hudson, who had stayed abandoned in her seat. She is a woman of considerable character, however, and was in no way inclined to hysteria on this occasion, unlike some of the other ladies in the theatre who were displaying, in various degrees, fits of the vapours.

Permission was soon given for all of us to leave the Hall, which we did, having first provided names and addresses to the constables and theatre staff. Holmes, Mrs. Hudson, and I elected to walk back to Baker Street, since any cabs we spotted were already taken. Although it was a cool and foggy night, we walked briskly and it was pleasant enough to be outside. In fact, I was glad of it, to clear my head. Of course, the conversation soon turned back to the terrible events of the evening.

"Did Veronique have anything to say about the substitution of the swords?" I asked.

"Only that they all look alike to her. In fact, she trembled at the thought that if the magician had picked up the real sword when she was in the box, it might have been she who was the victim." Holmes looked at me. "Think, Watson. Did anyone touch the swords between the two tricks?"

"Not that I saw."

"But of course, you weren't looking. I suppose that you only had eyes for the young person." Holmes recognised too well another of my weaknesses, that for a pretty face. "It is the traditional magician's ploy of diverting attention," he said.

"A man did appear from the side of the stage," Mrs. Hudson interpolated, "just as the young lady came down into the audience. "I noticed him fiddling around as if adjusting things. I cannot testify that I observed him place a new sword on the table but, as you say, Mr. Holmes, we were all distracted at the time. He may have done."

"Mrs. Hudson, as I have often remarked, you are a perfect treasure!" If Holmes had ever said such a thing, it was certainly not in my hearing, but never mind that. "I wonder," he went on, "if you can describe the man further."

"I am sorry, Mr. Holmes. Just that he was young and in a regular suit. Not a stage costume."

"A suit!"

"Rather a shabby suit. I remember thinking it a little strange at the time. In such a fancy place, you know. The men who wheeled the cabinet on to the stage previously were both in costume."

"You see," said Holmes, clapping his hands, "how it pays to be observant at all times."

"I have learnt it from you, Mr. Holmes." Mrs. Hudson smiled modestly. "You are an excellent teacher."

"Sad then," Holmes said, clapping my arm to offset the harshness of his words, "that Watson is such a poor pupil."

The next morning, Holmes and I set off to interview Mrs. Cecil Forrester, having first sent a telegram to warn of our imminent arrival. We took a train to Camberwell and from the station walked through that most delightful suburb to Addington Square and the elegant house wherein the lady dwelt. She expressed great delight to see us again, her plump features wreathed in smiles of welcome that soon turned to horror when she learned what was the matter.

"I haven't yet seen the newspapers," she said. "What a terrible business!"

She was dressed, I thought, somewhat too youthfully, given her age and shape, in a gown of mint green, festooned with ribbons and frills and perhaps rather too tightly laced, making bulges where there should be none. That said, we had always found Mrs. Forrester a lady of extreme good-nature, one who found it hard to see the bad in people – which had made her an easy prey for the villainies of her steward.

"I need to ask you some questions, Mrs. Forrester," Holmes said.

"Not hard ones, I hope." Her grey curls, under a lacy mop cap, bobbed coquettishly as she spoke.

"No, nothing to be concerned about. It is just on the matter of the tickets for the show."

"Well, Mr. Holmes, as I previously communicated to you, I had nothing to do with that." She rang a bell. "But let us discuss this further over tea. At this time of day, I always feel the need for some sustenance, you know, and I'm sure you would like to taste some of Cook's gingerbread. She made it fresh this morning, especially for you."

Since it was not long past breakfast time, Mrs. Forrester's hunger might be wondered at and yet, as I have mentioned already, she was a stout woman, whose girth flowed across the sofa upon which she was seated. The way she attacked the plate of cake subsequently brought in by the maid showed that her appetite was in no way diminished by bad news.

"The question," Holmes said, when he had finally managed to get the lady's attention back to the matter in hand, "is who might have appropriated your stationery." He produced the original letter and showed it to her. "If this notepaper does indeed come from your house."

She took it and studied it.

"Oh yes. It is identical. How very strange. Though it is not my hand, you know. Very like, perhaps, but I pride myself on the excellence of my copperplate."

She rang the bell again and asked the maid to send for Miss Sarah.

"I am sure I cannot think... Perhaps she will have some better idea, Mr. Holmes," she said. "You must have met my children's governess, Sarah Willis, at the time of the... er... unpleasantness."

"No," Holmes replied. "We have not yet had that pleasure."

"Ah, well," she replied. "As for pleasure... The poor girl isn't endowed with a lively personality, I am afraid, and as for her person... I have tried to urge her to make more of herself, you know." Mrs. Forrester paused thoughtfully to munch on her cake, and then continued. "Like myself, Sarah was greatly upset by the… the unpleasantness, you know. She seemed to have been under the foolish impression that she and Arthur had some sort of understanding." Mrs. Forrester smiled at some memory. "Oh, he could charm the birds off the trees, that one."

Holmes bowed his head as if in understanding, although I am sure he took both women for arrant fools to let their heads be turned by such a trickster.

"Is it not strange, Mr. Holmes," Mrs. Forrester went on, "how misfortune seems to follow some people around? Sarah is only now returned from visiting the death-bed of her mother and is understandably quite out of sorts. I was the same when Herbert died – you know, my dear dear husband." And she pressed a delicate handkerchief to her eyes. "But here she is…" She smiled at the newcomer. "Sit down, my dear. This is Mr. Holmes and his friend Dr. Watson. You will recall how they helped out when… well, you know…"

Mrs. Forrester clearly did not like to call a spade a spade.

The young woman nodded and sat herself down, no answering smile gracing her lips. As Mrs. Forrester had implied, Miss Willis was a person entirely without charm or attraction of any sort. Flat of figure, her colourless hair was pulled back in a tight bun, and she wore thick spectacles, surely too heavy for her thin face. Her black dress was so plain it might have suited a missionary. Indeed, a silver crucifix hung around her neck.

Her employer then explained the business and showed her the letter.

"How very strange," the girl said, in low tones, peering at it. "I cannot think…" She looked up at us, "unless… unless Mr. Alexander took some sheets before he left."

Arthur Alexander, the disgraced steward.

"Of course," said Mrs. Forrester. "It has to be Arthur. He was very bitter against yourself, you know, Mr. Holmes, and it would be quite in his character to play a trick upon you."

It was rather more than that, I thought, but let it pass.

"Perhaps," Holmes replied. "But surely Alexander left for South Africa. Did you yourself not provide him with a ticket to do so?"

"That is true," said Mrs. Forrester. "Well, in that case, I am sure I do not know…"

"We did not see him onto the ship," the companion cut in with some asperity. "He may not have gone at all. I am sure he didn't wish to, and only agreed because the alternative was Newgate Prison."

She regarded us with some defiance. Could she still have feelings for the fellow despite his villainy? Surely not, since, as Mrs. Forrester had informed us at the time, she had been as much a victim, in her own way, as the lady herself, having lent the man from her own meagre savings. All the same, if he had spoken soft words to her, the sort that a plain girl such as herself might never have heard before nor since, then maybe she forgave him on her own account.

"You are right, my dear," Mrs. Forrester was saying, "he may not have gone at all. Oh dear." And in her distress she took another piece of gingerbread, while Miss Sarah Willis sat rigid on her chair, hands neatly folded in her lap on top of her mourning dress.

It seemed to me that the case against the steward was convincing. He would have borne a bitter grudge against Holmes and myself, a bitterness that might easily have turned to an obsessive desire for revenge. Of course, there were questions remaining: How had the young man managed the change of swords, for instance? Had he obtained casual work at the Egyptian Hall? Was he the person spotted on stage by Mrs. Hudson? Had he disguised himself with a black beard, to bribe Veronique into picking out Holmes or myself from the audience? The answer to all these seemed to be in the affirmative. Oh, Holmes might deride my powers of deduction, and yet I felt this time I found my way to the bottom of the matter without any help from him.

An even more pressing consideration suddenly struck me. Alexander's murderous attempt against Holmes and myself had failed. It was of paramount importance, then, to lay hands on the scoundrel before he realised that he had killed the wrong man and came looking for us.

Holmes meanwhile was lost in thought. Suddenly he jumped up.

"Well Mrs. Forrester, Miss Willis, thank you for your time. Watson, we must be off."

Mrs. Forrester looked surprised. "But Mr. Holmes, you have hardly tasted the gingerbread."

"Indeed, we have," he replied. In fact, I had consumed my portion, but Holmes had not, the confection merely crumbled by his nervous fingers over his plate. "Our compliments to your most excellent cook."

Indeed, I thought – and yet Mrs. Hudson's gingerbread is most definitely superior.

"Well," Holmes said as we made our way back from Camberwell, "what did you make of that? Most enlightening was it not?"

"Indeed, "I replied. "It all points to the steward."

"You think so, do you?"

I looked askance at him, but he was merely smiling to himself, seemingly absorbed by the view from the window of the train.

We were not long back in Baker Street, considering what we had discovered – at least, Holmes was sunk into an armchair smoking his infernal pipe, while I tried to see what might be wrong with my theory and finding nothing – when the doorbell rang. Soon afterwards Mrs. Hudson showed Lestrade up to our rooms. He came in rubbing his hands and smiling broadly.

"It seems the case is solved," he said. "I thought you would like to know that we shall have no need of your skills on this occasion, Mr. Holmes."

"I am glad to hear it," my friend said. "But pray explain."

"The Frenchie and his girl have run off. A clear indication of their guilt, wouldn't you say?"

"Hmm," Holmes replied. "And you have them in custody, I suppose."

"Well no. Not yet. But we have it on good authority that they are making for Dover. No doubt to take the ferry back to France. The Kentish police have been alerted and are looking out for them at this very moment."

"I am afraid, then," said Holmes, "that your jubilation is somewhat premature, Lestrade. Of course, I don't know the source of your information, but I should be more inclined to congratulate you if the fugitives were captured, and had confessed. No, I fear there is a long way to go yet, my friend."

Lestrade looked momentarily abashed, but soon recovered. "You are merely envious, Mr. Holmes, that you haven't been able to solve the crime yourself."

"On the contrary," Holmes stated, to my surprise as much as to that of the policeman, "I rather think that I have. And yet there are certain points that I need to clarify before I am absolutely certain."

"Well, well," Lestrade replied. "We shall see. I expect to hear back from my officers in a short while and will certainly keep you up to date on our investigation."

"I suppose," I said, after Lestrade had left us, "that you meant that you were hot on the track of this Alexander fellow."

Perhaps Holmes had not heard me, for he picked up his violin and started scraping a few chords and arpeggios, my hint to leave him well alone.

Over the next few days, I had to spend some time at Barts Hospital. It was in truth quite a relief, after the excitement of the last while, to be in that humdrum world, attending to the sick, dressing wounds, and performing the occasional amputation, although I admit I was somewhat wary going about my business, and eyed askance any new patient if they happened to be a young man of attractive appearance. I had seen Arthur Alexander only once and could not recall his features with any precision. I certainly did not wish to find myself alone with him in case he persisted with his evil plan.

This peaceful time could not last, of course, and on the fourth morning I was hurried from my boiled eggs by Holmes insisting that I accompany him to Scotland Yard.

"I have received word from Lestrade," he said. "They have him."

"Alexander?" I asked.

"No, no, no," said with some impatience. "Fantôme. Lestrade has kindly invited us to sit in on his interrogation."

"You think he will confess after all?" I asked.

"To what?"

"Well, murder of course."

Holmes merely emitted a cynical harrumph and, in his excitement to be off, nearly pulled my arm from its socket.

The magician looked much reduced when we saw him again, in his shabby civilian suit, far from the splendours of the Egyptian Hall. The interview room provided a dismal enough setting, its bare plastered walls stained with rust – or possibly blood – its rough table and hard chairs set on a cold stone floor, the dim and flickering gaslight casting a mournful pall over all.

Holmes sat back in the shadows, the tips of his fingers joined, his head thrown back. Was he bored? Lost in thought? Was he listening intently? I am afraid even now I am often unable to read his mood. Lestrade meanwhile was leaning forward on the table, facing the Frenchman in a threatening manner and bombarding him with questions.

The little man, at first downcast and even sullen, soon reared up and protested his innocence with Gallic fervour. How could he, Fantôme, have committed such a frightful deed? Why? He did not even know this Monsieur Jameson. His hands flew about as he spoke, and I could tell that Lestrade was not one iota impressed with such a foreign carry-on. Yet as I thought back to my arrival on the tragic scene, I remembered how shocked Fantôme clearly had been at what he had done. I did not believe then that he had knowingly run the victim through with his sword, and I did not think so now. Lestrade, however, was not convinced.

"If that is the case," he asked, "why did you run away? Didn't you think that it would indicate your guilt?"

"But Monsieur," Fantôme pleaded, "I cannot deny that it was I who struck the blow that killed the man – in front of an audience of a thousand. I am guilty of the deed. So then Veronique…"

At the mention of this name, Holmes leant forward.

"Veronique said I must fly or you will send me to the guillotine."

"Not in this country, we don't," said Lestrade. "Not in England. Nothing so barbaric."

No, we hang you by the neck until you are dead, I thought.

"And where," Holmes cut in, "is the fair Veronique now, might I ask?"

Fantôme shrugged. "I do not know."

"She didn't flee with you."

"No."

"Ha!" And he leaned back again, Lestrade throwing him an inquiring look to which he didn't respond.

"But please to remember," Fantôme continued, "that it was Veronique who handed me the sword."

"You'll have to do better than to blame an innocent young mamselle." Lestrade was clearly intent on pursuing his quarry to the end.

"But she is not – ?" Fantôme started.

"What?"

Holmes rose to his feet. "She is no mademoiselle. She is not French. Isn't that the case?"

"*Oui.* Not French. No. Just for the act she pretends."

"Not French!" I exclaimed. "Well, I must say, she sounded French."

"Oh, zat is easy, *non*, to make ze pretence." Holmes had resorted to a terrible fake accent and Lestrade and I regarded him aghast. "But you see, my friends – " (back to the Queen's English, thank goodness.) " – when I spoke to her in what I took to be her native tongue, it was immediately clear to me that she understood not a single word."

"It is true," Fantôme replied. "She is *une Anglaise.*"

"And one I think that hasn't been in your employ long?"

"That is also true, monsieur. In fact, she offered her services to me just before the opening night. You see, my assistant, Claudette, had gone missing. At such a time! *Parbleu!*" He shook his head. "Claudette who has been with me for three years… Who is like a daughter to me! Gone! I am at the end of my wits. Suddenly, this Veronique arrives and tells me that she has experience as an actress. To be quite honest, messieurs, I took her on like that." He clicked his fingers. "I could not complain. She was not Claudette, but she worked well enough until that night so terrible."

"And then she impressed on you the need to run away. Good, good," said Holmes, rubbing his hands together.

"We must find this Veronique, or whatever her name is, as soon as possible," I said.

"I am afraid we have no leads on her," Lestrade remarked. "She seems to have disappeared into thin air, like in one of this fellow's trickeries." And he chuckled at his own joke.

"Not at all," Holmes said. "I know exactly where she is. If you're willing to accompany me, gentlemen, I think we can clear the matter up tonight."

Lestrade's jaw dropped. "And Fantôme?" he asked.

"Oh, you can let him go," Holmes said. "He has nothing at all to do with it."

"Well now, Mr. Holmes," came the gruff reply, "I don't think I can do that just yet. No, indeed. This fellow seems like a slippery customer to me, with his fancy French ways. I will keep him under lock and key for the time being, until you can prove his innocence to me beyond the shadow of a doubt."

Holmes gave a resigned nod. One cannot argue with Scotland Yard.

I had no notion at first where we were bound and Holmes was giving nothing away. He is something of a showman after all, producing solutions to crimes in the way a magician will pull a rabbit from a seemingly empty top hat. So it was only when we reached Blackfriars Station that I realised we must be returning to Camberwell. Indeed, the three of us – Holmes, Lestrade, and myself – soon boarded a train heading thither.

"I don't suppose," Lestrade said, "that you would care to enlighten us, Mr. Holmes."

My friend simply put on that rather annoying enigmatical smile of his and leaned back, extending his long legs across the carriage floor and placing the tips of his fingers together.

"All in good time, Lestrade," he replied. "All in good time."

It seemed that he was in a philosophical frame of mind and the subject of his musings on this occasion was the female of the species.

"Women, you know," he started, speaking out of what he no doubt considered his great experience of the sex, "are creatures utterly under the sway of their passions. They aren't rational the way men are. They let themselves be carried away by their emotions, and if those emotions are strong enough, then let mankind beware."

"Hmm," commented Lestrade, no doubt thinking of Mrs. Lestrade, a formidable woman, as I had heard say, who ruled her husband with a rod of iron, capable of reducing, in the domestic sphere, the lion of Scotland Yard to a meek lamb.

For my part, I could not keep silent. "I know of several women," I said, "who are quite as rational as men, and on the other hand men who are quite irrational and likely to be carried away by their passions."

"Of course you do. And yet I would argue that those are men who have given in to the feminine element in their psyche. Have you not read Briquet's treatise on the subject of hysteria?"

I had not, though I was aware of the fellow's arguments. Nevertheless, I stuck to my own opinions which were not gleaned from volumes of psychology, but from my own observations of the world.

The train soon pulled into Camberwell Station and again we walked the short distance to Addington Square. A pall of fog hung over all and the air, even in this usually pleasant suburb, was rank with the smell of coal dust. By the time we reached the Forrester house, our coats and hats were beaded over with droplets of moisture, as was my moustache, no doubt. I almost felt inclined, on reaching the refuge of Mrs. Forrester's hallway, to shake myself like a dog.

The lady of the house was again expecting us, so I presumed that Holmes had sent her another telegram. The presence of Lestrade, however, seemed to discommode her not a little – a frequent reaction, as I have noticed in the past, of even the most innocent when face to face with a Scotland Yard detective. Yet was she indeed innocent? Perhaps it was she after all who had sent us the letter to lure us to the theatre. For what reason I could not imagine, however, and despite Holmes's earlier disquisitions on the shortcomings of the female sex, I could hardly believe that the eminently respectable Mrs. Forrester had any great passions to hide, except perhaps in regard to gingerbread and other such tasty comestibles.

We had been shown again into her parlour, but this time Holmes insisted that we did not want any tea, answering for both Lestrade and myself, who might not have refused so readily. Clearly this was to be no social visit.

"I do not know what more I can tell you, Mr. Holmes," Mrs. Forrester said.

"It isn't you that I wish to question," he replied. "I wonder, could you send for Miss Willis."

This young person entered soon after, displaying a scowl of reluctance on her thin face that certainly added nothing to her attractions.

"Ah, Miss Willis," said Holmes genially. "So good of you to join us."

She nodded coldly.

"I might have expected," he went on, "that you would have returned to the theatre by now, to your acting career."

Mrs. Forrester gave a start of astonishment (as did Lestrade and I), but the governess regarded Holmes coldly.

"I have no idea what you're talking about," she said, fingering her crucifix.

"Come, come, Veronique – or whatever your real name is. That will not do, you know. Did you really think, no matter how skilled the disguise, that you could fool Sherlock Holmes? Did you not think that, despite those absurd spectacles, I would not recognise the same eyes that had wept so convincingly on the stage of the Egyptian Hall?"

Veronique! It could not be. I rather agreed with the young woman that my friend had, for once, to be mistaken. This skinny scarecrow, with her faded hair and pinched mouth, the fair and seductive magician's assistant? No, never!

"You are indeed a skilful actress," he continued, "able to switch characters in an instant."

"Mr. Holmes, I have to protest," Mrs. Forrester interrupted. "I really think you must be barking up the wrong tree, this time. Miss Willis came to me with the very best of references. Indeed, perhaps they glowed a little too brightly with respect to the poor girl, but Mrs. Standish is a woman of the highest integrity and wouldn't have sold me a pup."

"Can I remind you, Mrs. Forrester," Holmes said, kindly enough, "that references can be forged as much as letters containing tickets for the Egyptian Hall. I suspect that you did not contact Mrs. Standish personally to check if she had indeed had Sarah Willis in her employ. Although – " And here he looked across at the still expressionless girl. " – she is so devious in her ways that there might indeed be a Sarah Willis who once worked for Mrs. Standish as a governess – only, I can assure you, madam, this person is not she."

"Oh dear," said Mrs. Forrester, "oh dear, dear, dear."

At last, Lestrade, who had been sitting silently all along, broke into the conversation.

"What's all this about a letter with tickets?" Having received the explanation, he went on. "But why should Veronique hatch such an elaborate plan in the first place?" He shook his head. "I agree with Mrs. Forrester. This time you're being a bit too clever by half, Mr. Holmes. I still think the Frenchie is behind it."

"Remember, Lestrade," Holmes replied, "what we were discussing on the train?" (Hardly a discussion, I thought.) "The overpowering and all-consuming passions of womankind. I have uncovered evidence that Willis was in league with Alexander." He turned to Mrs. Forrester. "They entered your employ at about the same time, is that not so?" She thought for a moment, then nodded. "Their intent was to rob you, a trusting widow, of all that you possessed. Lucky for you, then, that I was able to thwart their devilish plan, although I admit that, at the time, I considered Alexander to be solely responsible."

Here the young woman shifted slightly in her seat and a smirk played over her features.

"But while Willis was devoted to Alexander," Holmes continued, "he for his part felt no obligation to her. He despised her and only used her of necessity. Once her usefulness was exhausted, he wanted no more of her and happily sailed off to South Africa, abandoning her here without a second thought."

"That's a lie!" The girl was as last stung into replying. She stood up, tearing off her spectacles and casting them from her. Her eyes blazed and at last I began to see that she might indeed be Veronique. "He loved me! Yes, he did. He loved me with all his heart. It was you, Mr. Sherlock Holmes, who took him from me. You!"

The quiet and plain companion was now quite transformed into a hellcat. She looked ready to jump on Holmes and scratch his eyes out.

"So he has written to ask you to join him in the colonies, has he?" There was a cruel and sarcastic edge to Holmes's tone.

"Damn you!" The oath broke from her lips. Mrs. Forrester exclaimed in shock, while Holmes smiled.

"I thought not."

I should have abhorred his harsh treatment of the girl more, had I not then recalled the fate of poor Mr. Hartley Jameson.

"The wrong man died, then," I said to her, "from your point of view, that is."

"Yes. It should have been him." And she pointed a quivering finger at Holmes. "Why was it not him? It is true," she went on, frowning, "I did not know exactly what he looked like except that he was tall and lean and often in the company of another man." Turning back to me. "You, Dr. Watson . . . So when I peered through the curtains before the performance started and saw you talking together like old friends, how could I not think that this is was the celebrated Sherlock Holmes? I rejoiced at the sight. You had fallen into my trap, and now I was to be revenged on the men who had ruined my life and taken from me the only person I have ever loved. I handed Fantôme a real sword – yes, I did, knowing its deadly power. But it is you two responsible for the death of Mr. Jameson, not me. Not me!"

She sank on the chair, exhausted and overcome. It was impossible for me to feel pity for her. Yet I detected an expression of sorrowful sympathy on the wide face of her employer.

Lestrade needed no more evidence – had she not confessed? – and sent forthwith to the local police station for a vehicle to convey the girl to the prison at Holloway.

There is little more to relate. Fantôme was cleared of all involvement in the crime. We had feared for a while for the fate of Claudette, his previous assistant, but as it turned out that she had simply been bribed by Willis to disappear. If the magician considered her like a daughter, Claudette apparently did not reciprocate with any sense of filial duty. Her loyalty was easily bought for a few sovereigns. Nevertheless, the magician forgave her and she returned to his employ where, for all I know, she has remained ever since.

Veronique – or Willis – was found guilty of the murder by proxy of Mr. Hartley Jameson, and still languishes in Holloway Prison.

The young man who had wandered onto the stage during the fatal performance, as observed so closely by Mrs. Hudson, turned out to have nothing at all to do with the business, which just goes to show that one can be too observant sometimes. Just as well that

Holmes did not allow himself to be distracted by that particular detail.

As for Mrs. Forrester? Her betrayal by trusted persons in her employ did not weigh on her for very long. She wrote Holmes a letter on her by now familiar crested notepaper in a fine copperplate informing us that she had found a most suitable replacement for the wretched Willis. This person had come with the most impeccable recommendations – although, the lady added, this time she had been sure to confirm them.

"*I do not think,*" the letter concluded, "*that I shall have any trouble with my new governess, a Miss Mary Morstan, a most attractive and intelligent young woman. Perhaps you and Dr. Watson will have the pleasure of meeting her someday.*"

As indeed we did, but that is quite another story.

"*I have come to you, Mr. Holmes,*" she said, "*because you once enabled my employer, Mrs. Cecil Forrester, to unravel a little domestic complication. She was much impressed by your kindness and skill.*"

"*Mrs. Cecil Forrester,*" he repeated thoughtfully. "*I believe that I was of some slight service to her. The case, however, as I remember it, was a very simple one.*"

"*She did not think so…*"

– Mary Morstan and Sherlock Holmes
The Sign of the Four

A Simple Matter

"I say, Holmes," I remarked over breakfast, while reading the morning paper, "Lord Giles is getting married. I took him to be a confirmed bachelor."

Holmes leaned back, shaking his head. "Another good man lost," he said.

I had to laugh, even though my friend's negative view of the state of matrimony inevitably brought back memories of the blissfully happy but all too few years I spent with dearest Mary, long since deceased, alas. If Holmes was insensitive to my pain, I had to forgive him, and even pity him – he who had never experienced the joy of loving a fine woman and being loved by her. Nevertheless, I could not let his words go unchallenged.

"Can you not accept," I asked, "that for many men, a good marriage is a rock on which to build a fulfilled life? Many eminent men, you know, owe a great deal to their wives."

"My dear Watson," he replied, "what a rosy-tinted world you live in. Who can say how much more those men might have achieved without the distractions of family, the increasing demands of their frivolous, small-minded wives, of their noisy brood of children? No, I will not have it. Mark my words, Lord Giles is lost."

Despite the forcefulness of his assertion, I noticed that he was at the same time absentmindedly fingering the gold sovereign that hung from his watch chain. The same sovereign which had been gifted to him so many years before by a woman. By *the* woman, in fact – Irene Adler, for whom I suspected, although never dared to say as much, he still carried a torch. In the photograph that Holmes begged from the King of Bohemia in payment for services rendered, and which he still kept by him, intelligence shines from her eyes.

But what eyes they are! What formidable beauty! No, despite the fact that "admiration" was how he termed his feelings for one of the few people who had ever got the better of him, methinks the gentleman doth protest a little too much.

Meanwhile, Holmes was opening a letter which had arrived by the morning post. He started to peruse it, a smile curling his lips. "Well now, Watson," he said, "we are to have a visitor shortly. Mr. Fairdale Hobbs. A most interesting young man, and the very exemplar of the merits of the single life."

"You know him, then?"

"Indeed. Our paths first crossed at the British Museum reading room. We wished to consult the very same volume on Nubian written texts – an astonishing coincidence, since the book had not previously been requested, so the librarian informed us, since 1863."

"He is a scholar, then."

"Precisely. Your perspicacity never fails to amaze me."

I decided to ignore the jibe.

"So which of you got the book?" I asked.

"The young man was polite enough to allow me to study it first. He was in any case working his way through several other tomes on Coptic and Egyptian writing systems."

"Fascinating," I commented drily.

"You would be surprised, Watson, at how truly engrossing the subject is. But I wonder why Mr. Hobbs wishes to visit me here. I hardly think it is to discuss hieroglyphs."

We did not have to wait long to discover the matter. It was less than half-an-hour later that Mrs. Hudson showed the young man up to our rooms. Mr. Fairdale Hobbs was over average height by a considerable few inches and, perhaps because of that, or perhaps because he spent much of his time hunched over books, he had developed something of a stoop. It was evident that he paid scant attention to his dress, for his suit was ill-fitting and worn at the cuffs, his shoes scuffed, and his hat, which he had removed from his head, decidedly rusty. Prematurely balding, poorly shaved, and wearing thick horn-rimmed spectacles, the unfortunate young man, a perfect specimen of an absent-minded professor, was far from presenting a handsome aspect. Despite this, there was something pleasing about him, a gentleness of mien, even though at that moment some strong emotion was clearly agitating him.

Holmes introduced me as a friend and colleague whose discretion was as impeccable as his own.

"Now, Mr. Hobbs," he went on, "pray tell what has brought you to me. Your letter provides little information, although your erratic orthography indicates a state of distracted anxiety."

"Oh Mr. Holmes," the young man said, in a voice that was deep and low, "You are correct. I am consumed with anxiety. It's quite dreadful to think what has happened to the poor girl. I am quite beside myself. Whatever can be done?"

He paced up and down, wringing his hands.

"Please be seated and try to collect yourself," Holmes said, with more patience than usual when faced with such a haphazard report. "You must explain more cogently, you know. Who is this 'she' of whom you speak, and what have you to do with her?"

Hobbs threw himself into the nearest chair which happened to have today's newspaper lying on it. I started to protest, but Holmes gave a warning shake of his head.

"Sally," Hobbs exclaimed, covering his eyes. "Dearest Sally."

"Sally who?"

The young man frowned. "I... I... It will come to me. If I ever knew it. I am not sure, you know, that I did."

I saw Holmes's patience starting to ebb away.

"Very well," he said. "Just tell me how you came to meet this Sally."

"Oh, at the Museum," Hobbs replied. "Just like yourself, Mr. Holmes."

"I see. In the Reading Room, was it? Over Nubian manuscripts?"

Hobbs actually emitted a hysterical little chuckle.

"Goodness no. I cannot imagine Sally there. Not at all. No, we met in the Egyptian Hall. She was contemplating the mummies, do you see." His expression softened at the memory. "She asked me about them."

"She spoke first, then?"

"I think maybe she took me for one of the attendants. I myself, of course, would never presume to address a young lady not of my acquaintance under such circumstances. Indeed, I had not noticed her to be there at all, because, you see, I was engrossed in trying to decipher a piece of papyrus in one of the cases. It seemed to be some sort of a love song, dating, I believe, from the Eighteenth Dynasty. Most absorbing, do you see."

He looked up at us, blinking.

"Yes, yes. Pray proceed."

"Well, I quite jumped when she spoke to me. She even had to repeat herself… You know, Mr. Holmes, she was so open and so truly interested in the subject. And yet at the same time so innocent. She could not believe that actual bodies lay swathed within the painted wooden cases, and thought that I was teasing her. I started to explain that they were indeed coffins, which quite shocked her. 'Are they not rotten and stinking?' she asked." He shook his head, smiling. "Ah, the sweet innocence of her."

"Yes, yes," said Holmes, a trifle testily.

"So then of course, I had to describe to her the way the ancients embalmed the bodies after removing the inner organs, placing a hook in the nose to draw out the brains, and so on."

"I am sure she enjoyed that," I said, intending irony.

"Indeed she did, Dr. Watson. She was enthralled, and even invited me to join her in the tea room, so that I could expatiate further on the subject."

"Rather forward of the young person, did you not think?" Holmes remarked.

"My fault for the way I am describing it, Mr. Holmes. If only you had been there, you would have seen how sweetly open she was."

"Hmm," said Holmes, frowning.

They had, it seemed, passed a pleasant half-hour over tea.

"She took such great delight in cream cakes," said Hobbs. "I cannot eat cream, you know, for it upsets my digestion, but it was quite charming to watch her consume so many. Not greedily, but so very delicately."

"At your expense?"

"Well of course. I could not ask a young lady to pay."

They had made an arrangement to meet again at the museum for the following day.

"She told me – or at least I thought she told me – that she worked in a florist shop nearby, and was free every lunchtime. She loved, she said, to spend that hour in the museum. Except that most of the time she was ignorant of that which she was viewing, and it was then that she expressed the wish to have me with her every day, because I explained things so well." A dreamy look crossed his face, and he sighed.

"And then?" Holmes tone, I noticed was getting sharper with each reminiscence from the young gentleman.

"So that was how we started meeting regularly. At first we spoke of ancient Egypt, progressing to the Sumerians and ancient Babylonians, you know. Then, one day... Oh, Mr. Holmes, one day when I was explaining cuneiform script to her, she took my hand in one of hers and placed the dear little forefinger of the other on my lips. 'Enough,' she whispered. 'Enough, Fairdale.' And then she told me that she had fallen in love with me. Me of all men. I could not believe it."

Neither, by his expression, could Holmes.

"I know it was forward of her, but after all, Mr. Holmes, she is a simple, unlettered little thing. When I asked whatever could she see in me – for I am not a vain man and am fully aware that my physical attributes are not generally pleasing to the opposite sex – she told me that she loved me for my mind and my great kindness. And then... oh I tremble to recount it, she placed my hand on her beating heart."

"In the British Museum?" I asked. "Surely not."

"Oh, did I not say? No, we were taking a stroll around Russell Square at the time – under the trees, you know. How very pretty she looked in the sunlight with her little fair curls."

Holmes leant back, groaning.

"These details are all very touching, Mr. Hobbs, but perhaps you can summarise quickly, and tell me what has befallen Sally."

"You also think something has happened to her, then, Mr. Holmes?"

"Well, my dear fellow, I presumed as much, since your first words on entering here were to that effect, were they not?"

"Yes, indeed. You are right. I am sorry... It was the note, do you see."

"The note? What note?"

"Somehow Sally and I had come to an understanding. I'm not quite sure how it happened, it was all so quick, and in truth, she is not the wife I should ever have envisaged for myself, and yet, when I think about it, how could I do better than a sweet-hearted young woman who would look after me? That's what she said: That I needed looking after, and that she would be the one to do it. I was deeply, deeply moved by her sweet words. We went and bought a ring for her finger right then. A little sapphire, to match her lovely blue eyes."

Holmes cleared his throat meaningfully.

"Yes, yes, the point. Well then for several days after that, I waited for her in our usual place by the Elgin marbles, but she didn't come. I waited and waited, and eventually started to worry. What if she were sick? What if – Oh God! – she had regretted her words of love and was even now avoiding me? I had to know, yet I did not have an address for her."

"You did not even know her last name," I pointed out.

"Well… I am sure I have that written down somewhere. Anyway, since she had told me that she worked in a florist's shop, I visited all such premises in the surrounds of the museum, but to no avail. No Sally to be found in any of them." He shook his head in puzzlement. "I must have got it wrong, do you see. It mustn't have been a florist after all."

"What then?"

"Well, on the fourth day, I found not my Sally but another young woman altogether standing by the statuary. She was in a state of extreme agitation. To my amazement, she asked if I were Mr. Fairdale Hobbs, and when I said that I was, she exclaimed 'Thank God!' and told me that she was Sally's sister, Iris."

"Excuse me, had you heard tell of this young person before?" asked Holmes.

"No, but then Sally and I did not talk of such things."

Only of mummification, cuneiform scripts, and love, I thought.

"Iris thrust a letter into my hand, saying it had been pushed through her letter-box that very morning. Mr. Holmes, Dr. Watson, what a terrible thing! What a terrible terrible thing!"

"Mr. Hobbs," Holmes said, "you must explain."

"I can do better. Here is the same missive."

He thrust it at Holmes who, having read it, passed it to me.

It was indeed shocking, as well as ill-written in a blocky print, with many atrocious spelling mistakes:

To hum it may kinsirn

If ye wish to see yor Sal agin put a hunnerd ginnys in a cloth bag an leeve it unner the big Dook statue in Russell Square at midnite on Wedsday . . . or she wil be soled to wite slavvers. Ye ave bin wornd.

A frend

"Extraordinary!" said Holmes. "Quite extraordinary."

"Indeed. I can tell you now, gentlemen, I near fainted away at the news. My darling Sally in the hands of white slavers! It was unimaginable. Iris had to support me to a nearby bench, where I tried to recover my wits. I was trembling all over, do you see. The horror of it!" His voice was breaking with emotion, though he managed to continue his narrative after a moment collecting himself. "Iris herself, a simple shop girl like her sister, was, of course, in no position to pay such a large ransom and, both their parents being dead, there was no hope to be had there. Iris told me how Sally had confided our love to her, and now expressed the hope that I could help out in some way. Oh, Mr. Holmes, Dr. Watson, the poor girl was distraught. As, indeed, was I, like I said. Trembling uncontrollably. I thought I would faint away... Even now..."

"I trust you told her that you have no intention of paying this preposterous sum, Mr. Hobbs."

"My goodness, sir, I have paid it already. Of course I have. I would pay anything to save my dear Sally from such a terrible fate. How can you possibly think otherwise?"

Holmes was about to reply, but the young man continued. "I have some savings, you know, so was able to raise the money. I took it to the appointed place – with some difficulty since the Square was closed and I had to clamber over the railings, fearing at every moment to be apprehended by a member of the constabulary. But I succeeded and left it as instructed. Oh dear, oh dear..."

The poor boy collapsed in floods of tears, his whole long body shaking. Even Holmes was taken aback.

"A glass of brandy there, Watson," he said. "Quick, man!"

"No, no, no," cried Hobbs. "I never touch spirituous liqueur. Perhaps a glass of water."

I poured some from a carafe on the side table and gave it into his trembling hand.

Holmes shook his head.

"Oh foolish, foolish young man. Let me guess. Sally has not returned."

"She has not."

"I am afraid she played you for a fool, Mr. Hobbs. So now, I suppose, you wish to employ me to recover your money."

Mr. Hobbs reared up.

"Not at all! What is money, after all, compared to love? To love, Mr. Holmes!" He gave us a challenging look and, though his words were naïve, the sincerity of them could not but inspire respect. In me at least. "No, I wish you to find Sally, to save her. I can pay you for your time, of course. Whatever it takes…" He struck an attitude. "Though it ruin me."

Holmes paused. He joined his hands together at the fingertips and pressed these to his lips, considering.

"Mr. Holmes," the young man cried. "You are my only hope. I know it looks to you as if Sally has made a fool of me, and yet if you met her, if you met her sister who is quite beside herself, I am sure you would change your mind. Pray speak to Iris, at least. She is to meet me as usual at twelve noon by the Marbles."

"Well," the reply came at last, "there are certainly elements of your story that intrigue. Let us go with you then to meet this sister, this Iris. After that, perhaps I will take on the case. However, Mr. Hobbs, if I do so, you must be prepared for the worst."

65

"That Sally has already been ruined? That I can accept, you know, for it would not be her fault, poor innocent child that she is. I would take her to my heart all the more willingly."

Was there no end to his heroics? Clearly this was a young man who had lived too exclusively in the company of books, the sort that deal in idealistic romance and self-sacrifice.

"No," Holmes said, "I rather meant that you must be prepared to accept that she is a cold-hearted fraud who has hoodwinked you, Mr. Fairdale Hobbs. That she has extorted money from you under false pretences, taking advantage of your generous and credulous nature."

"Ha!" the young man replied, "all I can say to that, Mr. Sherlock Holmes, is that you yourself must be prepared for once to be wrong."

Holmes simply smiled and shook his head.

The three of us thereupon took a cab to the British Museum, Holmes muttering to me that he would not be surprised if this Iris failed to turn up also, being most probably in league with the sister.

"They have his money. What more do they want?"

My friend, however, was mistaken in this respect, at least, for the girl was indeed standing as arranged by Lord Elgin's fine marble statuary, waiting for Hobbs. She looked most surprised to see that he was accompanied by myself and Holmes, but was not one whit dismayed, even though she recognised the name of the great detective. Indeed, she seemed pleased that we were there – a point, I felt, very much in her favour.

In fact, the impression the sister gave was altogether a positive one, being a neat little body, with smooth dark hair, lively brown eyes, and an olive complexion, as if she hailed from a place under the Mediterranean sun rather than from beneath the habitual foggy skies of London. A charming dimple appeared in one cheek when she smiled, which sadly, just then, was infrequently.

"Any news," she cried to our companion.

He shook his head. "None on your side either then, I assume?" he replied.

"None."

She tried then unsuccessfully to control her emotions, weeping into an already sodden handkerchief, and curious heads started turning our way. Holmes, ever discomforted by the sight of a woman in distress, suggested that we might repair to a quieter place to discuss the matter.

"I should like, indeed," he said, "to see where exactly you left the bag of money, Mr. Hobbs. In Russell Square, I believe it was."

We walked through the museum to the rear exit, hurrying past ancient Greeks and Romans frozen in heroic poses, past Grecian urns such as those described by the poet Keats, past the colossal carved column drum from the Temple of Artemis at Ephesus, not pausing for a moment to study these wonders. To have such a resource on my doorstep and not avail of it reflects sadly upon me. When dear Mary was alive, indeed, we were in the habit of frequenting museums and galleries quite regularly. I vowed, as we rushed past, that in her memory I must soon return at some more propitious time.

By now we had reached that doorway at the back of the building which provides egress into the Square. This is, for those not acquainted with the space, a large and pleasant garden park extending northwards to Woburn Place, with winding gravel paths between green lawns and flower beds, gracefully planted trees providing shade to those resting on the benches beneath them. The statue we sought soon came into view, for it was most imposing. Carved into the plinth were words identifying the subject as the fifth Duke of Bedford, Francis Russell, who gave the Square his name. The Duke was depicted with his hand on a plough and surrounded by sheep for some reason, I presumed symbolically, for he was assuredly neither a farm labourer nor a shepherd.

"This is where you left the money?" asked Holmes.

"Yes, indeed. Tucked up there in behind that cherub."

It was lucky, I thought, that Hobbs was so tall, for a man or woman of normal stature would have difficulty reaching so far. Holmes, tall himself, examined the place.

"Long gone, of course," he said, but continued to search the spot with some interest.

"Why here, I wonder?"

"This is where we plighted our troth," Hobbs replied with emotion.

"But how were the kidnappers to know that?"

The young man paused for thought.

"They must have forced the information out of Sally. Oh God! The poor poor girl!"

"Calm yourself, man."

"Can you help us, Mr. Holmes?" Iris asked. She looked so appealing, those brown eyes overflowing with tears, that I was sure even he was not cold-hearted enough to refuse.

"I confess there are elements here that pique my interest," the detective replied. "Yes, indeed, I have little doubt that I will find your Sally for you, and quite soon."

They were both full of gratitude, of course, though I wondered quite how Holmes intended to achieve this conjuring trick.

"Watson," he said, waving his hand in a vague direction, "perhaps you and Mr. Hobbs could comb the surrounding area in case the villains have left something incriminating behind them."

I glanced in some surprise at my friend. It was unusual indeed for him to assign such a search to myself or others, since he would ever doubt our ability to perform the task with sufficient assiduity. However, I understood that perhaps he wished to speak to Iris in private, asking questions the answers to which he might not wish Hobbs to hear. I duly led the young man out of earshot. We poked, fruitlessly enough among the bushes, finding only an empty bottle of porter, the remains of a pot of jellied eels, pages torn from an

Illustrated London News, and a lady's glove which Iris said did not belong to Sally.

I asked nothing further of my companion regarding the matter until the two of us were back in Baker Street.

"Well?" I said finally. "Did the charming little sister turn your head after all?"

"Such a remark, Watson," Holmes replied, sighing, "is beneath even you."

"What then? It seems a hopeless case."

"Not at all. It is a very simple matter."

"I can see no clues as to the thing at all. Can you really think Sally is in the hands of white slavers?"

Holmes laughed.

"Look at the note again, Watson. Does it not already tell you much about the case?"

He handed it to me and I studied it closely, even turning it over, without discovering any more from it than I had already observed.

"The paper is rough, the writer barely literate. It speaks of low-life villains to me. More than that..." I shook my head.

"I am afraid you have been led, Watson, as the author intended, up the garden path. The spelling of most of the words, it is true, is comically bad. And yet '*Russell Square*' and '*statue*', not the simplest of words, are correctly inscribed."

"Whoever penned it might have copied the name..."

"That will not do, Watson. No, the writer is as literate as you or me. He, or perhaps she, wanted there to be no confusion as to where the money should be left, which is why those particular words are correctly spelt. That raises another point: The note was delivered to Iris, and yet it is clearly intended for Mr. Hobbs, a man with more money than sense, a man who knows Russell Square intimately. He lodges nearby, you know. In Great Orme Street, I believe he told us.

Moreover, he has a sentimental attachment to the place and especially to the site of the statue where the money was to be left."

I could not argue.

"So poor Hobbs is indeed the victim of a trick," I said. "But I can hardly believe Iris to be involved. Unless she is an actress akin to Sarah Bernhardt, her worries for her sister seem genuine."

"Ah, that is another issue. You say 'sister', and yet when I quizzed her on the subject it turns out that they are not blood relations. Sally's mother married Iris's father, the two parents having been widowed and both girls already fully grown. I suspected as much when Hobbs described his *amour* as fair-haired with blue eyes, while Iris, as you saw, is dark with brown eyes. It can happen that way in families, of course – my brother Mycroft and myself, for example, being of very different physical types – but it is quite unusual."

"Yes, I see."

"You very astutely removed Hobbs from the scene," Holmes continued, "no doubt realising that I had questions for the girl. They were related to her sister's supposed work in a florist's shop. You will remember that Hobbs told us how he'd searched all around the museum for such places, but none knew of a Sally."

I nodded.

"Iris was able to inform me that it is *she* who works in such an establishment, while her stepsister is a dancer in vaudeville. Indeed, Iris, a sensible enough girl, had already visited the theatre, only to learn that Sally had not put in an appearance there for several days."

"But why would Sally lie about her place of work?"

"I suspect the theatre in question has a dubious reputation. Indeed, Iris suggested as much without actually saying it. It is in Soho, you see."

A notorious part of the city, and yet not far-removed from the Museum.

"So Sally might have become mixed up with a crowd of low-lifes after all. Perhaps they indeed, knowing she had become close to a man of means, abducted her."

"Perhaps," he replied, and chuckled. "We'll see."

The following day Holmes rather surprised me by expressing his intention of visiting the British Museum to pursue his interrupted studies of Nubian texts.

"What of the case?" I asked.

"Oh, that can wait," came the terse response.

Since I had pressing medical duties to attend to, our paths hardly crossed again for several days. Either he or I were gone in the early hours, and either he or I returned late.

It was not until the fifth day that we both returned for supper, he rubbing his hands and looking extremely pleased with himself.

"Your studies are going well," I remarked.

"Yes, indeed. It is all most satisfactory." He paused. "I know you have been busy, Watson, but are you by any chance free tomorrow?"

"I can be," I replied. "I think Colonel Lennox's gout might await my ministrations for a day or two more."

"Capital."

He did not explain further, but chuckled frequently to himself over the course of the evening, the which I admit I found somewhat irritating. However, Mrs. Hudson's fine mutton stew, and the warming glass of grog afterwards, put me in a better humour, and I was soon dozing off over my copy of *The Lancet*, able to ignore the occasional guffaw from the direction of the other armchair.

It was over breakfast the next morning, after I had presumed to ask at last what was the pressing matter that required my attendance that day, that Holmes made his astounding announcement.

"I wish you to come and meet my betrothed," he said.

71

I dropped the teaspoon I was using to decapitate my boiled egg.

"Good heavens, Holmes!" I replied, "You jest of course."

"Not a bit. I have taken to heart your words praising the condition of matrimony and have decided at last to take that giant leap into the darkness myself."

The wicked smile with which he accompanied his words led me to conclude that he was indeed joking, but that there was an ulterior motive at issue. I decided to play along.

"I shall be delighted to meet the lady," I replied solemnly.

"Excellent. I have invited our new friends Mr. Hobbs and Miss Iris Goodhart to join us as well. But now I must go and get ready. One must look one's best, you know, when one is courting."

And with a wink and another chuckle, he was off, only to return some time later, looking not at all dandified, but rather down at heel and dusty, and inexplicably sporting thick glasses.

"Not a word, Watson," he said, observing my face. "Let us go."

So it was that, just before noon, we arrived once more at the British Museum, where we found the other two awaiting us out front, wondering expressions on their faces.

"Watson," said Holmes, "not to terrify the young person with strangers, I plan to go on ahead. Please be so good as to accompany our friends here to the Hotel Russell and wait there for perhaps fifteen minutes."

"You will join us?"

"No. Then I should like you to take a turn in the Square, making for the statue we all know so well."

It was very strange, but I recognised that keen gaze. The chase was on and I began to have an inkling of the matter.

The Hotel Russell, only very recently completed, is a truly splendid building at the side of the Square. Its massive façade is of terracotta stone with arches and turrets and sculptures around its many scores of windows. Both my companions were in awe, and indeed young Iris looked almost afraid to enter through its imposing door, held open for us as it was by a uniformed attendant with a superior expression on his face. Inside we found it even more impressive, a lobby of Carrera marble of all hues, from pillars in charcoal grey to golden walls and a paler ceiling, while the floor sported in mosaics a flaming sun encircled by the signs of the zodiac, the whole place illuminated by a huge chandelier dripping crystal.

"Oh my!" exclaimed Iris.

We found a bench upholstered in gold velvet and sat upon it to wait out the fifteen minutes. My companions at first displayed a degree of unease, especially whenever one of the attendants passed by, fearing no doubt we would be asked what business we had there. When no such occurred, Hobbs at least relaxed somewhat and started to quiz me.

"I am most puzzled, Dr. Watson, as to what is afoot. Has Mr. Holmes given up the search for my Sally entirely because his own heart has been captured by another? It is hardly professional, sir."

"It is heartless," Iris said, "if it is so. Why should we be witness to his great happiness, when we remain bereft?"

"I do not think you need worry," I replied. "Mr. Holmes is a consummate professional. If he has invited you here, it is assuredly not to crow over you, but for a deeper purpose. However, he has not yet confided the matter to me, so I cannot enlighten you further."

The fifteen minutes being up, we left the hotel, I pressing a coin into the doorman's hand, since it seemed expected. He curled his lips in acknowledgement, and I wondered, as I have done many times before, at the arrogance of lackeys of all sorts who seem to feel they are in some way superior to those they are supposed to serve. That is by the way, however – simply an observation by one whom Holmes considers utterly lacking in that ability.

We crossed the busy thoroughfare and entered the Gardens. Approaching the statue, we soon perceived ahead of us a couple walking sedately arm-in-arm, one of whom I recognised as my friend and colleague Sherlock Holmes. The other appeared from the back to be a very young lady. She was wearing a jade green dress and jacket, her fair curls surmounted by a bonnet embellished with ribbons. At that moment, the pair turned around.

Hobbs started in astonishment.

"It cannot be!" he said.

"Good heavens!" exclaimed Iris.

"Here are my friends now," Holmes remarked jovially to his partner, "come to congratulate us on our happiness."

The young person had turned pale. She tried to wriggle away from Holmes, but he had her held tight.

"Don't be shy, my dear Sally," he urged.

"Bert!" she called out.

A youth suddenly appeared from behind the statue, stocky and with the damaged face of a pugilist. He made to attack Holmes, but the latter, being well versed in martial arts himself, and nimbler on his feet to boot, was soon able to overpower his slower, heavier opponent, and held him fast in an armlock. Meanwhile the girl had tried to run off, but I was able to catch her easily enough, for no woman can run fast in a long skirt, no matter how she tries.

Hobbs had slumped down on to the plinth of the statue, Iris beside him trying to comfort him, for his eyes were at last opened to the duplicity of the woman he loved.

"I almost wish," he muttered, "that you had not found her, Mr. Holmes, so that I could guard within my heart the pure unsullied image of her."

"Now, now, Hobbs," Holmes said. "Pull yourself together, man. You are not the first and will not be the last to succumb to a woman's wiles."

"How could you be so cruel, Sally?" cried Iris.

Her stepsister made no reply.

"Easily enough for one-hundred guineas, I suppose," replied Holmes. "As well as whatever sum they hoped to squeeze from me, or any other poor dupe who fell for her pretty face and flattering words."

Sally was trying to look remorseful. "I really cared for you, Fairdale," she murmured, blinking long lashes over those truly very blue eyes. "But you know, life is hard – and anyway Bert made me."

The young man in question then let forth a torrent of words not suitable for recording here, though the tenor was that it was all her idea.

"She said there was lots of boobs like Hobbsy here in that there museum," he concluded. "Noses in books, never had a woman. We could make a killing. That's what she said."

Hobbs looked as if he could make a killing right then, and Bert would be the victim.

"Right," said Holmes. "That's that then. A simple enough matter after all, as I informed you, Watson… So now let's get this pair of masterminds off to the nearest police station."

"That would be Holborn, I think," I said.

Hobbs, however, demurred. He was for letting them go – or rather, for letting Sally go.

"I should not like to see her in prison," he said.

"We can give you back your money, Fairdale," Sally said, with hope in her voice. "Well, most of it. Can't we, Bert?"

The young man gave a sullen nod.

"And your ring, too," she continued, reaching into her reticule and pulling out a pawnbroker's note.

Hobbs gazed at it aghast. Then shook his head.

"Mr. Hobbs," said Holmes, "I would most strongly advise against letting them loose. What would stop them from carrying on their wicked game?"

"Oh no, Sherrinford, I wouldn't do that. I have learnt my lesson," said Sally, weeping little pearly tears. "I have, Sherrinford, really I have."

"Sherrinford?" I asked.

"The name she knows me by," Holmes replied.

Back in Baker Street, over an evil-smelling pipe, Holmes said, "You know, Watson, I am utterly disgusted that, after all my efforts, Hobbs insisted on letting the miscreants go free."

"Let us hope," I said, "that you have put enough fear into them that they will not try that trick on anyone else."

"Of course," he went on, "it was obvious to me from the start that it was all a crude ruse to fleece the unwitting. White slavers, indeed. Only someone quite unworldly would be taken in by that."

"Scholars, you mean?"

"Precisely. Certain scholars, at least." He took a satisfied puff.

"But how did you know where to find her?"

"Oh, that was simplicity itself. I reckoned that if they succeeded once, so easily, they would try again. I took to hanging around various galleries of the museum, gazing intently at the various exhibits. My disguise as a single-minded scholar was rather convincing, was it not?" He smiled and I nodded, as I was expected to do. "It was in the Horology Department that I was eventually approached by a young woman who resembled the description of Sally given to me by Hobbs."

"Horology?" I asked.

"Yes. Luckily I am well versed in the workings of astrolabes, orreries, marine chronometers, and the like, and was able to explain them convincingly to Sally – though even if I had spoken nonsense, I doubt she would have been any the wiser. She is a foolish girl, though admittedly with a kind of animal charm. But you know, Watson, she did not even bother to change her name."

"Was she not fearful of bumping into Hobbs?"

"She knew, I think, that he would not wander from his established path, his interests being extremely narrow and confined to the ancient Middle East. It was a risk, of course, but I think the game diverted her as much as the result."

"The game?"

"Fixing to catch some poor impressionable dope in her net. 'Sherrinford' fitted the bill perfectly, a man obsessed with clocks and watches, and, though shabby, with a wallet packed with bankers' notes. I can concur with Hobbs that the young lady certainly enjoys her cream teas."

"And Bert?"

"I thought there had to be a confederate somewhere. You were right, Watson, about that at least. A low-life from the theatre – a doorman, I believe. Someone who comes heavy on anyone trying to take unpaid liberties with the young dancers. Something of a bonehead, too, whom she charmed into assisting her scheme."

"He composed the note, then?"

"More likely she did, for I doubt that Bert can even write his own name. You must have noticed how the letter was written, the words printed out, presumably to disguise her feminine hand."

"So she was the instigator, then?"

"Most certainly. Unluckily for her, Hobbs knew to call upon me, or she might have got away with it." He inhaled deeply on his pipe. "So Watson, can you now bring yourself to admit that I am right?"

"You are often right," I replied. "But in what specifically?"

I do not think he liked that "often", for he sniffed. "Always right" would be more to his taste.

"You must surely agree with me at last, as to the bad influence on men of all classes of the female sex. Mr. Fairdale Hobbs is much better off without his Sally."

That was indubitably so. However, some three months later we received an invitation to attend the nuptials of Mr. Fairdale Hobbs and Miss Iris Goodhart.

"That is capital news!" I said. "She is a lovely girl – sensible, as you yourself allowed. I am sure she will make him happy."

But Holmes only sighed, and cast the card from him.

"Another good man lost," he said.

"You arranged an affair for a lodger of mine last year," she said. *"Mr. Fairdale Hobbs."*

"Ah, yes – a simple matter."

"But he would never cease talking of it – your kindness, sir, and the way in which you brought light into the darkness. I remembered his words when I was in doubt and darkness myself.

– Mrs. Warren and Sherlock Holmes
"The Adventure of the Red Circle"

The Strange Case
of the Pale Boy

It was a peaceful Sunday afternoon in October – the calm, as it turned out, before a rather rough storm. I was engaged in reading a treatise on diseases of the digestive tract, while Holmes was bubbling up something unspeakable with his Bunsen burner. Outside, an autumn sunshine was slanting temptingly through Baker Street, and I had almost made up my mind to put aside my dry reading matter and go and stretch my legs in the nearby Regent's Park – though I rather despaired of dragging Holmes away from his experiments to accompany me, so intensely focussed was he on what he was cooking, and so satisfied the little grunts of "Yes, Yes," that escaped his lips from time to time.

Still, it is pleasant to amble on one's own sometimes, to enjoy in solitude the rusting of the leaves, to shuffle through heaps of the fallen ones, to pick up the odd conker and hold it in one's palm, relishing its silky surface and marvelling that from such small beginnings mighty trees can grow. To recall as well the conker fights of childhood: having amassed a prize collection, you would pierce each nut with a nail to make a hole right through the middle. You would temper them on the range to harden. Then string would be threaded through the holes, and knotted, to turn the nuts into formidable weapons. Whose conker would shatter first on impact with another's? Billy Brown's, Harry Meredith's, or my own? Whose would triumph? Ah, those happy, innocent, far-off days.

Such sentimental musings were, however, not to be shared with my friend, especially when he was in his most rational, scientific frame of mind. Lacking an eye for the beauties of nature, Holmes would probably start lecturing me on decay and death, and quite ruin my contemplative mood. No, far better to go off alone.

With this in mind, I closed the treatise I was reading, set it aside, and was about to stand up, when the most head-splitting racket was heard from below. Someone was pounding on our front door, and with far more force than required.

"For once," said Holmes, raising his head, "I hope that it's one of Mrs. Hudson's acquaintances and not a caller for us, Watson, for I have reached a delicate point in my analysis, and the female below would seem likely, if she makes her way up here, to prove seriously disruptive."

"You think it a woman then?" I asked, ready to hear Holmes's explanation.

"I do not think it, Watson. I know it. No gentleman would lose control of himself to such a degree on a Sunday afternoon to disturb the peace in such a manner, however pressing the matter. No, the caller is a woman, and like most of her ilk, one lacking all self-restraint."

I was amused, as usual, by Holmes's almost blanket dismissal of the fair sex, yet had to admit that in the present circumstances he was correct in his surmise. Not half-a-minute passed before we heard the thud of steps hurrying up the stairs, and then the door burst open, the lady not even pausing to knock. Sighing, Holmes turned off his burner and composed himself to learn what was afoot.

The apparition before us was large and purple, her hat waving ostrich feathers in her agitation. Behind her, Mrs. Hudson was clearly trying to apologise for not having prevented the visitor's trespass on our privacy, yet I doubt that anyone could have done so, given the whirlwind force that now faced us.

She looked wildly from one of us to the other.

"Which of you is Shylock?" she asked, peering with the screwed-up eyes of the short-sighted.

Holmes's lips curled in a slight smile. "Neither one," he said. "If you're looking for a money-lender, madam, there is an establishment displaying three golden balls just around the corner."

The Shakespearean reference eluded her.

"Moneylender?" she snapped. "No, I want Shylock the detective."

"If you mean Mr. *Sherlock* Holmes," my friend said coldly, "then I am he. But you know, madam, I am not used to receiving visitors in such a haphazard manner."

The air seemed then to empty from the woman, and, like a deflating balloon, she sank, uninvited, into one of the chairs.

"Mr. Shylock," she said, "I must apologise, but I am at my wit's end. I am indeed."

Mrs. Evadne Carpenter, for such, as we soon discovered, was the lady's name, was aged about fifty, with a large flushed face over several chins, and gingery curls that were possibly not quite the colour that nature had given her. Her purple attire was untidy and not in the very best of taste, being rather too fussy, flashy, and girlish for a person of her age and girth. However, the silk was of a good quality and the jewels that adorned her thick neck, wrists, and fingers were of gold, diamonds, and amethyst. I trusted Holmes would have been content with my conclusion that this was a person of considerable means.

A strange odour rose from her, the heat of her recent exertions being overlaid, not completely successfully, with a powerful perfume. Holmes later identified it to me as "Jicky", a recent concoction imported from France and by no means cheap.

(*"You may know, Watson,"* as he explained later, after the lady had left us, *"that I have made a particular study of perfumes, and in this case was able to isolate the different elements. Beneath the lavender and bergamot, it was simple to detect orris and vetiver, patchouli, vanilla, amber, and musk. And to my certain knowledge, Jicky is the only scent with this particular combination."*

"I'll take your word for it," I replied, musing that Mrs. Carpenter must have poured half-a-bottle of the stuff over herself, for the scent lingered on for the remainder of the afternoon.)

However, the above is a digression from the matter in hand. Following her arrival, we waited for our visitor to catch her breath and explain the reason for her abrupt presence, the rapid rise and fall of her stupendous bosom gradually subsiding as she calmed down.

"It's my pale boy, Mr. Shylock," she said at last. "He has disappeared."

If Holmes thought this a strange way to describe a missing child, he did not show it.

"Your pale boy... Hmm. When did you last see him, Mrs. Carpenter?"

"Last night. I'm sure it must have been last night. I'm sure I'd have noticed if he wasn't there... I would, wouldn't I?" She looked at us questioningly, as if we knew the answer. "But then this morning – well, he was gone. Utterly gone."

She sniffed and pressed a lacy handkerchief to her eyes.

"I see. And you have no idea where he might be?"

"If I did, sir, I would hardly be here."

"Quite so. And yet you might have some inkling. Is he with another relation perhaps?"

"Most unlikely. Which relation do you mean?"

As if we could know such a thing.

"So what is the little lad's name?" Holmes continued.

"His name?" Strangely, the query seemed to throw her. "If you must know his name, it is Edward de Vere Herbert."

"Not Carpenter, then."

"Certainly not."

So the child must not be hers. A grandchild, perhaps.

"And his age?"

"You do ask the queerest questions, Mr. Shylock... Let me think." She put her hand to her brow in a gesture of cogitation.

"About one-hundred-and-twenty years old, I suppose," she said finally.

Holmes took a deep breath. I could see how hard he was trying to be patient. "What exactly are we talking about here, Mrs. Carpenter?"

"I have told you already, sir." She too was finding patience hard to maintain, her face turning a deeper shade of crimson. "My Pale Boy. My Gainsborough."

"Ah, a painting!"

"Of course. What else? Everyone has heard of my Pale Boy, surely."

"Alas, no." Holmes spread his hands in a gesture of appeasement. "Not this poor detective anyway. So let us start again, Mrs. Carpenter. You have lost a painting by Thomas Gainsborough of a pale boy."

"That's what I said already." She paused, and then added. "Edward was my great-uncle. He died young. Though I never met him, the portrait has considerable sentimental value for me, as you can imagine."

Not to mention, I thought, the monetary value of it as a Gainsborough, an artist become very popular in recent times.

"Has anything else disappeared, apart from the painting?"

She regarded him blankly.

"Like what?"

"Other valuables. Other art objects, for instance."

"I have no idea. I only care about my pale boy." Again she pressed the lacy handkerchief to her eyes. "I came running here as soon as I was able, Mr. Shylock. My good friend and neighbour, Lady Wittering, you know, speaks most highly of you."

She looked around then and, catching sight of the disorderly piles of papers, the jumble of scientific equipment on the dining table, the Persian slipper containing tobacco by the fireplace, gave a dismissive sniff as if she found herself sorely disappointed in the recommendation.

"Ah yes," Holmes replied, "I was lucky enough to do her Ladyship some slight service."

He was being unaccountably modest. He had with considerable difficulty traced her Ladyship's prodigal daughter, who had eloped to the Continent with a lowly clerk. When the girl found herself with child, the bounder had abandoned her, taking with him all her money and jewellery, and leaving her destitute. Holmes had effected a most touching reconciliation between mother, daughter, and newly born granddaughter, little Penelope. As for the bounder, he was even now working a passage to the colonies, where he might as well rot for the rest of his life.

"So what do you think, Mr. Shylock? Can you find my Pale Boy?"

Holmes raised his eyebrows in thought. He made a steeple with the fingers of both hands and tipped it to his lips.

"Not the sort of case I usually take on," he said. "But Dr. Watson was about to take a walk anyway." (How did he know that? I hadn't even risen from my chair before Mrs. Carpenter arrived). "Since you live but a stone's throw from here, madam, we might as well take the air. Especially since," he gestured at the Bunsen burner and the cooling test tubes, "I shall have to restart the experiment from scratch anyway."

Mrs. Carpenter appeared unrepentant at the disturbance she had caused. Moreover, she showed herself not one jot amazed that Holmes knew where she lived, so he was unable for once to dazzle with his deductive powers. Perhaps she thought that everyone knew it, just as she imagined that everyone knew of her "Pale Boy". I supposed, having given the matter some consideration myself, that since she had said she was a neighbour to Lady Wittering, and since we knew where that personage lived, then all made sense. Holmes later explained that since Mrs. Carpenter had clearly hurried all the way from her abode on foot – arriving dishevelled and over-heated as she had been – then clearly it was at no very great distance, and not worth the bother of a cab.

"Did you happen to notice any signs of a break-in, Mrs. Carpenter?" Holmes asked, as we walked up Baker Street. I could tell by his tone that he did not hold out much hope of a useful reply.

"I didn't waste time looking around," she replied, puffing somewhat at the exertion of walking and talking at the same time.

"No, I suppose not," he said drily. "But can you think of any explanation apart from robbery why your painting should have disappeared into thin air? Or who might have taken it?"

"You are the detective, Mr. Shylock. Is that not your job to do the thinking? Is that not what I shall be paying you for?'

"Indeed it is, madam," he said, raising his eyebrows at me.

We had now arrived at York Terrace. This short street, adjacent to the Regent's Park and set with elegant white stucco dwellings, all of a piece, in the style of John Nash. However, Mrs. Carpenter rushed past these and turned down a side street, where the mansions, though still handsome, were far less imposing. Indeed, the one to which she led us was quite noticeably run-down compared to its neighbours. The plaster was flaking and the ionic columns on either side of the arched doorway were chipped. When we entered the spacious hallway, we found it gloomy, the murk attributable to the fact that the glass in the windows over and beside the door was thick with London soot.

The hallway featured a coffered ceiling inset with rather dusty stuccoed rosettes as well as a pair of tables, set facing each other over the grubby tiled floor. These tables, while evidently Chippendale, were piled higgledy-piggledy with papers and letters and gloves and what appeared to be the remains of some biscuits. We did not linger there, however, but followed our impatient guide up the staircase, she panting from the climb. Having earlier observed the way she gasped on our short walk, and adding in her high colour,

I swiftly diagnosed a heart condition, possibly combined with asthma. I could not help noticing, moreover, that the stair carpet itself was in dire need of a cleaning, and reckoned that the dust thereon would not be at all salutary for one in her state of health.

Mrs. Carpenter swept past a slatternly servant, who was evidently attempting to speak to her, and entered a large and stuffy room.

"Here," she said, gesturing histrionically to the wall over a marble fireplace, "Here is where my poor Pale Boy was hanging."

Somewhat taken aback, we looked where she pointed. Mrs. Carpenter looked too.

"But he's back!" she exclaimed. "He's come back, the darling."

For hanging over the fireplace in the spot indicated by Mrs. Carpenter's outstretched arm was indeed a fine painting of a thin boy, his skin almost translucent, dressed in pale blue silk, standing in a garden by a broken column and gazing sadly out at us, as if aware that his time on this earth would soon be cut short. I recognised the refined style of Gainsborough as well as I, an amateur, am able, though I mused that my dear late Mary would have been much more recognisant of the brush of the master.

"Consumptive, would you say, Watson?" remarked Holmes, ever the realist. "It is not a wonder that he died young."

Mrs. Carpenter, meanwhile, was still staring at the painting as if unable to believe her eyes.

"I fear, Evadne," said a hushed voice behind us, "that you have brought the police here on a wild goose chase."

Holmes and I turned to find a gentleman of slight build and wearing an embroidered smoking jacket, standing in the doorway smiling. Neither I, nor it seemed Holmes – even with his preternaturally sharp hearing – had been aware of his approach, perhaps because the man was wearing black velvet slippers.

"Look, Reggie!" exclaimed Mrs. Carpenter. "Edward's back!"

"Perhaps it would be more proper, my dear, to say that he never went away." The man moved forward, still smiling at us, revealing small teeth set apart from each other, like those of a young child. "You were in such a hurry to dash off, fearing the worst as usual, that you failed to enquire of the servants."

"But I did. I particularly asked Cissy."

"Oh, Cissy," he replied. "What does that silly goose know? You should have asked Monks, who, you know well, is on top of everything that occurs in this house."

"You know I don't like to ask Monks," the lady replied. "The man can be so short with me. Rude even. He really doesn't know his place, Reggie... Well, I've told you before how I feel about that. But he is your man and you like him. Anyway," she continued, "I assumed that Cissy asked Monks on my behalf."

"If she had done so, my dear, she would have discovered that Monks removed the painting on my orders, to have it measured."

During this exchange, Holmes and I looked from one of the parties to the other, more than somewhat perplexed.

The man turned back to us.

"Apologies for discommoding you, gentleman. I know you bobbies have more important things to do than go chasing after paintings that haven't been stolen."

"You mistake us, sir, "Holmes replied. "We are not from the police."

Mrs. Carpenter laughed. "I should think not, Reggie. This is Mr. Shylock and Mr... *erm*"

"Dr. Watson," put in Holmes. I was rather surprised that he didn't correct his own misnomer. Presumably, as ever, he had his reasons.

"I see." The man raised questioning eyebrows and frowned.

"Acquaintances of Lady Wittering," added Holmes.

"Ah, dear Lady Wittering!" Suddenly the man was all smiles again. He stepped towards us, little feet padding over the parquet like a cat's, to shake our hands.

"My dear wife is terribly remiss, I fear. And since she won't, let me introduce myself: Reginald Carpenter."

Although from the previous exchange between the two it was clear enough that they were close, I was still surprised. I had taken him maybe for her son, for, though prematurely bald, he was considerably younger than she.

"My second husband," Mrs. Carpenter explained. "Dearest Reggie. Such a support," adding a trifle sharply, "most of the time."

We were prevailed on to stay for refreshments. Surprise must have been the order of the day with me, for I assumed that Holmes, put out by the unnecessary break to his routine, would be in a hurry to get back to his test tubes. Not a bit of it. He wandered up to the painting and gazed at it as if he were quite the connoisseur of fine arts.

"Of course," said Mr. Carpenter, joining him, "it could do with a cleaning. And a new frame."

"What's wrong with the frame?" his wife asked. "It's the original."

"Quite so," came the reply. "That's the problem. Hardly *à la mode*, my dear Evadne. Hardly Pre-Raphaelite. Hardly Art Nouveau."

"Neither is the painting, Reggie... In future, dear, please do not touch my things without first referring to me."

He shrugged and gave us a contrite smile. "Just when I was planning to give my dear girl a delightful surprise. Ah well."

"What surprise?" Mrs. Carpenter simpered. "You are a sweet impetuous boy, Reggie." She tapped him on the nose. "And very very naughty."

Opportunely, to spare our blushes as witnesses to the couple's intimacy, the tea then arrived. It was served in a fine, if cracked, service of bone china, decorated all over in pink roses and edged with gold, and brought in by the same slatternly girl we had observed before, presumably the Cissy previously mentioned. I caught her giving a sidelong look at Reginald Carpenter. Was I wrong, but did he shake his head ever so slightly back at her, as if to give sort of a warning?

Conversation was strained. What, after all, did any of us have to say to the others? While Mrs. Carpenter burbled on, her husband gave us searching looks, clearly trying to figure out exactly why we were there, and breaking in, when the lady paused for breath, with probing questions. It was noticeable to me that Holmes parried them, for reasons of his own, repeating that we were merely acquaintances of Lady Wittering – letting it be thought, I suppose, that Mrs. Carpenter had run to her friend's in her panic and had met us there.

"Dear Cecilia," said Carpenter, as if he were on intimate terms with her Ladyship, which, knowing the dowager as I did, I doubted very much. "Quite my wife's confidante."

He turned to me, smiling as if finally he had it. "You are her Ladyship's doctor, then, sir?"

I was about to deny any such thing, when I felt Holmes give me a slight kick on the shins.

"I have indeed been honoured from time to time, to be of service to Lady Wittering," I said, inclining my head slightly. It was no lie, after all, given our previous involvement with her.

As for Mrs. Carpenter, she was far too distracted to explain fully, and the matter was left at that.

Following more apologies from Carpenter for wasting our time. Holmes and I set off for home, shown out of the gloomy hallway by an equally gloomy manservant, tall and cadaverous. This apparently was the all-knowing Monks.

"Well, Watson," said Holmes as we made our around Regent's Park, "whatever did you make of all that?"

"I hardly know," I replied. "The lady is certainly very scatter-brained."

"You think so? In some ways, maybe. But I am far more interested in Mr. Reginald."

"An unusual mate for her, certainly."

"On the contrary, Watson," he replied, "Carpenter is exactly the sort of insinuating young man a gullible woman like her would fall for. Yes, indeed. Sweet flattery has found him a soft berth."

"Goodness, do you think so? Is that why you don't want him to know who you are?"

He chuckled. "'Shylock' is a nice pseudonym, is it not? I shall remember it."

"I was astonished," I continued, "that despite the fact that Mrs. Carpenter is evidently a rich woman, the house showed so many signs of neglect."

"Indeed. Yet you may have noticed that the lady is very short-sighted and too vain, perhaps, to wear the spectacles that might correct her vision. It is possible that she fails to notice the state of things around her. Or else is simply too 'scatter-brained', as you described her."

"Well, anyway," I continued. "I suppose that is the last we have heard of Mrs. Evadne Carpenter."

Holmes just smiled. "Perhaps," he said.

I do not know what prescience he possessed, but it was less than a month later that we were called upon again, not by Mrs. Carpenter herself, but by her friend and our erstwhile client, Lady Cecelia Wittering. She requested us to call upon her on a matter that was troubling her greatly.

Again we made our way towards the Regent's Park and into York Terrace, this time to a house in an immaculate state of preservation, a vast contrast to the one we had previously visited in the area. Lady Wittering herself might also be said to be in a state of immaculate preservation. A personage in her late seventies, she presented the same upright and elegant bearing that I had observed at our previous encounters. Her stern yet handsome features were framed in a neat coiffure of snow-white hair, her skin was unblemished, and the wrinkles she possessed added to the sense of a strong character. Dressed simply enough in watered grey silk, she welcomed us into her parlour where again we took tea, this time served in delicate bone-china cups, none of which were cracked.

"It is so good of you to come," she said in that low, musical voice of hers that always reminded me of the sound of a *violoncello*. "I know how busy you both are," she added, graciously including me in her remarks.

She waved the maid away, pouring out the tea herself and offering us a plate of thin cinnamon biscuits. "I understand," she continued, "that you recently met my neighbour, Evadne Carpenter."

Holmes nodded. "Yes, indeed. She wished to consult me over a missing painting that wasn't missing at all."

"Typical of her. So feather-brained," Lady Wittering replied. I glanced at Holmes, but his face was inscrutable. "I am worried about her," she went on. "Very worried. You see, Mr. Holmes, Dr. Watson, it is only two years since her first husband, Alfred Garland, passed away, and barely one since she remarried this Reginald Carpenter fellow." She said the last name with considerable distaste. "Evadne, do you see, is the sort of woman who cannot seem to survive without a man at her side."

Lady Wittering, as we were aware, had managed perfectly well for the past many years without the support of a husband, her own having been tragically killed in the Crimean War.

"You have seen the house – how it has been let go to rack and ruin. Alfred must be turning in his grave, as I believe the common expression is." She sniffed. "You have seen the servants with whom the abominable Reginald replaced the existing staff. Cissy Grimes –

what an appropriate name for a maid who does no cleaning that I can see! – brought in when Evadne's beloved old housekeeper Maud was dismissed for stealing. Something I cannot credit, but Evadne let herself be convinced by her beloved spouse. As for Monks: What a sinister individual he is! Not to mention his wife."

"His wife? We met no wife."

"Mrs. Monks is the cook. She has replaced another old retainer. Reginald said that Nell Brady was getting too old. Too old! She can't be seventy yet!" She sniffed again. "He said that she didn't know how to prepare the latest dishes, whatever they are. French food, I suppose."

"Excuse me for interrupting, your Ladyship," Holmes said, "but are these merely bad feelings you have regarding the Carpenters, or has something specific happened that you wish us to know about?"

"Forgive me, Mr. Holmes, for beating about the bush, and Dr. Watson please have more biscuits. I can see that you like them."

I blushed just a little. Was my greed so transparent? But the biscuits were indeed very tasty. I helped myself to another.

"It is, of course, not simply dislike of the present members of Evadne's household that has caused me to bother you," her Ladyship continued. "There is something not right happening there. Indeed, without undue exaggeration, I have to say that I fear for my friend's safety... She is in many ways a silly woman, Mr. Holmes, but her heart is good – too good, too trusting. She is also, as you are possibly aware, extremely rich. Or she was, before that man came into her life. God only knows what inroads he has made into her fortune."

Holmes frowned. "You say you fear for her safety, Lady Wittering. That, I must say, is an extreme judgment, coming from you." He knew, as did I, that her Ladyship was not generally prone to hyperbole.

"The last time I met her," she explained, " – it must be a week or more ago – she did not look at all well and complained of stomach pains. She sat where you are sitting, Dr. Watson, and, although she usually has a perhaps rather too-healthy appetite, she put aside her biscuit and only took the merest sip of tea. She had lost weight, but not in a good way, you know. The flesh was hanging off her." Lady Wittering frowned. "Not having heard any more from her, I called in yesterday to see if she was feeling better. I was not admitted, Mr. Holmes, Monks informing me quite brusquely that Mrs. Carpenter was unwell and unable to receive visitors. The man actually blocked the door against me, and when I asked if his mistress was seeing a doctor, he more or less told me to mind my own business. I was shocked at his manners – or lack of them. If he were a servant of mine, he would be peremptorily shown the door for addressing visitors in those words and in that tone of voice."

Holmes shook his head sympathetically. "Just so."

"And then, as I was leaving, I happened to look up and saw Reginald Carpenter at a window, staring down at me, a nasty smirk on his face. And then he just turned away… I am very worried. I am sure there are dark doings afoot."

"You would like us to investigate?"

She inclined her head in the affirmative. "If you would be so good. At the very least to put my mind at rest."

"I wonder," I said at that point, "if I might pay a visit, in my capacity as a medical man."

"I doubt you would be admitted, Dr. Watson," she replied, "any more than I was, but you could certainly try. That is a splendid idea."

I smiled at this accolade and looked across at Holmes, but he had risen from his chair and was gazing down on York Terrace. After a moment, he smiled and turned back to us.

"The abominable Monks has just this minute passed, presumably on some errand. This would, I think, be a most opportune time to call. He cannot block the entrance if he is not there."

There was no arguing at all with that, and he and I hastened to set off before Monks should return.

We had to hammer on the door for a considerable time before it was opened. Young Cissy Grimes stood there looking sulky. She was a buxom girl and clearly not averse to flaunting her attributes, since the neckline of her dress was rather lower than modesty demanded. In fact, she seemed in the process of doing up some buttons.

"We have called to see Mr. Carpenter," Holmes said, putting a long leg over the threshold.

The girl regarded him in alarm. "I don't know about that," she said.

"Of course you don't, Cissy," Holmes continued. "Our business is with your master." He smiled and pressed a coin into the girl's hand.

"Well," she said, mollified, "I 'spect it's all right…"

Holmes pushed past her and started up the stairs, the girl hurrying after him and me at the rear.

"We can wait in here," he said, and entered the room where the Pale Boy was hanging. Heavy curtains were blocking much of the light, and I wondered they had not yet been drawn back.

"Right you be," Cissy replied, evidently still doubtful. She scurried off to fetch her master.

"So far so good," Holmes said.

"But why did you say our business was with Mr. Carpenter and not with his wife?" I asked.

"That approach had not availed Lady Wittering, so I hardly think it would have worked for us. In any case, I am curious to see the gentleman again. But look, Watson, what do you make of the painting?"

"It is rather hard to see in this light," I said. "Of course, it has been reframed, and certainly not, I think, to its advantage."

Holmes was staring at it, rather fixedly. "Hmm," he said.

"You don't approve?" Once again Reginald Carpenter had entered silently, as on cat's paws, wearing those same velvet slippers, though his feet, I noticed, were otherwise bare of socks. In November! I thought.

"The other frame was surely more handsome," Holmes said.

Carpenter smiled broadly. "I am sorry to hear you think that. Personally I consider the thing vastly improved. The modern taste, you know, Mr. Shylock, dislikes too much gilt and ornament."

Modern taste, however, as I privately thought, also dislikes crude and rough and ready, which the new setting most certainly was. But Carpenter gave us his most dazzling smile.

"I had it reframed and cleaned specially – you know, as a surprise for dear Evadne."

I recalled that she had expressed forbade him from doing any such thing, and wondered.

"How is your wife?" Holmes asked, knowing full well the answer to that. "Well, I trust."

"No, alas, she is most poorly," the man replied. "Very weak, Mr. Shylock. I'm afraid she will not be able to join us today. But she will be pleased to hear of your visit and interest."

"Oh, I am sorry to hear about Mrs. Carpenter," said Holmes. "Watson here, as you know, is a doctor. Perhaps he could take a look at her."

"So kind of you," came the reply, "but she is under our own doctor. Getting the very best of care, don't you know."

"A second opinion can surely do no harm," I said.

"Quite. But she passed a restless night, do you see, and has just taken a draught to help her sleep. I should prefer not to disturb her." He paused again and studied our faces. "Although on the other hand, it seems churlish to refuse your kind offer, gentlemen. Perhaps you would like to call by tomorrow or the day after, Doctor."

"I could most certainly do that," I replied. "Tomorrow, indeed. What time would suit you?"

He gave it a moment's thought, smiling at me. "The middle of the morning perhaps. If it doesn't conflict with your own engagements."

"Not at all. Tomorrow morning suits me perfectly well. At around eleven o'clock?"

"Excellent," he smiled again, and rubbed his little hands together. "*À demain*, as the French say. But, gentlemen, you still haven't told me the reason for your visit. Cissy told me you had business here? May I ask what is it?"

"Well," said Holmes, and I wondered what excuse he would come up with. "Given what you have just told us, I fear it is not an appropriate time to mention it."

He paused.

Carpenter waited, then said, "Appropriate or not, now that you are here, gentlemen, you might as well tell me."

"Very well," Holmes replied. "It is this. On our last visit, do you see, I quite fell in love with your Pale Boy, and was wondering if there was any chance at all that it is for sale."

Carpenter's eyes flickered in the dim light.

"I know that your wife is very fond of it," Holmes continued, "and seeing that she's unwell, it would of course not be a good time to bother her with the business. However," and he smiled back at the man, "everything has a price, as they say, and there is no harm in asking. Is there?"

There was a long pause. Carpenter seemed to be debating something with himself.

"I should prefer the old frame, however," Holmes said. "In fact, that would be a condition of sale."

"I see. Yes… Yes… I suppose that could be arranged… Well, what kind of sum are we talking about?"

Holmes laughed, "I won't say 'money is no object', sir. However, I imagine we could come to an arrangement most agreeable to everyone."

For some reason, Reginald Carpenter looked quite dejected at this, presumably because he knew that his wife would never agree to part with the picture.

"I… we… will have to think about it. Needless to say, I shall have to discuss it with dear Evadne, when she is feeling better. You understand, I am sure, Mr. Shylock."

"Of course, of course," Holmes replied. "So… unless you have changed your mind about Dr. Watson here visiting your wife today, we will take our leave and see you tomorrow."

"Splendid!" The man looked positively jovial suddenly, perhaps at the prospect of our departure. "Until tomorrow then."

He showed us out himself, padding down the stairs in his slippers, possibly worried that I would otherwise sprint up to the next floor to find his wife.

As we were traversing the street, we passed Monks, returning. The man gave us a blank stare, as if he had never seen us before.

"I was most surprised," I said, after he had gone, "that Carpenter agreed for us to return tomorrow."

"Indeed," Holmes replied solemnly. "There is no time to be lost."

Before he could explain this puzzling remark, we had reached Lady Wittering's mansion, and sought admission, having promised her Ladyship that we would report back on our findings. She was delighted to hear that we would be permitted to visit her friend on the morrow, Holmes omitting to express any dark forebodings to her.

We returned to Baker Street in silence. I could see that my friend was thinking hard, and I imagined he would reach for his pipe as soon as we were home, which indeed proved to be the case.

"I have to say that I'm most concerned," Holmes explained, settling into his favourite chair and going through the ritual of lighting up. "I fear we can do nothing before dark, and I only hope we won't then be too late."

"It is that bad, then?"

"Did you not see? Oh, how lacking you are in the most basic powers of observation."

Though I was used to being chided in this way by him, it still rankled me.

"What didn't I observe this time?" I asked, rather sharply.

"Did you notice anything at all about the painting?"

"That it was in a new frame."

"Patently obvious. Anything else?"

"That it seemed to have been cleaned. Perhaps a little too vigorously."

"Better. Did you notice the smell?"

"The smell?" I thought back. "Yes, a spirituous smell. From the cleaning fluid, perhaps."

"Turpentine and linseed oil?"

"Quite possibly. Yes."

"Which suggests what?"

I shook my head. What more than what I had said?

"One doesn't clean a picture with linseed oil, Watson, and turpentine has to be employed very lightly if at all for fear of damaging the work. But the smell was strong… For God's sake, man – the paint was still wet."

I remained in the dark. "The paint was *wet*? Some restoration work then?"

"You claim to be the art connoisseur, not me," Holmes went on. He seemed amused, not for the first time, at the cat-and-mouse game he was playing with me. "You yourself said the reframing was not to the picture's advantage, did you not?"

"I did. It didn't look nearly so fine as in the old frame."

"If you had looked more closely, as I did, you would have seen that it wasn't the frame that was at fault, horrid though it was. It was the picture itself. No wonder they kept the curtains drawn."

"What do you mean?"

"Up close, it was apparent that a crude copy of the Gainsborough has replaced the original."

"Good God!" I exclaimed. "Are you serious? How can that be?"

"Without firm evidence of motive, one can only speculate. Did you notice how chagrined Carpenter appeared when I suggested making a generous offer for the painting? I believe he has already sold the original, and presumably for much less than Mr. Shylock might be willing to pay."

"Mrs. Carpenter will surely recognise the deception when she recovers."

Holmes puffed on his pipe sending a plume of smoke into the air. Although I should be well used to it by now, and although I myself enjoy a pipe from time to time, I still found the pungent odour of Holmes's preferred tobacco sharp and unpleasant.

"You think she will recover, then?"

"I trust so – but Holmes, is the poor woman really that ill?"

"On the contrary. I don't believe that she is ill at all."

I gaped at him. "Not ill?"

"I think she is being poisoned. A sad, banal, and unfortunately not uncommon occurrence these days when poisons are so readily obtainable. And I'm afraid we may have hastened the final *coup* by our visit. When you arrive tomorrow to examine her, in all probability she will already be dead."

"Good heavens! We must act at once. We must call Lestrade."

"I go back to my earlier remark regarding evidence. There is none yet that would warrant the involvement of the police. Mere suspicions that a man as cunning as Carpenter will easily be able to bat aside. In any case, I imagine the lady herself wouldn't prove easy to convince. She is clearly besotted with her Reggie."

"So what is to be done?"

"Somehow or other," he said, and drew in and then exhaled a large puff of smoke, "she must be made to see the truth for herself."

The usual evil smelling fog of a winter night choked the November streets as we made our way back past York Terrace. I was surprised that we did not turn directly into the street where the Carpenters resided. Instead, Holmes gestured for me to follow him down a dark back alley. I sincerely hoped not to encounter any cutpurses there, for it seemed just the place for them to lurk.

"Why here?" I asked in a whisper.

"While you were otherwise occupied this afternoon – " (I'd had a patient to visit.) " – I returned to investigate the back entrance to the house . . . And, here it is." He pointed at a gate, set in a high wall. "See, I left a mark upon it."

A chalked stick figure, as if drawn by a child, adorned the gate.

"But what if it's locked?" I said.

"If it is, I have my little set of tools," replied Holmes. "In any case, I employed them earlier to make sure. And also to oil the hinges."

The gate swung open silently at his touch. As so often, I admired his forward planning.

"What if someone had spotted you? Monks perhaps?"

"I was disguised as a jobbing gardener, touting for work. Such a one would not try the front door." He paused and gazed through the gloom. "And, my word, this garden could certainly do with someone's services."

I could not disagree. The place was utterly overgrown, and as we pushed through towards the house where a light shone from a back room, twigs and small branches heavy with moisture brushed against us. Luckily the wet grass and leaves under our feet dulled any sound we might make.

However, we need not have worried on that account. The sight that greeted us through an uncurtained window into the kitchen of the house was one of unbridled merriment, not to say debauchery, most unbecoming and even shocking, particularly in a house of sickness. Reginald Carpenter was lounging back in a wooden chair, Cissy Grimes in a state of undress, her hair down, seated upon his lap. Beside them sat Monks, the tall manservant, together with a most ill-favoured dwarfish woman. Monks had discarded his jacket and his shirt was open, while his partner had quite evidently loosened her stays, allowing the other to take certain unseemly liberties. Horrid though it was to witness, I mused that if this was Mrs. Monks, at least the pair's intimacy was sanctioned by marriage.

The four were all laughing loudly and quaffing mugs of what had to be wine from the bottles standing on the table – excellent wine, indeed, as I could tell from the labels, presumably from the late Mr. Garland's cellar. On the table also, beside a hacked side of ham, a cheese, and a half a white loaf, stood a few bottles of gin. As we watched, Carpenter picked one up and drank directly from it, offering it then to Cissy, who was in no wise reluctant to partake.

Holmes backed off and whispered, "They are celebrating, Watson. I pray we aren't too late."

He slipped away from the kitchen to an adjacent dark window that thankfully proved simple to open with one of his tools. (I preferred not to know too much about these, but believe them to have been procured for him by Wiggins, the chief of the Baker Street Irregulars).

We slid through the window as soundlessly as we could manage and found ourselves in a kind of pantry, one door of which led into the kitchen – somewhere we did clearly not wish to go. The other opened on to a passageway that, as we traversed it, was found to lead up some steps and through another door into the hallway of the house. I felt Holmes sigh with relief. At least now we knew where we were.

Up the stairs we went, passing on the next floor the room with the forgery of the Pale Boy, and then up another flight to find Mrs. Carpenter's bedroom. It was a simple task in the end. Loud snores came from a room with its door slightly ajar.

"She still lives," Holmes whispered.

We crept into the room and saw, by the light of a gas lamp in the street outside, the bulky form of the lady lying in her tossed bed. Beside her, on a small table, stood a glass of cloudy liquid. Holmes picked it up, sniffed it, and pulled a face.

"I fear," he said in low tones, "that if Mrs. Carpenter had drunk this, it would all be up with her."

He passed it to me and I smelt a strong odour of bitter almonds.

"Cyanide!" I said. And replaced the glass on the table.

"To hasten the process, I think. Her symptoms before that suggested arsenic."

"My God!"

I stepped forward and endeavoured to rouse the lady without alarming her. Eventually she opened heavy eyes and looked up at me.

"Mrs. Carpenter," I said in soothing tone. "Do not be afraid. It's Dr. Watson, come to see how you are."

"Doctor," she replied in a cracked voice. "Is it morning already? It is very dark."

"Let me," I said, and turned on the lamp beside her bed.

"Oh," she exclaimed. "Mr. Shylock, too." She was more confused than shocked to find two men in her bedroom in the middle of the night.

Holmes stepped forward.

"Please forgive the intrusion, Mrs. Carpenter," he said. "I assure you it is a matter of the gravest urgency."

"Is it?" She tried to raise herself. "Has something terrible happened to Reggie? Oh, say it isn't true! Please say it isn't true, Mr. Shylock."

She showed such extreme signs of agitation that I shook my head in warning at Holmes.

"Calm yourself, dear lady," he replied. "Nothing has happened to Reggie."

At least not yet, I thought.

"Thank heavens for that. So what is it?"

"Well now, I am hoping that with our assistance you will feel strong enough to come downstairs. There is something you must see."

"Oh no," she exclaimed. "That is quite impossible, you know. Reggie says I'm too weak and must stay in bed."

"But it's Reggie who wants you to come down," Holmes went on. "He has a surprise for you."

This was a cruel trick indeed, and I wondered at Holmes for trying it. However, Mrs. Carpenter quite perked up at the news.

"Oh well," she said. "If it's all right with Reggie, but – " And she looked at the full glass on the bedside table, " – I haven't yet drunk my medicine. Reggie will be very cross with me if I don't drink my medicine, you know, Doctor." And she reached out for it.

"Reggie said not to bother with it tonight," I put in hastily. "He isn't sure after all that it is doing you good."

"Well, that's true. As I've told him many times, I always feel worse after taking it."

We helped her up out of bed then, and, while I fetched a robe for her to put on over her nightdress, I saw Holmes decant the contents of the glass into a vial which he then put in his pocket.

Mrs. Carpenter yet lingered. "I should brush my hair," she said. "I must look a fright."

"You look lovely," I told her. "Reggie said to hurry."

She was indeed very weak, and we almost had to carry her down the stairs, hushing her as best we could on the way. It would not do to alert those in the kitchen that we were coming.

To my dying day, I shall never forget the scene that confronted us when we burst through the door on that November evening. After a frozen moment, horror written on four guilty faces, Reginald Carpenter, flushed and dishevelled from Cissy's caresses, his shirt undone, threw the girl off and leapt to his feet, while the others remained paralysed.

"Evadne!" he exclaimed, then tried to recover himself. "Thank goodness you're better. Oh, my dear, my love."

He was bare of foot, as he moved towards her.

"How wonderful! It's a miracle!" And he made as if to embrace her.

But his wife had witnessed enough. The scales, as it says in the Bible, had fallen from her eyes. Cruel though it was to expose her to the truth in this way, the effect was finally to be kind.

"Get out!" she shouted, impressing me at least with her powers of recovery. This was a strong woman. "All of you – get out of my house!"

"You forget, my dear," Carpenter retorted sharply enough, "that I am your husband. I have rights here. Rights over yours…" She bristled at that, but he continued in oilier tones, approaching her and taking her hand. "My dear Evadne, you are upset. I don't know what these gentlemen – " (said with a snarl.) " – have told you, but it is all lies. You have taken us up wrong. We have been celebrating the fact that you seem so much better."

It was evident that she wanted to believe. Oh, how she wanted to believe.

Holmes stepped forward.

"You might try, Carpenter, to cajole your wife into swallowing your falsehoods, but what when I inform her how you have been poisoning her?"

The man laughed. "How ridiculous!" he retorted. "Poison my beloved Evadne! Light of my life. Whatever next!"

Mrs. Carpenter looked from one to the other in dismay. I drew up a chair for her to sit on, for she looked at last to be on the point of collapse.

Meanwhile, Holmes drew the vial from his pocket. "So when I send this medicine of yours to be analysed, it will be shown to be harmless. Is that right?"

Carpenter stared back at us.

"Or perhaps," holding it towards the man, "you would like to drink it yourself, to prove how harmless it is."

The villain recoiled, and Holmes pressed his advantage.

"And when I get an expert to examine the painting of the Pale Boy that hangs upstairs, it will prove not to be a crude forgery but an original Gainsborough. Is that also correct?"

"Not my Pale Boy!" cried Mrs. Carpenter. For her, this was the worst betrayal.

"Who are you really, Mr. Shylock?" The man's arrogant assurance was crumbling at last.

Holmes chuckled. "I'm afraid your wife has got my name slightly wrong. Permit me to correct her. I am Sherlock Holmes."

There was a general intake of shocked breath.

"Mr. Holmes, sir," said Monk, suddenly cowed. "As God is my judge, I know nothing about any murder and forgery. I am just the butler here."

"I don't know nothing neither," claimed Cissy Grimes. "Swear to God."

Mrs. Monks stayed silent, though her eyes looked daggers and her thin lips moved. I think perhaps she was laying a curse upon us.

Suddenly, with a howl, Carpenter made for the back door, for the garden. Holmes instantly drew a whistle from his pocket and gave several sharp blasts upon it. Then he looked at me apologetically.

"My dear chap," he said. "I did after all take the precaution of alerting Inspector Lestrade. The house is surrounded."

It was spring. We had weathered a nasty winter and survived. Since that November night, much had happened regarding the strange case of the Pale Boy. All four miscreants had been arrested, though the women soon went free, there being only hard evidence again Carpenter and Monks. But of that there was plenty, despite the "butler's" protestations of innocence. In fact, as it turned out, he was uncle to Carpenter and a true partner in crime. Over the course of the year of the marriage, the pair had systematically been stripping the lady of her wealth and assets. Monks had underworld connections, and many fine pieces had seen their way into the hands of these criminals, hardly now to be recovered. Some of them had, it is true, been replaced with crude imitations, but since Mrs. Carpenter had failed to notice anything amiss, the men had become careless. However, the attempted replacement of Gainsborough's Pale Boy was a step too far for its new owner, who proved anxious not to get further involved in the sordid business, and readily gave it up. I am pleased to say that it, at least, was soon restored to its rightful place over the mantelpiece of the withdrawing room, where I imagine it hangs to this day.

As for the attempted poisoning, Holmes was proved right. Arsenic had been administered to Mrs. Carpenter in increasing doses over a period of time and, on the night we broke in, a particularly powerful concoction of cyanide had been made up which would have killed her instantly, had we not intervened. We explained all this to Lady Wittering over tea in her delightful house.

106

"It is thanks to you, your Ladyship, and your acute observations," Holmes said, " – so unlike most others of your sex, I might add, and – " glancing at me with a slight smile, " – most of mine, too, that we were able to save Mrs. Carpenter from the evil schemes of her husband."

"It is, on the contrary, thanks to you, Mr. Holmes, for acting so swiftly and in such a dramatic way." Her Ladyship was all gratitude and forced Holmes to accept a substantial sum in recompense.

"But Mrs. Carpenter has already rewarded me," he argued.

"Nonetheless," she said, "I consider that it was I who hired you, and the labourer, as we know well from Holy Scripture, is worthy of his hire."

It was further to emerge over the course of the trial that this wasn't the first time Carpenter had perpetrated such a crime. He had been married twice before, each time to an older woman, and each of them had perished after a short illness. Exhumation of the remains found high levels of arsenic in both corpses. Carpenter was sentenced to be hanged.

On a day in late March, when the sun was dancing through new pale leaves, Holmes and I took a break from the new cases that were piling up for him to investigate and made our way to the Regent's Park to take a turn around the lake. As usual, Holmes cared little for the delights of the place, but had expressed the wish to clear his lungs of the winter fog – clear his lungs of the fug from his evil tobacco, more like, I thought, but said nothing.

"Good heavens!" A shrill voice broke through our companionable silence. "If it isn't Mr. Shylock and Dr... Dr..."

Mrs. Carpenter, for it was she – though, as she hastened to inform us, she had reverted to her former name of Garland – loomed up on the path in front of us, a vision in cherry red, the feathers on her large hat waving a greeting. She was hanging on to the arm of a most personable young man. We bowed to her and complimented her on her recovery and cheerful appearance.

"Thank you, gentleman. It's true, I am back to my old self, all thanks to you." She smiled happily. "This is Jonathan," she went on. "Jonathan Brewer, my new secretary. I needed someone, don't you know, after the mess Reggie made of everything, to put my affairs in order. And Jonathan is a perfect treasure."

The young man grinned. "Oh, Evadne," he replied in a smug voice. "Spare my blushes, do."

After a few more pleasantries, the two of them took their leave, giggling together like children, as they continued on their way.

Holmes raised his eyebrows and looked at me.

"Well," was all he managed to say.

The Mystery of
Maple Tree Lodge

"It has stopped snowing," I said.

There was no reply. I turned from the window and regarded my friend. Holmes was sprawled in an armchair, intent on a paper he was reading. I repeated the remark.

"I heard you the first time," he said with a sigh. "However, I didn't consider it of sufficient moment to warrant an answer. So it has stopped snowing, has it? No doubt it will start again shortly if a thaw doesn't set in. But what is all that to me when I'm engrossed in a treatise on the cuneiform script of the ancient Sumerians?"

Well, perhaps it was not the Sumerians. It may have been the Babylonians, or even the Assyrians. In any case, I said no more but turned back to my contemplation of the scene outside. The urban ordinariness of Baker Street had been transformed into an Arctic wonderland. I should hardly have been surprised to see a polar bear or two wandering by. It had, indeed, stopped snowing for now, but the precipitation of the last few hours had left a pristine carpet of pure white on the road and pavements, unsullied for the moment by the churning trace of any wheel or the tread of any passer-by. The inclemency of the weather had, it seemed, kept everyone indoors.

If a crime were to be committed under such circumstances, I mused, how straightforward it would be to track the perpetrator. One would only have to mark his footsteps in the way that Good King Wenceslas had instructed his page.

I suppose the Good King was particularly on my mind because Christmas was only a week away. Not that we would be celebrating it overmuch here at Number 221b. Mrs. Hudson would do her best with a roast goose and plum pudding, but I'm afraid that, with regard to the festive season, my friend and colleague rather shared the "*Bah humbug!*" opinion of Ebenezer Scrooge – before the latter's epiphany, that is.

My musings on the subject were brought to an abrupt halt by a tapping on the door, followed by the entrance of our landlady herself.

"There's a 'gentleman' here to see you on a matter of grave urgency, Mr. Holmes," she said, with an arch smile quivering on her lips.

I could not forbear.

"It is impossible, Mrs. Hudson," I said. "I have been looking out of this window for the last quarter-hour and can attest that no one has come up the street in that time."

"Now," Holmes said, suddenly alert, "remember what I always say about eliminating the impossible. If Mrs. Hudson tells no lie – and she isn't a woman given to lying – then quite clearly there is another explanation. Our visitor must have used the tradesmen's entrance at the back of the house."

Our landlady laughed. "There's no foxing you, Mr. Holmes. Yes, indeed. And here's the 'gentleman' himself to prove the point." She turned and addressed someone standing behind her. "Come up, now. Don't be shy. Mr. Holmes may look as if he is going to bite you, but here is Dr. Watson to stop him."

Thereupon a most extraordinary apparition sidled into the room, skinny as a broomstick, with a mop of unruly ginger hair escaping from under a battered cap. A face so covered in freckles that the pink skin beneath was hardly visible, the big ears that flapped out from his skull calling to mind those of an African elephant. The lad looked to be all elbows and sharp corners, and there was a lop-sided twist to his mouth. He was aged about thirteen or fourteen and dressed in the rough-and-ready attire that I associate with the Baker Street Irregulars who often help Holmes out in his investigations. However, he was cleaner than they were, and wasn't anyone that I recognised.

"This is Billy Higgins," Mrs. Hudson said. "The baker's lad. Every day, he brings us the fresh rolls that you like so much with your breakfast, Doctor. He's a good young fellow, Mr. Holmes, and you can believe what he says."

Holmes stood eying the young man, who by now had removed his cap, turning it in his big red hands as if to wring the very life out of it.

"Well, Billy," Holmes asked. "What have you to say to me that is so very urgent?"

The lad twisted his features into horrible grimaces, mimicking the torture he was inflicting on his cap. Clearly he was suddenly tongue-tied at finding himself in the august presence of the famous detective.

"Go on, Billy," urged Mrs. Hudson. "Tell Mr. Holmes what you told me."

"It about the boy, sir," Billy said at last with a rush, in a high-pitched voice that hadn't yet broken. "I seen him, I did, honest. But then they says there wasn't no boy. But I seen him, so I did. I swear to God, I did. With my own two eyes."

Eyes that were bright and blue and honest.

"Now," Holmes went on, patiently enough. "This won't do, you know, Billy. You must start at the beginning and tell me everything as clearly as you can. Mrs. Hudson, perhaps you could bring up some of your most excellent Scottish shortbread and a hot drink for our friend. He looks as if he could do with it."

Indeed, Billy's trousers were soaked almost up to the knees from wading through the snowdrifts, and he was shivering.

"Sit you down here, near the fire, Billy," Holmes ordered, as Mrs. Hudson most willingly went to get the said refreshments.

"Thank you, sir."

For my part, I was no little astonished at the attentive way in which Holmes was treating the lad. I could only assume that the particulars of the cuneiform script of the Sumerians were not proving as diverting as my friend might have wished, and that any distraction was thus to be welcomed.

Billy still needed coaxing to tell his tale in order, but here is what finally emerged.

Mr. McBean, the baker, being a man of pious bent, had, along with some of his fellow traders, organised their young employees and other youths into a band of carol singers, to go around the neighbourhood and collect offerings for the deserving poor of the parish.

I saw Holmes frown at this. Being musical himself, he was wont to rail against the abominations perpetrated in public at the present time of year on perfectly good melodies by those who could not sing a note.

"Do you enjoy that?" I asked Billy, before Holmes could make any disparaging remarks.

"Oh yes, sir," Billy replied, thoroughly relaxed by now and tucking in to the shortbread and other delicacies that Mrs. Hudson had promptly provided, along with a big mug of tea. "Yes, sir, I loves a good sing-song, me. And if I don't know the words, I just go 'La-la-la'."

Holmes shuddered almost imperceptibly.

The little band, as Billy explained, had duly set off with Mr. McBean supervising – presumably, I suspected, to keep the lads in order and make sure no farthings or ha'pennies went anywhere but into the designated little velvet sack.

"Well, all was well and good," said Billy. "Till we comes to this here Maple Lodge place. McBean tells us to sing 'While Shepherds Watched their Flocks', if you know that one, sir. It's a real beauty. Well, when we come to the line about the shinin' frong – "

112

"The what?" asked Holmes, startled.

"The shinin' frong, sir. Of angels praisin' God."

"Ah yes, the *throng*. Go on."

"Well, I don't know why, but didn't I look up just then. I suppose mebbe I was hopin to see the frong meself. Don't know. Anyways, what did I see instead but a boy lookin' down at us out of an upstairs window. I waved at 'im and 'e waved back. Then he was gone, like as if someone pulled 'im away from the window."

Billy paused.

"And that's it?" Holmes asked, rather sharply.

"Oh no, sir. No. If that was all I wouldn't have thought no more about it. No, indeed."

He paused again. A master storyteller in the making if ever there was one.

"Well?"

"That was the night before last. Next mornin', McBean tells me to make a delivery to that very same Maple Lodge. So when I gets there, I asks the maid about the boy. See, I thought perhaps 'e'd like to come out singin' with us."

"Yes? What did she say?"

"What did she say, sir? 'There ain't no boy 'ere.' That's what she says to me, comin' on strong and cross, like. 'There ain't no boy 'ere, young feller, and don't you be goin' around tellin' folks there is.'"

"That is indeed strange, Billy. You are quite sure what you saw, I suppose?"

"Well, o' course I starts to wonder if I dreamed it. I asked the others if they'd seen a boy, but they 'adn't. Not McBean neither. I was goin to let it go, but then I starts thinkin' – I know I saw 'im. And if someone says I didn't, then they're lyin. And if they're lyin, well, I wonder why, see. It bothers me, so it does, sir. And then I thought o' you, and 'ow as you could get to the bottom of it all, if anyone could. And Mrs. 'Udson, she said there was no arm in askin."

After this great speech, during which Billy had leaned forward so far in his eagerness I feared he might fall into the fire, he slid back into the chair, helping himself on the way to yet another piece of shortbread.

"Hmm," Holmes said, frowning. "You pose a pertinent question, Billy."

"Do I, sir?" Evidently Billy was unsure if this was a good or bad thing.

"Yes, indeed. If you are one-hundred-per-cent certain you saw the boy, and someone tells you that you didn't, and that there is no boy to be seen, the question indeed arises, *Why*?" He turned to me, "What do you think, Watson? Some new puzzle to divert us in this dreary weather?"

Billy was delighted. "You'll look into it then, sir?"

"I will, but without making any promises as to the result."

The lad nodded wisely.

"Can you tell me anything more about this boy?" Holmes asked.

"Like what, sir?"

"What age he was? What he looked like? What he was wearing? That sort of thing."

Billy scrunched up his face again in a frown of thought. "It's a bit difficult, sir. See, there weren't no light."

"You mean the boy was looking out of an unlit room."

"Yes, sir. That's it. The room was dark. 'E was younger n' me by several years, I'd say. About the same as our Tommy. 'E's nine." He thought a bit more. "I couldn't see what 'e was wearin', sir, but 'e had dark hair and a pale face."

Holmes rubbed his hands together. "That's very good to be going on with, Billy. Thank you for being so observant. If you think of anything else, please don't hesitate to come and tell me."

"Thanks, sir. I'll be goin' along then." He stood up, looking reluctantly at the last of the shortbread.

"Take the biscuits," I said. "To share with Tommy."

Billy didn't need telling twice, but stuffed what remained into his pocket. "Thanks ever so much, sir. We can share with Betty and Peggy and Wally and Francie, and baby Jimbo, too."

"Of course you can. In fact, ask Mrs. Hudson to give you some more cakes and biscuits for them all. For Christmas. Say the Doctor said it was all right."

He nodded, his face almost splitting in half with a grin, his big ears flapping. "Very good o' you, sir. They'll like that, sir."

Out of the corner of my eye, I could see Holmes looking at me askance. However, the lad appeared undernourished, and I could only guess at the privations he and the rest of his big family undergone.

"Oh, one other thing before you go, Billy," Holmes said. "The address of this Maple Lodge."

"O' course." He gave us directions to a place near Primrose Hill.

That done, he left, and we looked at each other in silence for a moment.

"There's probably a perfectly simple explanation for it all," Holmes said at last, reaching for his pipe. "On the other hand, Billy may have stumbled on a true mystery. Yes, indeed." And with a satisfied sigh, he started to stuff his pipe with that noxious weed that he likes so much to smoke.

The next day, I found myself sitting at the bar of the Queen of Spain tavern in that genteel suburb of London that is Primrose Hill, partaking of a rather fine luncheon of roast beef and Yorkshire pudding. I was there under instruction from Holmes to make enquiries of the landlord about the residents of Maple Tree Lodge.

"And keep it subtle, for goodness sake," Holmes adjured. "We don't want to arouse any suspicions that might get back to the Lodge."

The pretext for my curiosity was an intention to purchase a property in the area. I trusted I led up to the subject in a way subtle enough for Holmes. Luckily, my interlocutor was a man of a garrulous disposition, particularly since the continuing bad weather had kept most of his regular customers away from the inn. No doubt they preferred, like the sensible people they were, to stay home by a roaring fire. Not that that the place where I was sitting was cold – there was a fine fire there too – but the journey thither had been rather less than salubrious – the snow, which had fallen again in the night, being of a considerable depth. Holmes and I had been obliged, moreover, to trudge around first in search of the Lodge. It would hardly do, as he had pointed out, for me to express an interest in a property without knowing what it looked like.

We found the place at last, little thanks to Billy's imprecise directions. Maple Tree Lodge proved to be a large, somewhat fortress-like building, set far back from the road behind a high wall. One could glimpse it well enough through the gates, but I myself ventured no further than that. As for Holmes, he had donned one of his many disguises, intending to call at the house to offer his services as an odd-job man.

So now here I sat in the tavern, endeavouring to elicit information from my genial host, while uncomfortably aware of soaked boots and socks.

"Yes indeed," the landlord was saying. He might have sprung fully formed from the pages of Mr. Dickens's *Pickwick Papers* – a jolly round ball of a man. "You could do worse than move to our neighbourhood, sir. You'll find a very respectable class of person around here – very upright, if you know what I mean…" He regarded me with interest. "What line of business would you be in yourself, if you don't mind me asking?"

"I am a doctor," I replied.

He nodded. "I thought as much."

I was amused and curious. Evidently my new friend possessed, or at least boasted, powers of divination akin to those of Sherlock Holmes himself.

"How ever could you tell?" I asked.

"Well now, sir, I couldn't actually say 'doctor' as opposed to 'lawyer' or... or... whatever. But I knows a professional man when I sees one."

"You are just the observant fellow I need," I said, jumping to the matter in hand. "There's a particular house I very much like the look of, and I was wondering if there is any chance of it being on the market."

"What house would that be then, sir?"

I made a show of consulting a notebook. "Here it is. Maple Tree Lodge on Stanhope Walk."

He scratched his head. "I know the street. Can't say I knows anything about the house, sir."

That was a blow. I had hit a brick wall. Where I was to go from here, I had no notion.

Then, "Hang on a moment, sir," the landlord said. "Hey, Andrew!" He called to a skinny old individual seated at the far end of the bar, nursing what looked to be a hot rum. "You know anything about Maple Tree Lodge? This gent is minded to make an offer on it."

Andrew was nothing loth to join us. If this was a neighbourhood of genteel folk, this fellow was definitely on the margins. His clothes were old and patched and grubby, and his skin was ingrained with dirt.

"Maple Tree Lodge . . . Yes, indeed. 'Appen I knows it well." He grinned at me, revealing a mouth lacking most of its teeth. "Seeing as how they have so many chimbleys up there, sir."

"Andrew is a sweep," the landlord explained. "I always have him clean my own chimney." He gestured at the fire. "You see how it ain't smoking. That's the sign of a good sweep, that is."

His occupation partly explained the man's appearance. That was soot ingrained in his face, not dirt.

I offered Andrew another drink.

"Thanking ye kindly, sir, and I will accept. A body needs a hot drink on a day like today."

The landlord hurried to provide two hots rums with alacrity, since I concurred with the wise words of my new acquaintance, and decided to join him in that warming beverage. The landlord then moved off to serve a couple of men who had just entered.

"You be asking about Maple Tree Lodge, sir." Andrew looked thoughtful. "Furriners they be. From furrin parts. Mind you, I didn't know they was plannin' to move out."

"No," I said. "I don't know that they are. I just hoped they might be open to an offer. The house is exactly what I want."

Andrew's expression reflected the saying, "There's no accounting for taste."

"An elderly couple are they?" I continued,

"I wouldn't say old," Andrew replied. "Not young neither, mind you. No. In between. Like you and me, sir."

I guessed Andrew to be quite a few years older than myself, but let the remark pass.

"Do they have any children?"

"Children? No. None that I've ever seen. And you would see children, wouldn't you, sir? If they was there, like. If they was away, well, then you wouldn't see them. No." He paused and sipped his drink. "I wouldn't say they was plannin' to move out though, sir. No sign of that. Unless and all they wanted to go back where they come from."

"Where would that be, do you know?"

"Search me. All I knows is, they ain't British. See, I heared them one time, talkin' furrin.'"

"That's very helpful, Andrew. You wouldn't happen to know their name, by any chance?"

"I heared it but I couldn't tell you what it was. All spits by the sound of it.'"

"Spits?"

"You know, sir. All *esses* and *zeds* and that." He sniffed back a drop of water from his nose. "Furrin.'"

It seemed I had squeezed all the information I could out of Andrew. I ordered him another drink, paid my bill, and took my leave.

"You be back, I hope, sir, if you ever manage to close that deal," the landlord said, and I promised, readily enough, that I would.

My next destination was a nearby grocer's shop, where I made a few unnecessary purchases of tea and jam and anchovy paste and the like, and then repeated my question, in an offhand-enough manner, regarding the denizens of Maple Tree Lodge. It was to my advantage that the shopkeeper there was a woman, and one who proved only too ready to gossip. The trouble was that she had little to impart.

"I don't knows them to see," she told me, "but their maid, Edith Mott, comes here regular, like." She shook her head. "That Edith's a closed book, she is. All I know is what she buys for them." She paused.

"Yes?" I asked. It did not sound promising.

"They must eat funny food there, sir, that's all I can say."

"Funny food?"

"That Edith, she asks for things I've never even heard of, and gets quite uppity when I says I don't have it. Like rye bread. Or sour cream. Well, my cream ain't never sour, as I told her." She sniffed.

119

"And funny you should buy tea and jam." She pointed at my purchases. "Edith told me they puts jam in their tea instead of milk!"

She crossed her arms over her not inconsiderable chest and pursed her lips.

"Any nursery food? I heard somewhere they have a little boy."

She stared at me. "Where d'you hear that sir? Edith never said nothing about no boy. Mind you, now I'm thinking they get through a deal of porridge."

It seemed that was all the information I was likely to get, and, since I did not feel like plodding about any more on a wild goose chase, I decided to return to Baker Street. No doubt Holmes would heartily disapprove of my lack of progress.

"Well done, Watson!" my friend said jovially, later that afternoon.

I could hardly believe my ears. "I didn't feel I achieved very much."

We were sitting in our room over warming cups of tea and some more of Mrs. Hudson's most excellent shortbread.

"You achieved more than I expected," Holmes continued. "Think about it. What do we know now about the family? That they are middle-aged, foreign, probably from Eastern Europe."

"How do you work that out, Holmes?"

"A surname full of explosive sounds. The nature of the grocery purchases. The habit of taking tea with jam – a specifically Eastern European practice."

I nodded – wisely, I hope. I had never before heard of that particularly barbaric-sounding custom.

"In fact, you did better than I," he continued. "Except in one particular: the formidable maid that we now know as *Edith Mott* was certainly not inclined to let a disreputable-looking odd-job man over the threshold. Instead, she had me shovelling snow from the paths and driveway, and made sure I had done a decent job before giving me a miserable threepence for all my efforts. At least I was able to

120

peer through the downstairs windows and ascertain there was no sign of a boy."

"There we are, then," I said. "No one I spoke to talked of the possibility of a boy either. Billy must have been mistaken."

Holmes smiled and tapped the fingers of his hands together. "Not at all. Billy is absolutely correct. There is a boy. Or, at least, a child."

"How do you know?"

"Footprints, my friend, footprints. As I was engaged in shovelling snow from the path at the back of the house, I espied two pairs of prints in the snow. One set belonging to an adult, a man I should think by the size and depth of them. The other undoubtedly those of a child. I imagine the prints were made very early this morning, after the snow had stopped falling in the night."

The significance of this led me to only one conclusion.

"A child! A boy!" I exclaimed in great excitement, "He is being held in that house against his will. A prisoner! Holmes, we must act at once to liberate him!"

He laughed. "Not quite so impetuous, please, my dear Watson. Fools rush in, and all that."

"But the secrecy, the denials – What are we to make of it all, then?"

"I agree that something most unusual is afoot in that house. It may be, indeed, that you are right, that a child is being held against his will. However, I saw no signs of that in the footprints."

I gazed at him uncomprehending. "Whatever can footprints tell you?"

"A great deal to those who look carefully. The child – we may justly I think call him a boy – walked without reluctance with his companion. There was no dragging, no pulling away. The prints were regular and neatly spaced. No, he was trotting along happily enough."

I shook my head. The matter was beyond me.

"Think about it," Holmes continued. "Early morning exercise was taken before anyone else was likely to catch sight of the boy. He is being concealed in the house for a reason. Who knows yet what it might be?"

"Maybe he is an imbecile and the family is ashamed of him."

"Hmm. That's possible but unlikely. He waved back at Billy and walks normally. No, we need to tread here as carefully as angels. I should like very much to discover what is going on. And yet… You know, it may be that we should leave well alone – not to endanger the boy's safety."

"You think that a risk?"

"Well, let us say I am beginning to formulate certain ideas which I'm reluctant to share even with you, dear friend, until I have established more concrete facts. For the time being, I doubt there is any great urgency in the matter. The boy is secure where he is."

With that, he reached for his pipe and I for another piece of shortbread, not too pleased with his reticence, but having, as ever, to put up with it.

The following day I had various business affairs to sort out, as well as a Christmas lunch at my club, and thus only returned home in mid-afternoon. I was somewhat surprised to find Holmes comfortably ensconced with a person of a decidedly working-man's appearance. They were poring together over an album of some sort.

"Ah, Watson. This is Mr. Wicks. He shares my deep interest in philately."

I shook the man's hand, somewhat puzzled. This was the first I had heard of any such interest on Holmes's part, though the man was such a fund of useless as well as useful knowledge that I supposed a stamp-collecting mania might possibly have passed me by.

"I am showing him my collection."

Now this was definitely something I had never clapped eyes on before, a handsome leather-bound album packed with neatly arranged stamps. As such, an object could surely not have remained hidden from me, its sudden manifestation causing me to suspect some ulterior motive.

"Mr. Wicks is a postman," Holmes continued, "and in his line of work naturally has occasion to come across many very interesting stamps."

"Yes indeed," the man said, a zealot's glint in his eye. "And if I may say so, Mr. 'Olmes, your collection is about the best as I've ever seen."

"You are too kind," Holmes replied. "Imagine how lucky I was to fall into conversation this morning with Mr. Wicks as he did his deliveries."

Light was beginning to dawn even in my poor benighted brain.

"Would that be in the Primrose Hill area?" I asked.

"Yes, indeed, sir," Mr. Wicks said. "And a very good area it is for the more unusual class of stamps, as I was just telling Mr. 'Olmes. 'Specially this time of year when people receive Christmas cards from all over. Some of the people I deliver to know of my little 'obby and very kindly give me the stamps off their envelopes. Others . . . well." He shook his head. "What good they're to them, I don't know."

"Mr. Wicks was indicating to me some of the stamps he recognised from his rounds. I think you said you had seen these before, didn't you?" Holmes turned a page to show a collection of large, brightly coloured squares. He laughed. "We agreed the smaller the country, the bigger the stamps."

I looked over his shoulder.

"*Bzdva*?" I said. "Good Lord! What a name! I confess I have never heard of the place."

"It is, I believe," Holmes replied, "a small principality in the Carpathian Mountains. And interestingly enough, as Mr. Wicks tells me, one household that he delivers to regularly receives missives from that very country."

"I wonder what house that could be," I said, scowling at Holmes.

"The people what live there must be from them parts," Mr. Wicks offered in his innocence. "Their name ain't English anyway."

"No," said Holmes. "Mr. Wicks has written it down for me. What do you make of that?" He shewed me the paper.

What I saw penned was *Strzhcic*, a name I couldn't even begin to pronounce.

"They aren't too keen on vowels, are they?" I remarked. "But the stamps are pretty."

"One time I asked for them, sir, but the girl near bit me head off and told me to mind me own business. Unnecessary rude, she was... But tell me, Mr. 'Olmes, sir – where did you get these 'ere splendid stamps, if you don't mind me asking?"

I was wondering the same thing myself.

Holmes airily dismissed the query with a wave of his hand, and a vague answer that he had people who acquired them for him. Then he removed one of the Bzdovan stamps and presented it to Mr. Wicks with some ceremony.

"For your collection, my friend."

And when the other began to demur, Holmes went on, "It's the least I can do. For Christmas, you know. And please," presenting the man with a guinea to send him on his way, "buy something nice for your good wife and all the little Wickses."

I gazed at my friend in astonishment. Suddenly he had turned into Scrooge redeemed.

"Very much obliged to you, I'm sure," the postman was saying, pocketing the coin and gazing at his prize. "It'll be the flower in my little collection, so to speak."

When he had gone, Holmes smiled at me, rubbing his hands together.

"Well, we are making great progress. Now we know their name and where they come from."

My private opinion was that there might have been easier ways to find out. However, I merely gestured at the album. "And that?"

"Yes, indeed. I'm not quite sure how I'll explain to Mycroft how one of his precious stamps comes to be missing. He will not be any too pleased."

"Oh, it's Mycroft's collection, is it?"

"Yes, I visited him this morning with the precise intention of borrowing it for the purposes of which you have been a witness. Dear Mycroft," Holmes went on. "My brother would no more consider visiting any of the places designated by these stamps as try to fly to the Moon. They are the nearest he will ever get to 'abroad'."

"I'm surprised," I said, "that he would entrust such a valuable collection to you at all, knowing as I do how pernickety he is about such things and how careless you can sometimes be."

Holmes leaned back in his chair and stretched out his long legs. "Well, as to that…" He laughed. "He doesn't yet know that he has lent it to me."

"You stole it!" I exclaimed, horrified.

"Goodness, Watson, how you do exaggerate. But now," springing up and crossing to the bookshelf whereon lay an encyclopaedia, "let us find out all we can about Bzdva."

The answer was painfully little. We learnt where it was and a good deal about its troubled past history, and that the prevailing religion was Eastern Orthodox, but the encyclopaedia was sparse on anything to do with the present day. A subsequent visit to the British Museum Library the following afternoon, and a forage among the newspapers there, proved equally fruitless.

"There is nothing for it," Holmes remarked finally, "than to pick Mycroft's brains. If anyone knows anything about it, he will."

Holmes hadn't yet returned the stamp album, perhaps fearing the wrath of his brother, or else hoping for an opportune moment to slip it back without Mycroft noticing. As for the missing stamp, he had endeavoured to rearrange the page so that it wouldn't be noticed, but gave up. Mycroft had a precise system which couldn't be changed.

"I shall just have to acquire another Bzdovan stamp from somewhere," he said, "and hope my brother forgives me."

We duly made our way, album and all, to Mycroft's rooms in Pall Mall, hoping to catch him before he set off, as was his wont each evening, for the Diogenes Club. We were lucky. He was still at home, although he ostentatiously consulted his fob watch before permitting us to enter.

"I can give you ten minutes," he said.

Mycroft Holmes was taller and considerably stouter than his younger brother, his complexion florid, with tiny broken veins visible over his cheeks and nose, no doubt the result of an unhealthily sedentary life and a partiality for rich food and brandy. He was unlikely ever to consult me in my professional capacity, but if he did so, I should have prescribed regular exercise and a strict diet.

His abode always struck me as curiously impersonal. It might have been an office or an hotel room, with its utilitarian furniture and standard portrait of Queen Victoria over the mantelpiece. The one concession to individuality was a bookcase, and even that held only handsomely bound reference works. Not a novel, nor even less a volume of poetry in sight.

We sat ourselves down, and Holmes, conscious of the minutes ticking by and the knowledge that his brother would have no compunction in ejecting us at the end of the allotted time, asked straight away what Mycroft knew about Bzdva.

"A-ha!" the other replied. "How very interesting you should ask, Sherlock. That little place has been rattling around like billy-o the past while and causing all sorts of alarms."

"Really? In what way."

"As you have probably already discovered, it's a tin-pot principality in the wilds of the Carpathian mountains. A month ago there was a military coup – the ruling prince assassinated and his wife thrown into prison."

"Goodness!" I exclaimed. "I saw nothing about it in *The Times*, and they are usually prompt at providing news of that nature."

"I believe," Mycroft replied, "there was a very small notice in one of the papers. Who here, after all, would be interested in the fate of a country of which they have never heard? According to the editors of Fleet Street, not their readers, anyway. Our government, however, is become involved – and this is top secret – in that the son of the assassinated prince, his heir, was spirited away by a trusted servant of the family, and is at present somewhere in this very country. Indeed, the General now in charge, whose name I won't even try to pronounce, has sent a strongly-worded letter to our Prime Minister, demanding we hunt down the boy and return him, or, and I quote, 'Steps will be taken.'" Mycroft chuckled, his whole huge body heaving. "I'm not sure if the General intends to declare war on the British Empire, and if, therefore, we should be trembling in our boots."

"You don't know where the boy is at present, then?" Holmes asked.

Mycroft paused before answering, a faraway look in his watery grey eyes. "Despite the best efforts of our agents, they haven't been able to put a finger on him as yet."

"If you find him," I said, "will you send him back?"

"The General has assured us that the boy will come to no harm. Indeed, he has offered a large reward, albeit in Bzdovan crowns, for the return of the little Prince. Needless to say, we aren't about to publicise that fact right now. In any case, I think it most unlikely, *most unlikely*, Dr. Watson, that he will be found. Not by us, at least. So the question will never arise. Now, I think our conversation must end, for the ten minutes is up."

We rose to go.

"You may replace my stamp album where you found it, Sherlock," Mycroft said. "I shall hold you accountable if there is any damage to it. Or anything missing."

My friend had the grace to blush – a very rare occurrence for him, and something I had only ever seen before in the presence of his brother.

He babbled a confession regarding the missing stamp, and promised to replace it.

"I shall keep you to your word. In the meantime, please remember that there are persons looking for the boy, possibly to do him harm, so, in the unlikely event that you receive news of him, please keep it to yourself and don't think to become involved in the matter."

We walked a little way up the road with Mycroft until our paths diverged. Holmes was thoughtful.

"I'm somewhat surprised," I said at length, "that your brother didn't ask what was our particular interest in Bzdva, and that you didn't tell him about the boy at Maple Tree Lodge, who must surely be the missing prince."

"My dear Watson," Holmes replied. "I didn't tell him because he knows it already."

"But he said – "

"You should be aware by now that there is often a sizeable distance between what Mycroft *says* he knows and what he actually knows. I imagine the authorities are fully aware that the boy is safely hidden away at Maple Tree Lodge. They also realise that, once the General gets his hands on the little fellow, that will be the end of him."

"Good God! So what do we do?"

"I suppose we must stay out of it, as Mycroft instructed."

That however, was not to be. We returned to Baker Street to find a wide-eyed Mrs. Hudson in the hallway, informing us that a foreign lady wished very much to speak to us. This person was waiting at present, and impatiently, in our landlady's parlour, and in fact burst out of the room at the sound of our voices. We saw a woman not in her first youth but still attractively voluptuous, and of exotic appearance. She came accompanied by a strong and earthy scent of patchouli.

"Mr. Sherlock Holmes," she cried out in a thick foreign accent, looking from one of us to the other, "you must find him! He is in the gravest danger – if even it isn't already too late." At that point, she started howling and beating her breast, an action I had read about in novels but never before observed in practice.

Holmes gently urged the lady to come upstairs to our rooms. Once there he insisted she take a seat and begged her calm herself, to explain the matter fully.

Soon it emerged that this lady was none other than Madame Strzhcic, (approximately pronounced "*Strezh-chick*"), the same resident of Maple Tree Lodge of whom we had so recently made enquiries, and that the boy in her charge – "Dearest Mikel" – had been abducted that very afternoon.

"It is a catastrophe, Mr. Holmes."

"Yes, yes. But how did it happen, and how come you are here?"

"When I found they were gone, Little Mikel and that devil in women's clothes-es, I rushed into the street to look for them. But they were gone. Gone! I collapsed into the snow. It was there I was found by the kindness of a man – a man who delivers letters."

"Mr. Wicks?"

"Perhaps. I don't know. I told him what had happened and he advised me to come and see you."

"Not the police? I should have thought – "

"The police!" she almost shouted. "No, I will never speak to the police! Never! You cannot trust them. But Mr. Holmes... I hope I can trust you. I hope you can find our darling little Mikel."

She raised tearful brown eyes to look at him. Really, she was rather appealing, despite her melodramatic manner. My heart went out to her.

"You say it was a person known to you who took him."

"Yes. Mott. Edith Mott." She spat out the name. "I curse the day we brought that witch into the house."

"Let us proceed with all haste," Holmes said. "We have wasted too much time already."

The three of us travelled by cab back to Primrose Hill, Holmes enquiring for further details but allowing it to be thought, as the lady clearly intended, that we took little Mikel to be her own son.

The snow had stopped falling, but still lay thick on the ground. When we alighted from the cab, Holmes instructed me to accompany Madame Strzhcic into the house, while he conducted an examination outside.

"What is he doing?" she asked me.

"I presume he is looking for clues," I said. "For footprints."

"Ha!"

We waited in the comfortable parlour of the house – though just as with Mycroft's place, there was nothing much here of a personal nature – no photographs or knick-knacks to reveal the taste of the owners, if owners they be. Tenants more likely, I thought.

Soon we were joined by the lady's husband, a stiff stick of a man, his once-blond hair turning grey, his face haggard, and showing more wrinkles than one might expect in someone of middle years.

He said something to his wife in their language, and they continued speaking thus for a while in raised tones. Rather rudely, I

130

thought, though under the circumstances, perhaps niceties go out the window.

"No news yet," she said finally.

The man clenched his fists. "By Satan and all the devils, if I ever get my hands on that woman, she is dead! Dead!"

Madame again spoke in their tongue in what seemed to me to be in warning tones.

To break the uncomfortable silence, and though it was hardly the time for small talk, I asked how long they had been living in London.

"A month or two," the man replied, offering nothing more.

"Do you like it here?"

They both stared at me, as if astonished at the question, and I gave up.

As the minutes on the handsome grandfather clock ticked into three-quarters of an hour, I could see Madame getting more and more angrily restless, though her grief seemed to have dissipated.

"Where is he? What is he doing?" She paced up and down the room, stopping occasionally to stare out the window at the driveway.

"Trust him. Mr. Holmes has his methods," I said, but my words washed off her. Indeed, I was wondering myself at the prolonged absence of my friend.

Mr. Strzhcic, meanwhile, was sitting drumming his foot on the wooden floor, on and on and on. I tried to curb my irritation, but it was Madame who finally cried, "Stop! For God's sake, Hedrik!"

At last, the familiar form of Holmes could be seen approaching the front door. He was alone.

Madame flew to meet him, almost dragging him into the parlour.

"You didn't find them, then."

"Not yet. I was able to follow their traces for a way but then lost them."

"Lost them!" Her voice was sharp. "So much for the great detective. I hope you know that the boy's very life depends on you."

"Yes," Holmes said quietly. "Yes, Madame. I'm fully aware of that." He looked at me. "Come, Watson. There is nothing more to be done here. I assure you, Madame, Sir, that as soon as I have any news, I will let you know."

"Everything must be done in the strictest secrecy," she insisted. "No police."

Holmes inclined his head in acknowledgement.

Mr. Strzhcic rose to his feet, clicked his heels in military manner, and shook our hands with a curt nod. Madame, by then sunk in a chair, merely made a vague gesture of dismissal.

"One last thing," Holmes said, as if the idea had just come to him. "A foolish request, indeed, but I wonder if you could give me any stamps from your country. For my collection, you know. Dr. Watson will tell you what an obsessive philatelist I am."

The couple looked startled, as did I, though I soon gathered myself together and nodded agreement.

"Stamps?" said the man.

"Yes, I have none from your country and would love to add some to my album."

A rapid exchange followed in their guttural language, and finally Mr. Strzhcic crossed to a bureau and took out some envelopes. He was about to tear off the stamps but Holmes intervened.

"Oh no, please. Leave them in place. They need to be removed with care."

Mr. Strzhcic shrugged, and, after a moment's hesitation, passed three envelopes to Holmes, who thanked him warmly.

"How beautiful they are," he said. "Look."

I nodded, but stamps are stamps and of no particular interest to me.

Holmes was sunk in thought as we headed away. I supposed he must be very worried at the fate of the poor boy, but when I said as much, all he replied was, "There is great evil here, Watson. Very great evil."

"No one seems to have a good word to say of Edith Mott, anyway. What a hellcat she must be to abduct an innocent child. I suppose she did it for the reward money."

"The money is key, quite evidently."

He said no more, and I could tell he wanted quiet to order his ideas, and so we continued in silence, until of a sudden he turned to me, shaking his head.

"You go on home. There is something I must do."

I was about to protest, but he insisted.

"It's cold, my friend," he said. "Take yourself to Baker Street and get Mrs. Hudson to make you a hot punch." He laughed. "To put you back in the Christmas spirit."

I knew better than to argue further, though once more I was disappointed. His nose was twitching, a bloodhound keen to be off on the hunt, and he wanted rid of me.

Now the business is all over, I can look back and see clearly what he observed and I missed. At least, I could see it all clearly once he explained it. I only wish I had been there when he found the boy.

That fateful day, while I obediently sat by the fire, enjoying the hot punch so aptly provided by our landlady, and trying to concentrate on the newspaper, he was bringing the saga of the boy at the window to a conclusion.

As evening drew on and no still sign of my friend, I became ever more restless. Hearing carol singers in the street outside, I put on my greatcoat and wrapped a thick scarf around my neck to go out and join them, to try to muster up the joyful glow associated with the season.

The little group was clustered under a street light, flakes of snow starting to fall upon them, turning them into veritable snowmen. Nothing daunted, they next launched into "Hark the Herald Angels Sing" with more gusto than tunefulness, though it was impossible not to be moved. When the carol was done, I gladly contributed to the fund for the poor of the parish. Our friend Billy stood amid the "frong", for all the world like a ragamuffin angel. He waved at me, raising questioning eyebrows. What could I tell him? Nothing, without putting little Mikel in even more danger.

As the group started to move away, a hansom cab drew up to our door. It was with utter astonishment then that I descried the persons descending from it. Holmes of course, but accompanied by a small boy and a woman. He hurried them into the house.

I stood gaping for a second. Then Billy ran up to me.

"That's 'im, Dr. Watson. That's the boy what I seen. That's 'im."

He was calling too much attention to the matter.

"You'd better come up, Billy," I said.

He made his excuses to the man I took to be McBean and gladly followed me into the house.

Upstairs, we found Holmes standing by the table, and the boy and woman huddled round the fire, her arm round his shoulders.

"That's 'er," Billy exclaimed. "The 'orrible ol' devil from the 'ouse."

"Edith Mott?" I asked, looking at the stout, red-faced woman in front of me. Whatever was going on?

"Indeed," Holmes replied, "this is Mrs. Mott, and she is very far from being a horrible old devil, Billy. She may well have saved this little boy's life."

"You're my darling, aren't you, Mikel?" the same woman said, holding the boy even tighter. He smiled up at her, a beautiful child with black hair, olive skin, and long lashes over dark eyes.

"I knew I had to get him away," she said, "when I heard them talking. They didn't know, but I've picked up quite a bit of their language, minding the child. They were planning to sell him to the General. My little boy!"

She was deeply moved and started to cry, so now it was Mikel's turn to comfort her.

"I don't understand," I said.

Holmes started to explain. After becoming aware that the General was planning a coup, Mikel's mother, the Princess, had entrusted him to her maidservant, Adele Strzhcic.

"Take him to England," she had said. "He will be safe with my sister in Gloucestershire."

The Strzhcics, however, had other ideas. At first they had no fixed plan to enrich themselves at the expense of Mikel's welfare, but decided to keep him with them to see what transpired. Then, on learning that a large reward was being offered by the General for the boy's return, they had entered into correspondence with him.

"You noticed, of course, the official nature of the envelopes given me by Mr. Strzhcic, embossed with the palace insignia," said Holmes. (I had not. My eyes were on the colourful stamps). "The letters couldn't be from the Princess, because she is in prison. Therefore, they had to be from the rebels."

"Well spotted," I said, rather lamely.

"I was already suspicious of the couple before that," he went on. "Why had they not informed the British authorities of the young prince's whereabouts – surely the first thing blameless people would do?"

"But," I said, "the envelopes show that the General knew well where the boy was being kept. Could he not just send emissaries to pick him up and avoid paying the reward?"

"Excellent. You are thinking at last. However, it isn't so easy to abduct a child from the beacon of civilisation that is our fine country, especially with the authorities looking out for him. I

135

imagine the idea was for the Strzhcics to travel back to the Continent with Mikel, hand him over there, and collect the blood money."

I shivered at the thought and looked across at the boy. Billy was now crouched beside him, chattering nineteen-to-the-dozen and clearly puzzled that Mikel had difficulty understanding him. However, Mrs. Mott translated and soon merry laughter could be heard, a most pleasing sound. More delights were to follow as our landlady entered with a laden tray.

"Mrs. 'Udson!" Billy exclaimed. "You're a right treasure, you are!"

On tracking down the runaways to Edith Mott's mother's house in Southwark – the safest place the good woman could think of to take the child – and having established from her the truth of his suspicions, Holmes had straightway sent word to Mycroft, along with the envelopes from the Strzhcics, as evidence, and also, of course, those three fine stamps to replace the missing one. As we were to learn later, the treacherous pair were soon arrested, though not without some resistance. Strzhcic drew a pistol but was disarmed by a well-placed blow from a truncheon, while Madame inflicted deep scratches on the face of the unfortunate constable who was trying to restrain her. However, they were soon safely locked away in Newgate.

Our concerns just now, however, were for the safety of the boy. Where could he stay for the moment where he could not easily be found? It was Billy who came up with a plan.

"'E can come to ours for now, Mr. 'Olmes. No one'll notice one more among the lot o' us."

It was such an absurd solution that, as Holmes remarked, it might just work.

"Me ma and pa won't mind, honest. Better than shuttin' 'im away, like 'e was before."

The appropriate consultations were made forthwith, and indeed the Higginses proved happy to welcome Billy's little friend, an orphan as he was described, into their large and jolly family, without needing to know more about him.

"We'll make an 'appy Christmas for the pore little chap," said Mrs. Higgins.

Holmes, as I know, pressed a good few guineas into her hand, even though none was asked for, and what was offered only reluctantly accepted.

A few days after Christmas found us dining on cold roast goose and pickles. Holmes, reading the paper at the table – a most regrettable habit of his – gave a sudden start.

"Good heavens, Watson – Listen to this. An item dated December 25th:

> *Bzdva. Royalist colonels have engineered a counter-coup against the Republican generals who recently ousted and executed the ruling prince. Princess Denissa has been released from prison and will, it is hoped, soon be reunited with her son, Mikel, and have him recognised as ruler of the country. General –* (Some unpronounceable name, Watson) *– and his co-conspirators have been beheaded and their heads placed on spikes around the royal palace to warn off any others who might be tempted to rise up against the sovereign ruler.*

"My Lord! How very barbaric!" I said. "Of course, I'm delighted to hear that the General has been deposed, but I should not wish such a grisly fate on my worst enemies."

"Indeed. The Strzhcics are lucky to find themselves in the relative civilisation of Newgate."

"I must say, though, I don't like to think of that dear little boy returning to such a country. As ruler, indeed! Who knows when there might be yet another coup?"

"Nevertheless, go back I'm sure he must, and just in time for Christmas."

"Whatever do you mean? Christmas is well over."

"I presume that Mikel is of the Orthodox faith practiced by the rest of his countrymen. They celebrate the Nativity according to the Julian calendar, on 6 January. No, Watson, this year little Mikel will have *two* Christmases to put up with."

He shuddered at the thought, one season of goodwill being more than enough for Mr. Sherlock Holmes. *Bah, humbug!*

The Strange Case of the
Man from Edinburgh

"I tell you, gentlemen, someone is trying to kill my wife!"

To say Holmes and I were taken aback at this blunt outburst would be putting it mildly. The bearing and sober dress of Mr. Ramsay Ballantyne, for that was how the man had introduced himself, spoke of one not given to wild imaginings. He was a stern-looking Scot in the cast of a Presbyterian minister, tall and lean, almost entirely bald, and yet not elderly by any means.

"If that is so, then surely it is a matter for the police," Holmes remarked, but his nostrils quivered as if already scenting an interesting case.

"My wife is adamantly against such a procedure," Mr. Ballantyne replied, in the lilting accents of an Edinburgher. "She will not take the threats seriously and claims the whole thing is a prank played by one of her friends or relations."

"A strange sort of a prank," Holmes said. "But pray explain the nature of the supposed attempt on her life. And please do sit down, Mr. Ballantyne. We will all be more comfortable."

The man took a seat reluctantly, staying poker-upright in the hard chair he had selected, as if fearing any concession to comfort might detract from what he had to say.

For his part, Holmes stretched out in his usual armchair, as if ready to be entertained. I took a seat across from him, also facing our visitor.

"I have to confess that the matter did at first seem to be some sort of a twisted joke," he began. "The letters she received being of such a ludicrous nature, so badly spelt, and with such a mangled syntax." He shook his head in disgust.

I began to think: Not a minister, but a teacher. I could well envisage Mr. Ballantyne in front of a class of boys, keeping their grammar and spellings in order with a switch.

"I trust you have brought the letters to show me," Holmes said.

There was a pause. "Alas no. They are destroyed. Before I could stop her, Hélène, my wife, tore them up and tossed them in the fire."

"All of them? I think you have one at least with you."

Mr. Ballantyne looked surprised, but reached into his inside jacket pocket and brought out a missive.

"I will not ask how you knew it, Mr. Holmes," he said. "I have heard of your methods. I suppose you noticed that, at the first mention of the letters, my hand made an involuntary movement towards my breast."

Holmes nodded and smiled. Clearly this Ramsay Ballantyne was a person of no little perception. For my part, I hadn't noticed the gesture. He now handed the said letter to Holmes, who scanned it and then passed it to me. In a cursive hand, in red ink, it read as follows:

Hélène you have been worned. You cannot escape the fate. Your days are short. Blud must to be spilled for your duplicite.

"To the point," I said. "Though I see what you mean, sir. The writer is not an educated person."

Holmes held up his hand to silence me.

"On the contrary, Watson, we can make no such assumption."

"You think the note has been written that way deliberately in order to mislead us?" Mr. Ballantyne asked.

"Perhaps." Holmes leant even further back, making a steeple of his fingers. "However, might I assume that your wife isn't British, sir? She is perhaps French? Belgian?"

Ramsay Ballantyne now evinced astonishment. He nodded.

"French. But how – ?"

"Tut tut, sir. Not a difficult deduction. The way you pronounced her name is one clue. And see how the writer has placed the accents correctly over her name. There are many signs that he, or she, isn't a native speaker of English. '*Warned*' and '*blood*' are misspelt as if transcribed by someone who has only heard them spoken aloud and has guessed at the spelling. However '*duplicity*', a more unusual word, is correctly spelt, apart from the final letter. And that is how the word appears in French, though usually with an accent *aigu* over the final '*e*'."

Mr. Ballantyne nodded. "Of course. I should have noticed that, too."

"And then," continued Holmes, "there is the handwriting itself. You see how it flows to the right with many looped letters. I have made quite a study of graphology, and can tell you that the note is written in the calligraphic style taught in French schools."

Mr. Ballantyne took back the letter and studied the handwriting. "It is indeed an educated hand," he conceded. Definitely a teacher.

"However, that raises an interesting question, does it not?" Holmes said. "If the writer is French, writing to your French wife, then why write in English?"

"He knows she will show it to me, who cannot speak the language."

"Hmm." Holmes was thoughtful. "But I am sure, Mr. Ballantyne, that this crude little missive cannot comprise the sum of your concerns. What else is there?"

Again our visitor paused, looking solemn: A man who liked to underline the significance of his actions.

"This," he said at last.

He produced a box from an outer pocket and laid it before us. Holmes reached towards it.

"Stop!" Ramsay Ballantyne exclaimed. "It must be opened with the greatest of care, Mr. Holmes. You will understand why in a second."

He first drew on to his right hand a grey leather glove, and then slowly lifted the lid. Holmes peered in.

"Ah," he remarked with satisfaction. "Yes, indeed."

I, however, could see nothing of the contents, being at too great a distance. However, I hadn't long to wait for the horrid revelation, for Holmes straightway reached into the box, and drew out a huge and hairy spider, placing it gently on the back of his other hand.

"Mr. Holmes," whispered Mr. Ballantyne, as if fearing to disturb the monster. "It is deadly poisonous."

"That is something of an exaggeration," Holmes replied calmly. "*Steatoda nobilis* can indeed give a nasty bite, but very seldom does it prove fatal. Still, I will put her back in her box. For now... Indeed, you may leave the little lady with me if you wish, Mr. Ballantyne, for I am sure you aren't comfortable carrying her around with you."

"I should be much relieved, Mr. Holmes. But tell me, is the creature indeed less dangerous than I understood it to be? I thought it a tarantula."

"No, no – As you may imagine, spiders have been yet another of my fields of interest. *Steatoda nobilis* isn't harmless, far from it, but its venom is unlikely to cause more than the pain you would get from a bee or wasp sting. Still, it is an unpleasant gift to receive. How did it arrive?"

"In a package addressed to my wife. Luckily, I was with her when she opened it, and was able to prevent the creature escaping from its box and biting her."

"This box?"

"The very one."

"Nothing distinctive," Holmes said, examining it. "And the package itself?"

"Nothing distinctive either. Just my wife's name and address inscribed upon it."

"You didn't bring the wrappings with you."

"I didn't think to."

"A pity. Did you notice the handwriting? Was it perhaps the same as in the threatening letter?"

Mr. Ballantyne thought for moment, frowning.

"No," he replied finally. "It was printed in capitals. I am sure of it."

"Nonetheless, I should like to see it," Holmes said.

A slight smile of relief lightened the man's grave face.

"Of course. I should like nothing more than for you and Dr. Watson to accompany me home, to convince my wife, as I have failed to do, that this is no trivial matter."

The three of us took a cab to Paddington Station, whence we boarded a train to Wimbledon, and then another cab carrying us thence up the steep hill to Mr. Ballantyne's residence, a solid Georgian house on the edge of the Common. At first, I took the person who came forward to greet us to be Mrs. Ballantyne, a tall, stately woman in a black dress, quite the counterpart to the husband. However, this turned out to be the housekeeper, a Mrs. McDuff.

"Your wife is in the library," she told Ramsay Ballantyne in answer to his query, thereby revealing herself, in case her name did not, to be a Scot like her master. "She is reading, I believe."

Why her tone should express disapproval was strange. Surely reading was a most acceptable pastime for a gentlewoman, particularly in a library. Perhaps she thought her mistress should be occupied with something more practical – like sewing, for instance.

"Thank you, Margaret," Mr. Ballantyne replied. "Please arrange for some refreshments to be brought us."

"To the library?" Again that disapproving tone. "Would the withdrawing room not be more suitable?"

"We will take it in the library, thank you, Margaret," he replied, somewhat impatiently. I suppose such domestic details seemed irrelevant under the more urgent circumstances.

Mrs. McDuff nodded, unsmiling, and withdrew. She was evidently as dour as those of our race are often reckoned to be.

Hélène Ballantyne, on the other hand, wasn't at all like that, and not, I have to confess, as I had imagined her. Her husband being so upright and stiff, I had thought his wife must be of a similarly serious character, as well as slender, elegant, and restrained, in the typical way of French ladies. But Hélène was round and bubbly, with mischief in her eyes. And very young. Laughing aloud and merrily at the sight of the three of us, so solemn and concerned, she put down the book she was reading. Its yellow cover revealed it to be far removed from one of the classics, which perhaps explained the housekeeper's tone of censure. The lady's taste was clearly for sensational reading matter.

Mr. Ballantyne introduced us.

"Mr. Holmes, the great detective!" She smiled broadly. "What an honour! But my dear Ramsay," she continued, "you have brought your friends here to chase the wild goose, I think." She possessed the lightest and most charming of French accents. "The more I consider it, the more sure I am that it is my cousin, Adolphe, who is sending the letters. He is a silly boy who would think he is being funny."

"But the spider? That is no joke, Hélène."

"Did it bite anyone? No. It is probably quite quite harmless."

She shook her head and her dark curls quivered as if they shared her mirth. I noticed that she missed off her "aitches", so that Holmes became "'Olmes", and the spider, somewhat comically, "'armless" (Eight legs but no arms!). I shall not, however, attempt to reproduce her accent here for fear it might prove tedious for my readers.

Holmes coughed. "Not quite harmless, Mrs. Ballantyne. As I have informed your husband, though seldom fatal, that particular spider's bite can be very painful."

She shrugged. "But who would want to hurt me? You know well, Ramsay, there is nothing true in these silly accusations. You know that, my dearest." She took his hand and pressed it to her lips. Then she turned to us. "You can see, gentlemen, just what a very old fogey my husband is…" She laughed again. Ramsay Ballantyne was, I guessed, barely forty. "He married me when I was sixteen, five years ago. Since then, I have lived a life without blame in Edinburgh and here. And before my marriage – *Mon Dieu!*" She threw her little white hands up in the air. "What evil can a young girl from Lille do in a convent school, that years later causes someone to want to kill her? No, it is a joke. In bad taste, yes certainly, but nothing to worry about. See, I am not worried."

At that moment, Mrs. McDuff entered, every line of her face expressing discontent.

"Please take care not to spill anything," she said, setting the tray down on the desk, from which papers had swiftly to be moved.

"Coffee, Ramsay! In here?" Mrs. Ballantyne looked wide-eyed.

"It's tea, actually, Madam," the housekeeper said.

Mrs. Ballantyne laughed merrily. "Of course it is. You British and your everlasting tea-drinking! A cup of Darjeeling, and all is well, is that not so?" She turned to the housekeeper. "A big coffee with cream for me, please, Margaret." Her warm smile wasn't returned, the woman merely nodding and stepping out of the room.

"I will be *maman*," our hostess then said, holding a pretty porcelain jug over matching cups. "Milk, Mr. Holmes? Dr. Watson?"

I nodded. "Just the merest amount," I said, for I like it strong.

Holmes shook his head with impatience. He wasn't here to drink tea.

"This cousin of yours – Adolphe?" he asked. "Where does he live, Mrs. Ballantyne?"

"As far as I know, he is still in Lille." She passed me my cup.

"But the last letter sent had a London postmark."

"You kept one of the letters?" Hélène asked her husband. "I thought we had burnt them all. Well," she shrugged again, "maybe not Adolphe, then. It must be someone else. Unless…" A smile burst over her face as if the sun had suddenly emerged from behind a cloud. "I have it! He is come to London to surprise us! Ramsay, there will be a knock at the door one of these days, and it will be Adolphe!"

"My dear girl…" There was an unmistakably patronising tone to Ballantyne's voice, "that is too great a leap of the imagination, even for you."

"Not at all. It is just what he would do, the silly boy."

"I suppose," Holmes drawled, "it is too much to hope, Mrs. Ballantyne, that you still have the wrappings in which the spider was delivered."

A charming little frown appeared on her forehead. "I think… I think…" She rang a bell, and a young maidservant soon appeared. The two women spoke in French for a few seconds, and then the maid withdrew.

"Claudine has gone to look. I think maybe you will be in luck, Mr. Holmes."

Indeed, shortly after, the maid returned with a pot of pungent-smelling coffee, as well as a quantity of brown paper on which was clearly printed, as Mr. Ballantyne had told us, the name and address of his wife.

"Margaret forgot the cream. No matter, I will take milk."

Holmes was examining the wrapping paper closely. As far as I could tell, there wasn't much to see, but then, of course, I am not gifted with his powers.

"I thought it was the lace collars I had ordered," the lady remarked.

"Well," he said finally, "I will retain this if I may. And Mrs. Ballantyne, although you are convinced there is no real threat involved here, I beg you to stay alert and not to open anything that looks in any way suspicious."

She nodded, a little smile trembling on her lips.

"I promise, but really, Mr. Holmes – "

"As for you, sir," Holmes turned to her husband, "the same instruction. Open nothing if you don't know the source. And please keep me informed of any developments."

He stood up.

"You are leaving so soon?" the lady cried. "But Mr. Holmes, you have had neither tea nor coffee. And the poor Dr. Watson hasn't had time to drink his."

Holmes turned to me. I knew that look.

"I am ready to go," I said, draining the cup, which anyway contained little more than a thimbleful. "Thank you, Madame." I too stood up, and inclined my head.

"Another time then, gentlemen," she said smiling, "I hope."

Little did we realise how soon and under what circumstances our return would take place.

Mr. Ballantyne accompanied us to the door.

"What do you think, Mr. Holmes?" he asked. "Can it all be just a silly prank?"

"You were right to consult me. It may well be as your wife thinks – that her cousin is behind it all. On the other hand, there is certainly enough here to cause alarm. I beg you, please be very very careful."

He agreed that he would.

The early spring day that had started misty when we first set out had by now turned into a pleasant and sunny afternoon. As we walked down the drive-way, I looked back at the house. Mr. Ballantyne was still standing in the doorway. I raised a hand to wave farewell, but he seemed lost in thought and did not reciprocate.

"A fine house for a teacher," I remarked. "He is doing well at it."

"A teacher?" Holmes chided me. "Whatever gave you that idea? Surely you could tell instantly. Did you not observe the handsome stick pin in his cravat."

I had not particularly.

"It was in the form of a thistle – the insignia, of course, of the Caledon and Dunedin Merchant Bank."

"Of course," I replied sourly. Neither a minister nor a teacher, then, but a banker – and a prosperous one at that.

Holmes grinned at me.

"And of course, his position was indicated on the card he sent up this morning. I am sorry, Watson, for teasing you. Even I, sometimes, have the need for concrete information, you know."

I laughed with him, though still somewhat peeved.

We were strolling down the hill towards the station. Already the leaves of the plane trees lining our route were unfolding, dressing the bare branches in pale green.

"Do you think Hélène Ballantyne's life really is in danger?" I asked after a while.

"As to that – Well, what did you make of the lady?"

"Quite delightful. And not 'French' at all!"

He smiled. "Your eye is so easily turned by a pretty face, my friend. I suppose by 'not French', you mean that she is not aloof and proud. But you know, that is just a prejudice based on the manners of certain Parisian ladies. Mrs. Ballantyne is a provincial. It is quite a different matter."

"Whatever caused her to marry Ramsay Ballantyne? They appear such an ill-matched pair. And yet, she seems happy enough."

"I am flattered you would ask me that," Holmes replied, although my question was, in fact, a rhetorical one. "However, on the subject of matrimony, and indeed on the general nature of relationships between the sexes, you are in a much better position that I to speculate."

I was silent. Although it was some years since my dear Mary had passed away, I considered his remark insensitive, recalling as it did my lost, happiest times. However, I could not expect him, whose heart had never been so engaged, to understand.

It was barely a week later. Holmes and I were sitting over breakfast when Mrs. Hudson appeared holding a telegram which had just been delivered.

"You take it," Holmes said. "I find I have butter all over my fingers."

I opened the grey envelope and almost turned that colour myself.

"Good Lord! What terrible news!"

"What is it?"

"Ramsay Ballantyne is dead!"

Buttery fingers notwithstanding, Holmes snatched the message from my hand, as if to find other words written there. "Sent by Mrs. McDuff," he said. "Oh, I am very much remiss. I should have stopped it."

"I don't see what more you could have done."

He was already on his feet.

"Come. There is no time to be lost."

"Where are we going? To Wimbledon?"

"Of course. Put down that slice of toast, man, and hurry."

I would not even be permitted to finish my breakfast.

The door was opened to us by the French maid, Claudine, looking pale and anxious. She showed us into the withdrawing room, already occupied by three persons, two of whom we recognised. The third, a thin young man, stared wild-eyed as we entered. Beside him stood Mrs. McDuff, who nodded a grim acknowledgement to us, while poor Mrs. Ballantyne, reclining on the sofa, looked utterly distraught, her curls a-tumble, her face swollen and pink from weeping. She was wearing a loose robe, a tea-gown in a pale blue, silky fabric, the sort of garment my own dear Mary would have worn in the morning before dressing to go out. It was, even under the sorry circumstances, most becoming.

"Thank goodness you are here!" she exclaimed, and, jumping up, threw herself into Holmes's arms.

I had almost to smile, my friend looked so discomfited. He patted her back and gently withdrew from the embrace.

"You will find out who did this terrible thing, Mr. Holmes," she stated rather than asked.

"My dear Mrs. Ballantyne," he replied. "It will be for the police to do that. I see Inspector Lestrade is already on the case. You can ask for no one better than him."

The same man was now approaching us.

"I might have guessed you'd turn up, Mr. Holmes," he said genially enough, "given the extraordinary nature of the crime."

"It is a crime then, and not an accident?"

"It was supposed to be me. *Me!*" Mrs. Ballantyne cried, and then again subsided into grief. Luckily, I caught her before she fell, and kept firm hold while leading her, staggering, back to the sofa. She looked up at me with eyes the colour of forget-me-nots, and clutched at my hand.

"Thank you, Dr. Watson," she said. "You are so kind."

"It seems a parcel arrived for the lady," Lestrade explained. "However, it was her husband who opened it. The box contained a venomous snake. The enraged creature shot out, biting him, and he succumbed almost instantly."

More sobs from the sofa. "It was so terrible," she muttered. "Poor Ramsay!"

Holmes shook his head. "The foolish, foolish man. I told him to be cautious."

"Did you, now?" the inspector asked. "When was that, then?

"Mr. Ballantyne consulted me recently regarding some threats directed at his wife," Holmes explained, continuing, "I trust you have caught the snake. I should not like to think it is lurking around here somewhere."

"Yes, thankfully, it is dead," Lestrade replied. "The servant – Claudette?" He consulted his notebook. "Claudine – a most resourceful young person, ran into the room on hearing the lady scream out. She seized a poker and succeeded in smashing it over the head of the creature."

"May I see?"

"The thing is in the breakfast room where the tragic event took place."

We followed him out.

"The – er – victim is still there, too."

The breakfast room turned out to be pleasantly airy, east-facing, and so chosen no doubt for the sake of the morning sun that was even now streaming through the window. Remains of a breakfast very like our own still lay on the table, toast and eggs and a pot of coffee. However, the porcelain cups and saucers lay smashed, and the milk jug had toppled over, spilling its contents across the damask tablecloth, the stain dark from the wood beneath.

Between the table and the window lay the body of the unfortunate Mr. Ramsay Ballantyne, his face frozen in a contortion of horror. I recognised the man who crouched beside him as Dr. Merry, a colleague who was frequently called upon to assist the police in their investigations. He looked up at me, shaking his head.

"A bad business, Watson," he said. "Once bitten, the poor man didn't stand a chance."

"There's the guilty party," Lestrade said, gesturing to a box on the sideboard, presumably the same which had held the living snake. Holmes crossed over to it and drew out the dead reptile.

"A-ha!" he said. "You will recognise it at once, I think."

Its speckled markings indeed looked familiar.

"Is it swamp adder?" I asked, recalling a previous occasion when another such was employed as a fiendish agent of death.

"Indeed, it is. And here is the paper that wrapped the box. Inscribed, as you will see, by the same hand that sent the spider."

"What spider?" asked Lestrade.

Thereupon, Holmes had to expand on the matter as we knew it.

"Hmm," said the inspector. "A nasty business altogether. Sending poisonous insects and snakes through the post! That's a first in my experience. Whatever next?"

"Might I examine the body?" Holmes asked.

"Of course, though there isn't much to see."

Dr. Merry made way for Holmes, who crouched down beside the corpse.

"Look here," he said, raising his head. "Is this not rather strange?"

He pointed to a pair of puncture marks on the victim's neck, evidently the snake bite.

"What's strange about it?" I asked.

"Perhaps nothing," he replied. "However, I am imagining Mr. Ballantyne opening the box. Surely the snake would have gone for his hand, his wrist. The nearest uncovered piece of flesh."

"Unless he was again wearing gloves."

"As you can see, he is not, which is strange in itself. He was so careful before."

"Perhaps he was bending over the box to see what was in it," I suggested.

Holmes clapped his hands. "Of course. Sometimes your voice of common sense cuts through my suspicious imaginings. Mr. Ballantyne bent his head low over it. Well, all that remains now is to track down who sent it."

"This 'Adolphe' you talked about?" put in Lestrade.

"Hmm," Holmes muttered. "Yes, by all means try to track down Adolphe, though... Well, we'll see."

"Since Mrs. Ballantyne was the intended victim, should measures not be taken to protect her?" I asked.

"I have already spoken to the housekeeper, and more especially to the lady's personal maid about it," Lestrade put in. "This Claudine is utterly devoted to her mistress, and has promised to exercise the greatest caution until we discover the callous villain who has done this deed."

"Did the girl have anything to add to what we already know?" I asked.

"Not really," Lestrade replied. "The box arrived by special delivery first thing. Claudine brought it in to her mistress, who had just come down, as you can see, to breakfast with her husband. The maid left the room. Shortly after, she heard the scream and rushed back in. Seeing the snake on the table, she seized the nearest implement, a poker, and managed to batter it to death."

"I see."

That accounted for the broken cups and saucers.

"And Mr. Ballantyne?"

"By that time, Mrs. McDuff, the housekeeper had arrived on the scene. She could tell that her master was already in his death throes. Nonetheless, she sent for the family doctor as well as the police."

"Is that the young man in the withdrawing room?" Holmes asked.

"No, the doctor left when we arrived with Merry. That young fellow is Mr. Ballantyne's secretary. Name of – " Lestrade again consulted his notebook, "Mr. Frederick Page."

"How does he come to be here?"

"He was bringing Mr. Ballantyne some papers for them to work on this morning."

"Was he indeed? Interesting, most interesting… Shall we rejoin the others for now?" Holmes said, adding, "I hope you will permit me to pursue the investigation, Lestrade. Since Mr. Ballantyne had commissioned me to do so, I feel I owe it to him."

"I am always grateful for your help, Mr. Holmes," the inspector replied, a little drily, adding, "Well, almost always."

The scene in the withdrawing room was much as before, although now Mr. Page was standing by the window, looking out. He was a pale young man with fine light hair. His appearance, along with the dove-grey suit he was wearing, gave the impression of a shadow, rather than of a full-bodied individual, and one, I suspected, who at that moment would have liked to be able to dematerialise altogether. Meanwhile, Mrs. McDuff still stood by, motionless as a statue, while poor Mrs. Ballantyne remained prostrate on the sofa.

"It is all my fault!" she was saying as we entered. "I shouldn't have dismissed it as a joke. It should have been me, who died, not Ramsay… My poor, poor Ramsay!"

Lestrade shook his head. "A tragic business," he said. "But you, Madam, are in no way to blame. You couldn't have known."

"I am amazed," Holmes added, "that he opened the box so carelessly after my warnings."

"He snatched it from me," Mrs. Ballantyne said. "I told him not to touch it, but alas, he was too curious." She collapsed in tears, her whole body racked in shudders.

"I wonder if the lady might go to her room to lie down," Holmes said. "It is clearly all too much for her. Perhaps there is something she can take to calm her."

154

Lestrade nodded.

"A good idea."

Mrs. Ballantyne stood and took a step, but nearly fell again.

"Claudine," she said. "Please send for Claudine."

"You go with her, Watson," Holmes said. "I should like a word with the maid."

Somewhat surprised at this instruction – to which, however, Lestrade made no objection, I offered the lady my arm and, she leaning heavily on me, we ascended the stairs to her room. As a doctor, I am, of course, well used to visiting ladies in their bedrooms. On the present occasion, I was, however, unaccountably uncomfortable. It was instantly clear that Mrs. Ballantyne didn't share sleeping quarters with her husband. The room was entirely feminine in its appurtenances, with pretty throws and cushions in delicate colours, and I felt I was intruding on the lady's private domain. Perhaps my confusion showed on my face, for she explained, "Ramsay sleeps fitfully, and often reads late into the night. He kindly decided to spare me his restlessness, and stays in the adjoining room."

The poor woman, speaking as if her husband were still alive!

She threw open a side door to show me. It was a different world, a monk's cell in its austerity. A single iron bedstead stood against a wall, a small table beside it on which lay a Bible.

She laughed through her tears at the expression on my face. "Despite what you might conclude about this, Dr. Watson, my husband and I loved each other dearly. He was one of a kind. There can be no one else like him."

"I am sure of it," I said, seeing she was about to break down once more. "But please, rest now."

We returned to her room, but instead of lying down, she crossed to the window. I followed her.

"What a wonderful view," I remarked. We were at the rear of the house, its fine garden backing onto Wimbledon Common.

"I love to look at the trees in all seasons," she said. "They calm me. See how the leaves begin to unfurl. Spring is such a wonderful season, is it not? A time of new beginnings. *Oh, God!*" She clutched at the window sill.

To distract her thoughts I asked, "How long have you lived here?"

"Only just over a year. Before that we were in Edinburgh. Then Ramsay was asked to take over the London branch of the bank. I thought…" She smiled sadly. "You know, Dr. Watson, in Edinburgh we lived in the New Town. There was always lots to do, to see, people to visit."

"Yes, I know Edinburgh well," I replied. "I have family there." I regarded her tear-stained face. "You are lonely here, I think."

"A little. But I am getting used to it."

She must have imagined life in London would be the same, or more so, as life in the busy Scottish capital. Instead, she found herself far from the centre, in this remote place. Her husband had his work, but she would know no one, would have nothing to do.

Five years married and no children, I thought but didn't ask. Most women in her position by now would have one or two little mites to care for.

She sighed deeply, her words echoing my suppositions.

"Now I have no one at all." Again she took my hand. "Promise me you will stay my friend."

Taken aback at the intensity of her tone, I replied in some confusion, "I promise. But your cousin – "

She flared up. "If Adolphe did this, then a thousand thousand curses upon him! But no, I cannot believe it. I cannot. Oh, Dr. Watson, please find out who killed my husband."

I stammered that Holmes would undoubtedly get to the bottom of the matter.

"I pray to God he will. Now, I will rest. Leave me please." She subsided on to the silken coverlet of the bed.

"Can I fetch you anything?" I asked. "I have no potions with me, but perhaps I could ask Mrs. McDuff to send up a soothing cordial."

She shook her head and buried her face in her pillow. I left the room quietly and descended the stairs. Holmes was no longer in the withdrawing room.

It turned out he had been talking to the same dour housekeeper.

"It was like trying to squeeze water from a stone," as he told me later.

"Even though it was she who summoned us to the house?"

"Yes, that is interesting, isn't it?" He paused. "From what she said, it became clear, finally, that she was utterly devoted to her master, and rather less to her mistress."

"I think that even I could have deduced that much," I said. "To be sure, she was in love with Mr. Ballantyne."

"Ah, you are ever the romantic. But what of Mr. McDuff, then?"

"Is there such a person?"

"There is, indeed." He looked at me quizzically. "The lady's father. Currently resident in Fife."

"I see. The 'Mrs.' is a title of convenience."

"Yes, but she is considerably older than her employer. Perhaps her feelings might be said to be more maternal than amorous."

"Still, she heartily dislikes his wife."

"That might be putting it too strongly. I get the impression that she considers young Hélène a silly goose, far too frivolous for such a man as Mr. Ballantyne."

"Perhaps that was what he liked about her, Holmes. Given the strange ways of the heart and all that."

"Again, I bow to your better wisdom on such matters."

He was teasing me again.

"Unforthcoming as she was in general, however, she was happy to tell me that the couple have separate bedrooms." He looked at me. "As you must have noticed just now."

"Yes. That's true." I described the arrangements, adding Mrs. Ballantyne's explanation as to why it was like that.

Holmes made no comment.

"What of the secretary?" I asked. "Does he come into the picture at all, do you think?"

Holmes regarded me with even more amusement. "You are determined that he should be in love with Hélène Ballantyne, and that perhaps the strength of his feelings led him to an extreme. Let me see… Ah, yes. Either to kill the woman who had rejected him, or the husband who stood in his way?"

I had to admit that such thoughts had indeed crossed my mind, the young man's arrival that morning being rather too much of a coincidence.

"But what a dangerous proceeding in that case," Holmes continued. "The plan might have misfired terribly, with the wrong person slain. Still, we won't rule out Mr. Page entirely. There is something about him that raises questions in my mind. I don't think he has been completely honest with me."

"In what way?"

"He claims to have arrived with papers for Mr. Ballantyne to go over this morning, and yet did you notice what the corpse was wearing?"

I tried to remember: Nothing out of the ordinary, surely.

Holmes cut in on my musings somewhat impatiently. "He was dressed as if preparing to go out. In addition, Mrs. McDuff had been quite taken aback at the arrival of the secretary, which occurred shortly after the terrible event, for Mr. Ballantyne had said nothing to her about it. This, she said, would have been most unusual, for he was generally very precise in his arrangements. She had assumed that he was preparing to set out for the office after breakfast as was his custom. When I challenged Mr. Page on the matter, he mumbled that there must have been a misunderstanding. He showed me the papers he had brought, as if they proved anything, except to give him an excuse to be there."

"Then you think he came to see the lady."

"Or perhaps the maidservant, Claudine. Surely it hasn't escaped your notice that the maid is quite as fetching as her mistress."

"Ah."

"Perhaps you are too smitten with *la belle Hélène* to notice." He waved a dismissive hand in the air. "In any case, we will leave Lestrade to pursue the matter for now. Let us go home and finish our own breakfast, for I find I am suddenly very hungry."

Time passed, as time is wont to do. Lestrade seemed to believe that cousin Adolphe was the key to everything. However, the boy was nowhere to be found, neither in London, nor Edinburgh, nor even at his home in Lille, his very elusive nature, in the eyes of the inspector, underlining his guilt.

"If he is innocent, then why is he hiding, Mr. Holmes?" Lestrade remarked, standing one morning in front of our fireplace. "I am inclined to Mrs. Ballantyne's view that it was a prank that went disastrously wrong – for why would young Adolphe want to hurt his cousin? And now the lad is terrified out of his wits."

"Hmm," Holmes said. "You may be right, Lestrade." He drew on his pipe as if utterly bored with the subject.

Meanwhile, I was keeping my promise to Hélène Ballantyne to be a friend to her, not an onerous undertaking by any means. There was, after all, something in Holmes's earlier insinuations, though to say I was "smitten" was going too far. I enjoyed her company, especially when she forgot her troubles and shewed herself to be the lively young woman of our first acquaintance. To distract her from her sorrows, I would meet her in Wimbledon to take tea (or coffee in the lady's case) in one of the delightful establishments in the village, or if the weather was fine to go for walks on the Common. She had a true love of nature, explaining that, growing up in an industrial city, she now revelled in the delights of the countryside.

"Yet you miss Edinburgh," I said.

"But in Edinburgh, you always have nature nearby. The times I have climbed Arthur's Seat or taken a turn in the Meadows or even in the Botanical Gardens!"

Another time I asked how she had met her husband. For an instant she looked stricken at the painful memory, then rallied.

"My papa has business interests in Scotland. I accompanied him one time and liked it so much I prevailed upon him to let me stay on there to learn English. Don't you think I have a 'fine wee Scots accent'?" Her face lit up. "The nuns in the school were horribly strict, but we were occasionally allowed to go out to cultural events – the theatre and so on. Oh, how I love the theatre!" She clapped her hands together. "I was even thinking of becoming an actress, though papa would have been terribly shocked! But I took part in some of the school plays, you know. It was such fun. I was Helen in *Women of Troy* once." She smiled at the memory. "But you asked about Ramsay. I met him through one of papa's associates at a reception in the French Consulate. It was quite the whirlwind romance, as they say."

Perhaps the fact that I found it hard to reconcile such a whirlwind with the serious gentleman I had met shewed on my face, for Hélène, as I had come to call her at her request, laughed merrily.

"Oh, but you have a saying in English, do you not, that still waters run deep." We were walking on the Common at the time, and she took my arm. "Ramsay was like that, and I think it is the same with you, Jean."

Good heavens! I admit that I was much attracted to her, but she was a widow of only a month or so, still in the black weeds that suited her so well. On the other hand, I mused, she was French.

160

Let me state now that I remained, and remain still, devoted to the memory of my dear late wife. However, Mary would have been the last person on earth to begrudge me happiness. One day I might expect to remarry and maybe even to raise a family, although I wasn't anticipating anything of the sort so soon and in such a way. Now I was conscious of Hélène's closeness, the light scent of her lavender water, the touch of her little hand on my arm, the faintest pressure of her breast. My heart started to beat faster. Was this then what was meant by a whirlwind romance?

"You are silent," she said. "I hope I haven't offended you, Jean."

"Not at all," I replied, a little shakily, and we talked thereafter of more inconsequential matters.

I had not divulged to Holmes the extent of my involvement with the lady, but no doubt he suspected it.

"A good thing you are looking after her," he said one day. "It is strange, though."

"What is?"

"Well, since the death of her husband, Mrs. Ballantyne has not, to my knowledge at least, received any further threatening letters, nor indeed any unpleasant parcels. It is possible, of course, that she has simply omitted to inform us. You might ask her about it, the next time you meet her. I hardly think the danger can have passed so completely."

To tell the truth, that she might yet be attacked had quite escaped my mind, and I chided myself for the oversight. When I put the matter to her at the earliest opportunity, she became thoughtful. We were sitting in Wimbledon's pleasant little Cherry Tree Café, with its flowery wallpaper and pretty cups, a favourite place of hers. She particularly loved their cakes, and was daintily partaking of a slice of Victoria sponge, using a small two-pronged fork to carry each bite to her lips.

"Mr. Holmes is right," she said finally, putting down the fork. "It is indeed strange. Of course, if Adolphe or another is behind it all, they are possibly too shocked at the fatal outcome to pursue their vendetta."

"So now you think Adolphe may have had a sinister motive after all?"

"Oh, Jean, I don't know what to think any more." She pushed her plate away. "My appetite is quite spoiled."

Of course, I apologised profusely. She forgave me, and even finished her cake. I forbore to tell her of the tiny blob of cream on the corner of her mouth, it looked so charming.

A few days later I called back to the house as arranged. The lady had taken a fancy to go on an excursion to the famous windmill. I confess that I was rather neglecting my medical obligations, and Holmes too, who, however, seemed caught up in some new study, for he was preoccupied with his Bunsen burner and stinking vials, and hardly acknowledged my frequent departures.

On being shewn into the withdrawing room by Claudine – and yes, I could agree that she too was very pretty – I found Hélène still in her blue morning robe.

"Oh, Jean, I am so lazy this morning. Forgive me."

"Of course," I said. "We can postpone our outing."

"No, no. I will get dressed in a moment. But, Jean dear, I was delighted to receive your gift. Thank you so much. How did you know they are my favourites?"

My gift? I had sent no gift. I espied an open box of chocolates upon the table. A sudden shiver went through me.

"I hope to God you haven't eaten any," I said.

"No, my dear. I was waiting for you." She picked up the box and offered it to me.

"Hélène, they aren't from me. I didn't send them."

She stared at me in shock, dropping the box. The confections rolled over the carpet.

162

"Oh, *mon Dieu*," she cried. "They are from *him!* – *The killer!*"

I started to pick them up, carefully, replacing each one in its little paper bed.

"We must get them analysed," I told her. "It's very possible they are poisoned. Where is the wrapping in which they came?"

She called for Claudine and gave her rapid instructions in French. The girl nodded and disappeared off, soon returning with the papers. The address had been printed as before, though the hand and ink looked to be different, no doubt to avoid raising suspicions in the lady's mind.

"Why did you think they were from me?" I asked.

She shewed me a card. It read simply, "*Sweets to a sweet, J.*" Far too sentimental to be something I would ever have written.

Of course, there was no more talk of windmills that day.

"With your permission, Hélène," I said, "I will take all this to Holmes. He has the means to analyse the chocolates. Let us hope we are fearful for nothing, and that they are harmless."

"Perhaps." She looked very small and vulnerable, and I longed to be able to comfort her further.

I instructed her to stay home and told Claudine to keep an eye on her. The girl had been promoted to housekeeper, since Mrs. McDuff had not wished to stay on after the death of her master. In any case, I do not think Hélène would have let her.

Instead of looking concerned, Holmes surprised me by rubbing his hands together gleefully, exclaiming, "Ha! I expected as much!"

He set to immediately to analyse the chocolates, cutting each one in half carefully, extracting a small crumb and placing it into a vial containing clear liquid. He then added a drop of another solution from a pipette, shook it and observed the reaction. The first six so tested proved to be unadulterated, and his good humour waned somewhat.

"I have better hopes of this one, Watson," he said at last, examining the seventh. "See, there's a tiny puncture mark underneath."

Surely he shouldn't hope to find anything. Still, Holmes had his notions and I kept silent. At last, his investigation done, he turned to me in triumph, holding up the vial. The liquid within had turned bright red.

"Cyanide."

"My God."

"Of course, no one was meant to eat it."

I looked at him, uncomprehending.

He sighed. "I have to apologise to you, dear friend."

"Why, Holmes? In what way?"

"I am afraid I have used you cruelly."

"I don't understand."

"Of course, I suspected the woman from the start. But how to prove it? I had to make use of your affections, in order to trap her."

A chill of fear overcame me.

"Hélène?"

He nodded. "It was almost unforgiveable of me, I know. But the woman is a monster. She and her accomplice."

"Frederick Page?"

"Not at all. That poor fool was another dupe, summoned, not as he thought, by Ballantyne but by his employer's wife, in a crude attempt to confuse. No, her accomplice was her sister, Claudine Dutoit."

I suppose my mouth dropped open, for Holmes couldn't help but chuckle.

"Oh, my poor Watson. How I have left you out of things. The women thought they were being so clever, but Claudine didn't even use a false name. An application to Lille soon revealed that Hélène and Claudine are siblings. Indeed, did it not strike you that they look very alike?"

164

"But how could you know about the chocolates?"

"I deliberately mentioned the lack of further suspicious packages to you because I knew it would get back to the lady, and that she would be likely to act quickly to avoid, as she would think, suspicion falling upon her. I therefore commissioned young Wiggins to activate the Baker Street Irregulars and keep an eye on both Mrs. Ballantyne and Claudine, which they did admirably."

The Irregulars were a gang of street urchins whose ability to blend with the crowd had enabled them frequently to assist Holmes in his investigations.

He popped a chocolate into his mouth. I started.

"Fear not. It is one I have already tested and found harmless. He pushed the box towards me, but I shook my head, shuddering.

"You will have noticed the name on the box, that of a well-known chocolatier in Piccadilly. Wiggins followed Mrs. Ballantyne there and observed her purchasing it, getting a clout on the ear by the doorman for his trouble." Holmes chuckled. "A necessary hazard for which I reimbursed the lad well. Anyway, the lady returned home and, early the next morning, Claudine was followed by one of Wiggins's foot soldiers to the General Post Office near Charing Cross, where he observed her posting a parcel of a similar size to the box of chocolates. You see the animal cunning of the pair, acting out the charade far from home."

"They poisoned the chocolates themselves and then sent the box to themselves?"

"Precisely."

"But how did you come to suspect them? Hélène seemed so genuinely upset at her husband's death. Indeed, it might have been she who was bitten by the snake. As you said before, a great risk to take."

"Another charade, my friend. Did you not tell me of her predilection for amateur dramatics? I strongly suspect that Ramsay Ballantyne didn't die of a snake bite at all, but, as I think a full autopsy will discover, of the same cyanide used in these chocolates. The symptoms being similar, the doctor would have had no reason to doubt but that the swamp adder caused the victim's death, particularly given the mark on the neck, probably made while the man was dying by something like a small two-pronged fork. I noticed such an item on the breakfast table."

I felt sick to the heart, and sank into my chair. A two-pronged fork – just like the one with which the cold-hearted woman had used to eat her cream cake.

Holmes continued. "To be sure, I prevailed upon Lestrade to let me examine the snake more thoroughly, and found it was certainly already dead before its head was smashed in."

I was angry with Holmes, though I supposed I could understand why he had kept me in the dark. He wished to use me to trap the murderers but couldn't trust me, if I knew all, to act out my part convincingly.

"But why should she do it? She had been married to the man for five years. Why now?"

"Life in Edinburgh was gay. No doubt a merry round of parties, dinners, concerts, theatres, of flirtations even, while the older husband, immersed in his work, indulged his pretty bride. Then they move here, where there is nothing to distract her. She is bored to death, with a man who has turned out to be far from the passionate lover of her favoured reading matter. I imagine she only married him to escape from the strictures of the convent school."

That thought had occurred to me too.

"She starts to think that life would be better as a rich widow," Holmes went on, "no doubt again getting ideas from the sensational novels to which she is partial. She calls for her sister to come over from France to pretend to be her maid, and eventually share the loot. Did you know that Claudine only started working for her recently, after the couple moved to London? They hatch the plan, thinking themselves terribly clever. I can only imagine the shock when you and I turned up, though the lady disguised it well. She had thought only to be dealing with plodding London policemen, and not the foremost private detective in Britain."

Preening himself, he took another chocolate. I hadn't known him to have a sweet tooth before, though I understand that particular brand of the confection is highly valued by connoisseurs. At that moment, to tell the truth, I felt so darkly about the whole business that I could have almost wished he would take a poisoned one by mistake. Not to die, of course, but to be sick. He had used me very badly.

"My heart is broken," I said.

"Nonsense. Your heart is perfectly intact. Anyway, the baggage would have thrown you over as soon as you had outlived your usefulness." He laughed. "You know I am right. If you really want a new wife, find yourself a nice comfortable woman, nearer your own age, one you can trust. One who won't put poison in your cup of Darjeeling. Or preferably, stay a contented bachelor, like myself."

Was he contented? It was not an adjective I should readily apply to him. Only sometimes, when he played his violin, did I guess him to be perfectly at one with himself and with the world.

We conveyed our discoveries to Lestrade, and duly accompanied him and his team to Wimbledon where we found the sisters blamelessly playing cards together.

"Jean," Hélène said, rising up, and looking in puzzlement at my companions. "I fear you have found something amiss with the chocolates. Is it so? Thank God, neither of us ate any of them."

How she was transformed, moments later from the sweet, pretty young woman before us. When faced with the truth, she became a snarling maenad, and cursed me and Holmes in a French which I imagine would never be found in school books. Claudine, for her part, shewed no sisterly solidarity, but tried to make out that she had nothing to do with the affair, that she was as astonished as the rest of us. But soon the pair of them turned on each other, each maintaining her own comparative innocence. They were taken away still screaming.

"You know, Watson, what first alerted me, by association of ideas, to the lady's involvement," Holmes said, that evening as we sat over glasses of a fine port wine. I had decided to forgive him, for after all a friendship like ours is to be cherished above a passing fancy. "It was," he said, "the arachnid."

I waited for him to expand.

"*Steatoda nobilis*. Known in English as the 'False Widow Spider'. Cheers."

He laughed, and we clinked glasses.

The Mystery of the
Murderous Ghost

"Dr. Watson! Dr. Watson!"

I knew that voice. My heart sank. However, I could hardly pretend to be deaf, common courtesy requiring me to turn with a smile on my face.

"Miss Pyne!" I exclaimed. "What a pleasant surprise! Whatever brings you to the Regent's Park?" For the woman had been a neighbour of Mary's and mine in Paddington, some distance from where we now found ourselves.

She returned my smile with a twisted one of her own that did nothing to enhance her thin, yellow face.

"Like yourself, I suppose, Doctor. Enjoying the clement weather."

It was indeed a fine day in early spring, bright but with an invigorating nip in the air. I had decided to escape from Baker Street, where, for he had nothing else to do, and no new case to investigate, Holmes was furiously playing some discordant piece of modern music – Russian, I think – on his Stradivarius, or when he gave up on that, slumping back in his armchair with a dark frown, puffing his vile pipe fumes into an already-stuffy room.

The park, up to that moment, had lifted my spirits, along with the spears of daffodils I could discern rising from the earth, fat buds ready to burst open on the cherry trees, young leaves about to uncurl. Truly spring is a glorious season, casting off the gloom of winter and giving rise to hopes and expectations for the future. It had been difficult for me near the anniversary of losing my beloved Mary, and then – unable to bear living any longer in the house where, for but a too brief time, we had been so happy together – returning bereft to Baker Street and Holmes. Yet on this March day nature's balm had proved even more soothing than the understanding sympathy I received from Mrs. Hudson. Precious little of the same, I might add, from Holmes himself, though, since I wasn't expecting any, I could hardly be disappointed at my friend's lack of empathy. How could he, whose heart had never been given to another, share my feelings of loss?

But now the lightened mood that had descended on me evaporated like a morning mist.

"Dear Dr. Watson." The woman hurried forward, her sharp little face avid. "I cannot tell you how very, very sorry I was to hear about poor Mary. I can only hope she was peaceful at the end – that she didn't suffer too terribly much."

I thought of my wife in her last hours, fighting for each breath, and myself unable to do anything more for her except to hold her hand and tell her that I loved her. I wasn't about to discuss this with my present interlocutor, however.

"It is kind of you to ask," I replied. "Yes, it was very peaceful."

"Thank the Lord for that," she said. "You know what a very dear friend I was to Mary. I was distraught not to be able to attend the funeral. I only learnt about it, you know, when it was quite over."

"According to my late wife's wishes, it was a very private affair."

"Yes, but surely she'd have wished her dearest friends to be there."

The pain was too much. Overcome with emotion, I prepared to walk on, courtesy be d----d. This woman, Eliza Pyne, despite what she claimed, was no great friend to Mary, who spoke of her as a busybody of the worst kind, always pleased to spread scandalous and usually unfounded gossip. I had no desire to prolong the conversation. However, I was not to be permitted to get away so easily.

"You poor, poor man!" Miss Pyne continued, actually catching hold of my sleeve. "But you know, you must believe Mary isn't truly gone. She will always be with you."

I nodded. "I will never forget her."

Again I tried to shake her off but the woman was as tenacious as a dog with a bone. Short of physical violence, I couldn't detach her.

"Ah, yes," she continued. "But you are in need of more solace than memories alone can provide, Doctor." Her darting eyes were bright. "And it just so happens that I know where you can get it." Her voice held a triumphant note. "This chance meeting of ours was assuredly meant to be."

I had a sudden dark suspicion that perhaps there was no chance at all in this meeting. Eliza Pyne might expect that, living so near, I would be in the habit of taking a turn in this park of all places. Was it possible that she had been lying in wait for me? Surely not. Yet it was a disturbing coincidence.

"Dr. Watson," she went on. "I must tell you that I have recently met with a truly amazing woman. She has great powers, you know – Signora Alma Contini. Well, you have no doubt already heard of her, for she is proving to be a great sensation in London."

No, I replied, I hadn't heard of the lady.

"That's a great pity. And it surprises me. Her name should be shouted from the rooftops." Her voice sank to a hoarse whisper. "She is able, you see, to communicate with those who have... *gone before*."

"Oh, you mean a medium. Miss Pyne, I hardly think – "

"Stop right there, Doctor. I know what you're thinking, a rational man like yourself. I was sceptical too before my dear friend, Miss Wraggs – you no doubt know her, another great friend of your Mary's..." I shook my head. "Well now, I am most astonished at that, Doctor. I should have thought – Sally Wraggs rings no bells?" I shook my head again. "No matter. Dear Sally induced me to attend a séance with la Signora – against my better judgment, I must say, for I am an even more rational being than yourself, you know. However, I went and was completely won over. The woman has powers over and beyond any other medium I have ever consulted. Here, take this." She thrust a leaflet into my hand, crudely depicting the image of a woman with penetrating eyes and Medusa-like curls, ghostly forms wreathed in ectoplasm peering over her shoulder. Inscribed upon it were the words *"Signora Alma Contini speaks with The Dead every Friday at eight o'clock at the Scriveners Hall, Chelsea."*

I started to explain that I had no wish to try and summon my late wife from whatever realms she now inhabited. Heaven, I had to assume, given Mary's goodness.

The woman refused to give up.

"Just promise one thing: that you'll attend a séance as an observer, and make up your mind then. What harm in that?"

I was tempted to tell Miss Pyne that I found a lot of harm in such activities. I abhorred them and fully believed that those who practised them were nothing more than quacks and charlatans, preying on the susceptible and needy. However, I simply demurred again, a little more forcefully, though still, I trust, within the bounds of politeness.

"Well," she said at last, more coldly, "I have to confess I am quite taken aback, Dr. Watson. I rather understood your feelings for your wife to be stronger. I imagined you, like Orpheus, would have travelled even to the Underworld itself to catch a glimpse of her again."

With that riposte, she turned on her heel and walked away from me, leaving me my mouth open. Orpheus, indeed! Wherever had that come from? I couldn't even be offended. It was too ludicrous.

I continued my walk around the lake, trying to distract myself from the unpleasantness of the recent encounter, and paused to watch three small children who were feeding the ducks, laughing delightedly and jumping up and down each time one of the birds made off with some crumbs. It was a pretty sight, yet I couldn't but recall how my dear wife and I had planned to have children – a whole tribe of them, as Mary used to say smiling. A fury rose in me then at Eliza Pyne's suggestion that I hadn't loved enough. I sat down to compose myself and try to shake off the meddlesome woman's remarks, the way the ducks were shaking water off their backs.

"What's this?" Sherlock Holmes was lifting the leaflet I had carelessly cast on the table. "Notice of a séance! Watson, have you become credulous in your old age?"

I explained about my encounter in the park.

"You see!" he replied, shaking his head. "As I have often tried to tell you, it is dangerous to indulge in unnecessary exercise. And yet…" He peered more closely at the paper. "Alma Contini. I have come across that name quite recently in some connection." He paused to think and then clicked his fingers. "I think I have it."

He rummaged through a pile of newspapers until he found what he wanted, an illustrated publication entitled *Il Secolo XIX*. He turned the pages, scanning each with eagle eyes.

"Here," he said finally, thrusting the paper towards me. "Read that."

"You are joking of course," I replied. "It's in Italian."

"A-ha, yes. You have not yet mastered that mellifluous tongue. Ah well, let me translate." He took the paper back.

Mysterious occurrence at séance [he read]. *On Tuesday last in the crypt of the Abbey of St. Carlo Borromeo, during a séance conducted by Signora Alma Contini, a young girl, Guilia Molinaro aged sixteen, fell unconscious, the near-victim of a murderous ghost who*

173

threatened her with Hell, fire, and damnation. In resonant tones…

Holmes looked up at me. "*Toni risonante,* mark you, Watson." He read on.

…in resonant tones, the imperturbable Signora Contini ordered the ghost to be gone, thereby it is believed, since the thing dematerialised immediately, saving young Guilia's life.

"Good Heavens! How melodramatic!"
"Indeed. But, wait, it gets even better:

When she regained consciousness, Guilia spoke of being dragged by a multitude of ferocious demons towards a dark tunnel – the entry as she understood, to the Kingdom of Hades. Despairing that all was lost, she then heard faintly at first but in crescendo, *the resonant tones* (Mark those tones again, Watson!) *of Signora Contini. Whereupon the demons ran howling from her and she returned to the land of the living, swearing to mend her ways and live a purer life. The powers of Signora Contini are truly amazing, a witness said later. She saved not only Guilia's life, but also her soul.*

Holmes put down the paper and looked at me, a smile playing over his lips.

"Well," he said, "after all that, are you still telling me you have no interest in making the lady's acquaintance?"

"Even less than before," I replied. "I have no interest whatsoever in involving myself with the Dark Arts."

"The Dark Arts indeed. A telling phrase. Well, let us see. Every Friday. So the next session with the resonant Signora will take place in three days' time. I should like very much for you to be there."

I laughed. "For *me* to be there? I don't think so. Go yourself if it interests you so much."

"It's true I am bored to death just now, with no juicy case to interest me. Indeed, while you were gone, I had a visit from some wretched woman who actually wanted me to find her chambermaid. The girl has made off with the family silver. How unutterably tedious!"

"She should contact the police."

"That's what I told her, but there's more to it. The family the silver belongs to is that of her husband, and as yet he knows nothing of the theft. She fears he will blame her. An angry and violent type of a man, by the sound of it. Discretion is what she wants and is willing to pay for. I have sent her to Rayfield."

Joshua Rayfield was a young man and admirer of Holmes who had just set himself up in the private investigation business.

"He will be glad of the work," I said.

"Yes, indeed. Though I doubt he's up to it. Well, no matter. However, you asked just now why I wouldn't attend the séance myself. A naïve question, Watson, if I might say so. That I, probably the most rational being in the whole world, should be seen consulting a medium! I should never live it down. You, as a widower, however, have the best excuse in the world."

I rose up, mortally offended.

"Holmes, if you think I would stoop to exploit my grief over Mary's death for your idle amusement, then you are an even colder fish than I took you for! How can you even suggest such a thing?"

He had the grace to look chastened.

"My dear fellow," he replied, "I had no such motive. It wouldn't be for my amusement, I assure you. Not at all. No, I have a feeling there is more to this Signora Contini and her activities than meets the eye."

"A feeling? You are generally not inclined to follow your feelings." If you even have any, I thought, still angry with him. "Unless, of course, there is evidence to back them up."

Holmes tapped the newspaper.

"This story intrigues me. One might imagine the lady would use it to advertise herself and her powers." He picked up the leaflet I had been given by Eliza Pyne, "But she does not. Hardly anyone in London has heard of her. Why is that? Are you not intrigued, too?"

"If I go," I said, already hating myself for giving in, "it will be as an observer pure and simple. I shall not let Mary come into it at all."

Holmes actually shook my hand.

"Capital, Watson!" he said. "Capital!"

The Scriveners Hall was a surprisingly dingy building, at least from the outside, set in an unprepossessing street that bordered rather on the working class district of Fulham than the prosperous Chelsea of the given address. I was surprised, the Scriveners Guild being a worthy and prestigious organisation.

The interior of the building, at least, bore out my preconceptions. The entrance hall was handsomely appointed, with a marble floor inlaid with the crest of the guild, and banners bearing the same hung from fine oak-beamed rafters.

I was accosted by an ancient with an alarmingly dark-red complexion – a sure symptom of Bright's Disease – in some sort of frogged uniform, complete with breeches and gaiters. I took him to be the gatekeeper.

"Your business, sir," he asked briskly, though politely enough.

"I am here to attend the séance," I replied.

At that, he frowned and muttered something, directing me to a room at the rear of the hall with a door that stood slightly ajar.

"In there," he said.

I tapped on the door, waited a moment and, hearing nothing, entered.

The place was dimly lit, its gloom only relieved by a few guttering candles, but I soon discerned a crowd of people seated in rows before a stage. A woman approached me, modestly dressed in black, a large silver crucifix around her neck. Was this Signora Contini? If so, she looked nothing like her printed image, with her smooth, prematurely grey hair and pale complexion and eyes.

When I asked, the woman laughed lightly.

"Good Heavens, no," she said. "The Signora is preparing herself. Mentally, you understand. I am Miss Violet Beynon, her humble assistant. But you are most welcome, sir. Please take a seat."

She tried to usher me to the front, but I slipped into a chair at the rear.

"As you please. I wonder," and she produced a notepad, "if I might take your name." She smiled. "Unless, of course, you prefer anonymity."

"Not at all," I replied, and identified myself. But when she asked for my address, I hesitated, reluctant to reveal as much. "Paddington," I said, which was not exactly a lie for my old house was still my property, though now rented out.

While sitting waiting for the show to begin, I took care to observe as much as possible, knowing I would be thoroughly quizzed by Holmes on my return. The low stage in front of us was screened off by a black curtain. The walls of the room were panelled in dark wood, topped by dusty-looking plaster mouldings depicting the accoutrements of the scriveners' trade: Quill pens, ink wells, open tomes, and the like. An unlit chandelier hung above us. The place was cold and smelt musty. It was all rather dispiriting, and I wished I had not come.

A few more shadowy people had entered after myself, to be greeted in the same way by Miss Beynon. By then I estimated that about forty people were in the room, most of them identifiably female by their bonnets. We waited on, some of the ladies starting to fidget and murmur.

Abruptly and without warning, the black curtain slid back. The whole audience, including myself, gasped, for now revealed in an intense shaft of light, a tiny woman sat huddled on a chair, her head down, arms crossed over her breast, hands lightly resting on her shoulders. From that attitude, I reckoned, she surely could not have drawn the curtain herself, and yet who else could have done it? No other person was near, the assistant standing behind us. And whence came that light where previously there had been none?

Now, slowly, the woman raised her head. I caught my breath. Before me was perhaps the most beautiful woman I had ever seen, delicately featured with skin of a porcelain whiteness, jet black curls piled high on her head. For some time, she stared out at us, motionless and silent. At last she stood up, extending her arms above her head and then letting them fall in a graceful gesture of welcome, the sleeves of her loose black robe, falling back at first almost to her shoulders and then down, to cover her lowered hands. It was a piece of impeccable stagecraft.

Holmes was to remark as I later described the scene that I had quite clearly become so besotted by the woman that my account of the séance was less than useless.

"Can you never be trusted not to have your head turned by a pretty face?" he asked, exasperated.

I was annoyed with him, reckoning I had given a fair description of what had happened. Signora Contini was beautiful, so why should I not say so? Of course, I had no belief in the woman's channelling of the voices of those who had passed over, as she described them. In fact, it had turned out to be an unremarkable, even disappointing evening from the point of view of spiritualist manifestations, of which there were none. No ectoplasm. No poltergeists. Yet there was no doubt in my mind that Signora Contini was a consummate professional, and even perhaps worked some good by bringing comfort to those she singled out. I could mention in particular a mother whose only son had recently died of consumption. Young Bertie told his mother, through the Signora, that he dwelt in a delightful garden of eternal summer, at peace, surrounded by the splashing of water, sweetly-aromatic flowers, and the song of birds.

"All a bit general," Holmes said, when I recounted the same to him later. "I could have invented something better than that."

"Yes, but then Bertie asked his mother if she remembered the Paradise Gardens at Littlehampton, which they had visited together years before, and she said she did, clapping her hands with joy. Well, it is just like that here, he told her. Now, how could the Signora have known such details, Holmes? The boy's name. And then Littlehampton of all places! I ask you that?"

"Beware, Watson. You are in danger of falling into the bottomless pit of credulity. If Signora Contini was aware that the woman was likely to be present, she would have investigated her in advance. That is how these quacks operate. I should expect to learn that the mother had attended a previous séance and, like you, had given her name and address."

"I didn't give my address."

Holmes made an impatient gesture. "No, but the mother probably did."

"I don't deny absolutely that trickery is involved. I just can't see how it works."

"It's elementary," he replied. "Ask any magician. In fact, I imagine I could do as well myself if I could be bothered to try." He threw back his head, revealing his noble profile. "Yes, indeed. It might be quite amusing. What do you think, Watson? The Great..." He clicked his fingers. "The Great *Cialatano*, perhaps." He turned

179

back to me. "In any event, I trust you will respond to the lady's invitation."

For, at the end of the séance, after the Signora had disappeared again behind her curtain and we were all making our way out, dropping our monetary contributions into a tray positioned for that purpose by the door, Violet Beynon had hurried up to me.

"The Signora particularly requests that you attend a more intimate meeting, Doctor," she had whispered. "A private séance with just a few chosen ones. She senses that you have experienced a loss and wishes to help you."

How the woman had even known I was present, sitting as I had so far from the stage was one mystery, and why she should have singled me out from all the others there present was another.

I had mumbled something non-committal, being torn. On the one hand, I had no desire to cheapen my grief over Mary with conjuring tricks. On the other, I admit the beautiful Signora intrigued me. When Violet Beynon pressed a note into my hand, inscribed in a flowing hand, it turned out to contain a date, time, and an address in Hampstead.

"You must come," she had said. "The Signora wishes it, you know."

It was almost an order and, despite myself, I had nodded.

Now Holmes rubbed his hands together.

"I might have expected as much," he remarked.

"Really?"

"Indeed, Watson. Your status and evident prosperity make you an attractive catch."

The population of London had been congratulating itself prematurely on the advent of spring, since, on the night that I set out for Hampstead, an icy wind was blasting the hill, howling through trees and causing them to hurl their still bare branches towards the Heavens as if pleading for mercy. Only a few hardy souls had ventured out, and those I saw looked barely human, scurrying by, bundled up and bent against the elements. By the heath, a fox crossed my path, stopped and turned and looked at me, its eyes flashing in the trembling glimmer of a street lamp. I shivered with a sense of foreboding.

Once again I wondered how Holmes had managed to talk me into such an enterprise. Even the prospect of again seeing the Signora could hardly make up for the ordeal of such a journey. If I were a superstitious man, I might even have thought that nature was conspiring to prevent my arrival, that the wind was crying, "Go back! Go back!" Or perhaps it is only writing this after the event that I imagine such a thing.

Worse was to come, however, for I soon realised that I was hopelessly lost, and now there was none but shadows to ask the way. The warren of dark little streets offered no guide. I must have been walking in circles, for again I found myself on the edge of the heath, its lumpy bushes darker against the dark like lurking hunchbacks. I turned away, and then nearly cried out in shock, for right behind me loomed an apparition in the shape of an old tramp, his hand stretched out.

"For pity, sir, on such a wild night."

His voice, though low and coarse, reassured me that this, after all, was no creature spun of mist but one of flesh and blood. My cold fingers fished a coin from my pocket and, as I gave it to him, I asked the way to Steeple Street.

It seemed I must have given rather more than I intended, for his gratitude was such that he insisted on conducting me to the steps of the very house that I sought, a tall building in a narrow street of similar edifices. When I looked back to thank him, he was nowhere to be seen. My sense of foreboding returned. I hammered on the door.

"A bad night and no mistake." Suddenly everything became normal again as the door opened on a bright hallway. The woman who greeted me was a homely body with a mob cap perched on grey curls, and a wide smile over her broad face. "You'll be here for the meeting, sir?"

I told her that I was. The housekeeper, I thought.

"This way then."

She bustled ahead, soon showing me into a well-lit and thankfully warm room with nothing sinister about it, just the usual appurtenances of any well-appointed parlour: a thick Persian carpet surmounted by several armchairs and a chaise longue, all most tastefully upholstered in dark green velvet, a fine marble fireplace within which embers yet glowed. A glass-fronted cabinet displayed a collection of china figurines – sentimental shepherds and shepherdesses, a boy in a sailor suit, crinolined ladies, a gallant in a three-cornered hat. A grandfather clock stood against one wall, an upright piano, sheet music open upon it, against another. Above all were hanging portraits in heavy gilt frames of worthy but rather grim gentlemen and ladies, perhaps the earlier denizens of the house. The only somewhat out-of-place feature was a large and highly polished round mahogany table in the centre of the room, around which eleven upright chairs were set, on which several persons were already seated.

If the wind continued to howl outside, in here we were unaware of it, protected as we were by heavy drapes that hung over the windows.

I had feared to be late but from the number of empty chairs, it seemed that not all were yet present. Of the Signora there was again no sign. However, her assistant stepped forward to greet me.

"I am delighted you have come, Doctor," she said. "Alma will be so pleased."

Just then I heard a squawk from one of those already seated. One of the women twisted herself round in her chair and fixed me with a quizzical eye.

"Dr. Watson! And you claimed not to be interested in such things!"

That rasping voice again! I might have expected Eliza Pyne to be one of the chosen. She made me sit next to her, something I could hardly refuse. Wedged in on her other side was a woman of grisly aspect and astounding girth, whom she introduced as Sally Wraggs, the other supposedly dear friend of my late wife's. The unfortunate woman's moon face was disfigured with a number of hairy warts, and several chins hung over her massive bosom.

"But of course you already know each other," Miss Pyne asserted.

I could truthfully say that I had never met the lady before, since, once seen, such a personage would only with great difficulty be forgotten. In any case, Miss Wraggs confirmed it.

"No, Lizzie," she said in a strangely high-pitched and somewhat childish voice, "I have to say I've never had the pleasure."

"Well now, I am astounded to hear that," Eliza Pyne retorted. "I could have sworn you and the Doctor here were acquainted. The recital in the town hall. Hubert Parry, you know."

"Alas," I replied, recalling the event. "I missed that concert. I had to attend a patient that night. In the end, Mary went with her cousin."

Miss Pyne shook her head and sniffed as if doubting my word and that of her friend over her own convictions.

More people were now arriving, including a fragile young girl who was shown to the seat beside me. I smiled at her but she looked away nervously. Perhaps, I thought, it was her first séance.

Now with only two seats remaining empty, including a throne-like one directly across from me, no doubt for the medium herself, Miss Beynon started to prepare the room. She placed a screen in front of the fire and extinguished the lights until only one candle remained, that in the middle of the table. The sudden gloom blotted out everything that had made the room familiar. All that could be seen outside our circle were flickering shadows. All that could be heard was the steady ticking of the grandfather clock, and soon enough Miss Beynon dealt with that as well, opening its front panel and halting the motion of the big brass pendulum.

Once again, most of the visitors here were women. Apart from myself, the male sex was represented only by a stout man of advanced middle age, dressed in tweeds, with a large walrus moustache and thinning hair, who looked to be more at home striding across the heath with a large dog than dabbling in the occult. In addition, a youth sat hunched in his chair as if hoping to disappear into it. This individual was skeletally thin and phthisic-looking, purple shadows under his eyes, lank hair long over his collar. A poet or some such, perhaps, dying for love of the Signora.

Silence hung uneasily over us until Eliza Pyne, unable to restrain herself, made some remark *sotto voce* to her neighbour. At which, Miss Wraggs started to shake with laughter, setting the whole table, against which her enormous bosom was pressed, trembling and vibrating. A cold "*Shh!*" from Miss Beynon soon brought the pair to order again, apart from a couple of quickly repressed final snorts.

The Signora clearly liked to keep people waiting – I suppose to increase the nervous susceptibility of her audience – but at last she entered, or most exactly floated in, all in black as before, wearing a loose garment that revealed nothing of her form, a mantilla over her head and face. She arrayed herself upon her throne – Miss Beynon taking the empty chair beside her, to her left – and stayed thus for a while, presumably regarding us all, though exactly where her gaze was directed could not be told through the black lace. Finally, raising her arms – this time encased in long, tightly-cuffed sleeves, so that we were sadly not vouchsafed a view of those slender limbs – she lifted the veil from her face, revealed now as lovely as ever, with, it struck me, the mature beauty that comes to some women in

184

their middle years. She had to be forty at least, and yet seemed to be without age, youthful and ancient at the same time, like a Greek statue. (How Holmes would laugh at such a notion. I often thank my lucky stars that he isn't able to read my mind. At least, not completely.)

Signora Contini now informed us in that charmingly low-pitched Italian accent of hers that she would endeavour to summon her spirit guide, a Roman slave from the eastern Empire named Puerus. Miss Pyne helpfully whispered to me that such guides – mostly of ancient and exotic origin – are common among mediums.

"Now," the Signora said, frowning at Miss Pyne, "please take the hands of the persons on each side of you, and, no matter what happens, hold tight not to break the circle. Do not forget. This is very important for all our safeties."

For my part, I was happy to keep hold of the cold little hand of the young girl to my left, though less pleased at having to grasp the damp paw of Eliza Pyne.

At a signal from the Signora, Miss Beynon blew out the candle and we were instantly blanketed in a total and unnerving blackness, until a faint gleam from the partially screened fire restored some shape to the room and particularly illuminated the white face of the Signora. I wondered indeed if she had anointed her face with some sort of luminous cream to enhance the effect.

Several times she called on Puerus, and at first there was no response. Then, at last, a boyish voice, quite unlike that of the Signora, replied that he was indeed present. A shiver of anticipation rippled through our circle.

"Have you any messages for anyone here?" That was Miss Beynon speaking.

Yes, it seemed, speaking through the Signora, that Puerus had messages – just like, I couldn't help thinking, some sort of astral telegraph boy.

The first was to an elderly woman, Mrs. Grace Herbert, from her late husband, Horace. He told her not to trust the man with one leg.

It sounded an unlikely piece of advice, but Mrs. Herbert squealed.

"That's Alfred!" she cried. "He's talking about Alfred Smith! Oh dear oh dear oh dear! But Alfred is always so kind and helpful."

"He is after your money," Puerus said flatly. "Have nothing more to do with him."

There were a few other similar and rather trivial sounding messages to others in the circle. Miss Wraggs, for instance, was chided by her mother for forgetting to keep the aspidistra watered, to which Sally replied in her childish voice, "Sorry, mama." Once again, I wondered what the devil I was doing there.

Then Puerus said, "*M... M...* there's an *M* here with an urgent wish to contact the living."

Eliza Pyne squeezed my hand, but I said nothing.

"*M...* a lady... she suffered much. Who recognises her?"

I frowned and clamped my teeth together. Eliza Pyne made nudging motions with her elbow but I refused to respond. I just hoped she would not answer on my behalf.

"No one wants M?" The call sounded plaintive.

Then the stout gentleman said, "I suppose it could be my maid Molly, who died from a kick in the head from my horse, Arion. A beauty, but such a nervous beast, you know." Presumably referring to the horse. "Well," he continued, "if the silly goose would go into the stable yard, she was asking for trouble. However, what urgent message she could have for me, I cannot think."

Maybe to care more for humans than for beasts, I thought.

But no, it was not the unfortunate Molly. Puerus finally gave up and moved on. I let out a deep breath. Forgive me, Mary, I thought.

"A man – a father, I think – wishes to warn his daughter," Puerus said. I felt the cold little hand of my neighbour tremble in mine.

Suddenly, shockingly, another voice, a hoarse and brutal male voice shouted out, "*It is too late, Annette, to repent your evil ways! Too late! You have shown yourself heartless and must in punishment lose your heart! Hell has opened its doors wide for you. Prepare to meet your doom!*"

Immediately, Hell broke loose quite literally. A cacophony of false notes crashed from the piano, the grandfather clock started chiming, objects flew about the room in all directions, the fire flared up behind its screen, casting writhing shadows, then died down as quickly. A portrait fell with a heavy thud. But far worse than all, a horribly decayed face, as of one long in the tomb, loomed huge and ghastly through the murk above us, only to swoop down upon the girl at my side. She uttered a long-drawn out shriek and then collapsed head foremost on to the table in front of her. Some of the women started to scream, Eliza Pyne among them, gripping my hand as though her life depended on it.

"Stop!" It was the Signora, in her own voice again, in what were undoubtedly resonant tones. "Stop this at once. Begone foul fiend!"

A sudden silence and a thickening of the darkness. Then, at last, someone lit a candle, revealing the table to be strewn with broken china ornaments, the now headless gallant in front of me. Amidst all this, the girl still lay prone, I still holding her limp hand in mine, though the circle must already have been broken by whomever lit the candle – someone I soon recognised as Violet Beynon hurried round to us. To give her space, I relinquished my hold on the girl's hand, and the assistant bent over her, trying to rouse her.

"What has happened?" the Signora called over to us. "Is the child all right?"

Miss Beynon looked across at me, horror on her face, and almost imperceptibly shook her head.

"You tell me, Doctor," she said in a shaky voice, moving aside. I felt for a pulse in the girl's neck. There was none. I gently lifted her head. Her eyes were wide and staring, staring but unable to see anything ever again.

"She is dead!" I said finally.

The moment of horrified silence was broken by a mighty scream from the Signora, who leapt up and rushed over to us. The mantilla fell from her head and her black hair streamed loose about her shoulders.

"No! it cannot be!" she cried, and held the poor corpse to her. "You are wrong, Doctor, cruelly wrong. There is life here yet. Her heart still beats."

She pulled the girl back and tore open her dress as if to prove it. Eliza Pyne, leaning over my shoulder, shrieked out and pointed.

"Look! The hand of the ghost." Indeed, bloody imprints of clutching fingers were branded on the ivory skin over the left breast. "The ghost snatched out her heart. Like he said he would!"

Could the foolish woman not hold her tongue!

The assembly gasped. As for the Signora, she fainted away into my arms.

A murderous ghost! It was absurd – and yet I could honestly attest that no living person had approached the girl before she collapsed. The circle had remained unbroken, I holding the girl's hand on one side and the surely blameless Mrs. Herbert the other. Indeed, the poor old lady was quite overcome, as were the other females present, particularly the wretched pair to my right, while the phthisical young man moaned and trembled as if about to have a fit.

The rational mind says that ghosts do not kill people. Sometimes, it is true, people die of shock, though not usually healthy young girls. But what of the marks on her breast? Oh, how I wished Holmes were present to tell me what to think!

188

Meantime Violet Beynon was taking care of the Signora, now conscious again but paler than ever, while the stout man seemed to think it incumbent upon himself to take control of the situation.

"A bad business," he said, shaking his head. "The police will have to be notified, of course."

"What! So that they can arrest a ghost, I suppose," Eliza Pyne put in tartly.

"And we must call an ambulance," I said.

"Isn't it a little late for that, Doctor?" Eliza again.

"The poor child will have to go to the morgue to be examined further," I said gently. "Does anyone know who she is?" I looked at Miss Beynon.

"She just gave her name as Annette de la Roche," she replied. "Of Paris."

"Oh, a Frenchie!" exclaimed Miss Pyne, as if that explained everything.

"That is most unfortunate," I said. "What is to be done?"

"The police will no doubt accomplish what's necessary, ambulance and all, without further help from us," the stout gentleman said, glaring at me as if I questioned his better knowledge.

"Well, now," Inspector Lestrade was chuckling a while later. "This is the last place I should have expected to find you, Dr. Watson. Is your esteemed colleague present, too?"

"He is not."

"Not yet, eh? I don't suppose he'll be able to keep away from a case like this." He laughed. "They're all telling me a ghost did it."

We were ensconced in the small study off the main hall that Lestrade had taken over for his interviews. It was a pleasant, book-lined den, with a handsome roll-top desk. I should, under other circumstances, be pleased to pass time there.

"Now I've always taken you for a reasonable man, Doctor," Lestrade continued. "Perhaps you can describe what happened here tonight in terms that don't include supernatural killers."

I shook my head.

"I have been trying," I replied, "to make sense of it all, but I'm sorry to say that the evidence indeed points to the ghost." Lestrade was about to interrupt. "Let me explain. We were all sitting in circle, holding each other's hands…"

Lestrade consulted his notes. "Yes. In the dark."

"In the semi-dark. It was possible to make out shapes. I had on one side of me Miss Pyne and on the other, the unfortunate victim. Not only can I be absolutely certain that we kept hold of each other throughout, but also that no one approached the girl until the ghost swooped down on her and she collapsed."

"You'd swear to that, Doctor."

"I would. However, I shall be most interested in the results of the autopsy. Then it will be clear if the girl died of shock – not an impossibility. The experience was, even for me, a frightening one, and perhaps the poor child had a weak heart. But, of course, I should also like to know whether there is evidence of some human involvement."

"We all would. I can't see my superiors being too happy if I told them I'm to arrest a ghost." He again turned to his notebook. "But perhaps just now you could take me through the events of the entire evening as you recall them."

I did so, in the knowledge that Holmes's training had sharpened my powers of observation to a creditable extent. At least, Lestrade seemed satisfied, making the odd note and nodding frequently while I spoke, confirming that my account tallied with that of the others. At last I reached the climax.

"Less sensational on the whole than that provided by certain of the ladies," Lestrade remarked. "And doubtless more accurate for that. But what do you make of this business of pianos playing by themselves, stopped clocks chiming, and china flying about the place? I have to say it sounds very peculiar. Very peculiar indeed."

"Nothing more than a clever magician could engineer, Inspector."

The new voice belonged to Holmes. I am not sure who was the more astounded at his sudden entry, Lestrade or myself.

"Apologies for my intrusion," he added.

"I thought you said he wasn't here." Lestrade regarded me accusingly.

"He wasn't."

"No, I just happened to be in the neighbourhood," Holmes said airily, "and observed the commotion outside this premises. Hey ho! said I to myself. Isn't that where Watson is attending a séance?"

Happened to be in the neighbourhood, indeed! I regarded him suspiciously, but his face revealed nothing.

"The housekeeper, Mrs. McDuffin, kindly let me in, when I told her who I was. She has of course heard of me." Spoken with a degree of smugness. "Since I'm here," he went on. "Perhaps I might be permitted to have a look at the location of the – Can we even call it a crime if the suspected perpetrator is... er... *disembodied*?"

Lestrade frowned. "I'd like to say no," he said. "I'd like that very much. But this one's a puzzler, and no mistake." He sighed. "Perhaps you can see things in that room, Mr. Holmes, that have escaped the rest of us mere mortals."

"Show me the way," Holmes replied.

In the hall we were accosted by Miss Beynon, who addressed herself to Lestrade.

"Inspector," she said. "The Signora's in a most dreadful state. Can she not go to her room?"

It was Holmes who answered.

"In a little while, after I have spoken to her, Madam."

She looked at him queerly but, since Lestrade didn't contradict him, nodded her acquiescence.

"This is the Signora's assistant, Miss Beynon," I explained to Holmes, who regarded her keenly. I had mentioned her to him before.

We then made our way to the parlour. It was empty of all but poor Annette – now laid out on the chaise longue and covered with a shawl – as well as two burly constables, the rest of the company having decamped to the breakfast room.

"No, no, no," Holmes said. "This will not do. Lestrade, please ask your fellows to leave. They are trampling all over the scene with their big flat feet, destroying evidence as they go."

Lestrade sniffed his displeasure at being thus ordered, but duly instructed the constables to withdraw. Holmes then commenced his investigation, getting down on to his knees to examine, painstakingly and most particularly, the floor around the table. Meanwhile, he questioned me. Who sat where? I reconstructed the space as well as I could remember.

"Ah! So the victim was next to you there, Watson. The Signora directly opposite. Good."

He rose to his feet. If he had found anything, he didn't share the intelligence.

"What was the precise sequence of events?" he asked. "For instance, how long after Signora Contini dismissed the ghost was the death discovered?"

I closed my eyes to prompt my memory. "The ghostly head swooped. The girl collapsed. The Signora spoke. Then silence…"

"Excuse me, Watson. Did the other manifestations – the music, the clock, the poltergeists – did they continue throughout while the ghost made those threats?"

"No. They had stopped. I think. Well now, it was definitely silent after."

He sighed. "Thank you. How long was this silence before anyone moved?"

I was about to say no time at all, but that wasn't correct. "Some moments," I said at last.

Holmes shook his head and tut-tutted. "Moments! How many? Think Watson."

"Not long, but maybe half-a-minute."

"Half-a-minute is long enough."

"Someone lit a candle. The one on the table."

"I see. And then you say the assistant – "

"Miss Beynon, yes. She came round to see what was wrong with the girl."

"On your side or the other?"

"On my side. I had to shift my chair back. Miss Beynon soon realised something was terribly wrong and asked me to confirm her worst fears."

"And then and only then the Signora started to scream."

"Everyone started to scream. Well, all the ladies."

Holmes picked up the headless china gallant, still lying on the table in front of my seat. It seemed to amuse him. The he moved to the chaise longue and gently lifted the shawl from the girl's body.

"A pretty child," he said, with more emotion than I had heard him express for a long time. "So where is the mark of the hand?"

I lifted the torn dress from the girl's breast. The ghastly red imprint still corrupted the white flesh. Lestrade shuddered.

"Hmm," Holmes said. "If it were blood it would have turned black by now." To my horror, he drew a dampened finger across the mark and lifted it to his nose. He sniffed and then tasted it. "No taste or smell. Cochineal, unless I'm very much mistaken" he pronounced.

"*Cochi*-what?" asked Lestrade.

"A red dye derived from insects."

"I don't understand," I said.

"Come now, Watson. It is surely simple enough. Remember the Italian newspaper article. This is quite certainly another trick employed by the delightful Signora to fool the credulous."

"A trick that went badly wrong, then."

"Well, that depends on your point of view. The ghost no doubt thought it turned out perfectly."

I disliked his levity. "But you don't believe in ghosts."

"Of course not. For one thing, if the girl is French and her wicked father the same, why did he speak English?"

"How did you know that?"

"Because you, Watson, who speak nothing but English, told me what he said. Maybe he even spoke English with an Italian accent, eh?"

He smiled at me archly.

For his part, Lestrade had been looking more and more puzzled.

"What newspaper article are you talking about?" he asked. "Don't tell me this has happened before?"

Holmes had then to explain his earlier discovery.

Lestrade scratched his head. "All most peculiar. So what do you make of it then, Mr. Holmes?"

"Clearly the masquerade was part of the show put on by the Signora, without intending, we may assume, the girl's death. She was assuredly to have been saved in the nick of time, as on the previous occasion, with the Signora as the heroine of the hour, and worthies like Watson here as witnesses. All present would then make a sizable donation to the lady, and spread the word of her powers. But someone had other ideas. The question is, why should this surely blameless child fall victim?"

"Unless indeed she died of fright."

"Unlikely if she was in on the trick, as she must have been."

"Well, I can only repeat that no one came near her." I threw up my hands. "I give up. It is an impossible murder."

"Hardly impossible," Holmes replied drily, "since we have the plain evidence before us that it indeed took place. Tell me everything again, Watson. Leave out nothing. Not a single nuance. And then I should like to meet the rest of the company."

As we made our way to the breakfast room, we met the housekeeper coming away with an empty tray. She had clearly been providing tea, or perhaps something stronger, to the shaken company.

"Ah," Holmes said. "The very woman. Please tell me, Mrs. McDuffin, does the Signora own this house?"

"God bless you, no sir. It belongs to Mrs. Grace. Mrs. Herbert, that is. Didn't she invite the Signora to visit her here after attending one of her séances, the first time the Signora was over from Italy, just after Mr. Horace passed on. Now she stays whenever she's in town." Mrs. McDuffin shook her head. "We've never had nothing like his happen before, sir. That poor little girl..." She sighed deeply. "I can only thank God Mr. Horace isn't here to see what them spirits have done to his lovely parlour. All Mrs. Grace's lovely ornaments broke. I told her no good would come of it, but would she listen? Not to say that the Signora isn't a nice enough lady. It's the rest of them."

"The rest of them?"

"The ghosts, sir. In my opinion," and she tossed her head with its little mob cap on top of it, "the dead should be left rest in their graves, where they belong."

"Amen to that," said Holmes piously. I threw him a suspicious glance.

"Mrs. Herbert," Holmes whispered to me as Mrs. McDuffin withdrew. "Wasn't that the person sitting on the other side of Annette?"

I nodded.

As we entered the room, all eyes turned towards us. Many of the ladies had been weeping, none more loudly than Miss Pyne and

Miss Wraggs – their faces red and blotchy. None more desolately than the Signora, with Violet Beynon sitting beside her, holding her hand.

"When will we be allowed to go home, Inspector?" the stout gentleman asked irascibly, consulting his fob watch. "It's getting very late. And," looking at my companion, "who the devil is this fellow?"

"Well, if it isn't Sherlock Holmes," exclaimed Eliza Pyne. There was a gasp of surprise, or perhaps dismay, from somewhere. "Oh, Mr. Holmes, please tell me we aren't all about to be murdered by that horrid ghost."

"No, no," Holmes said. "You're safe enough."

"How can you be so sure?" It was Sally Wraggs who spoke in that baby voice of hers. She put a hand to her stupendous bosom. "My heart's still thumping at the memory of that awful apparition."

"We will get to that in a moment," Holmes said. "But first I should like to commiserate with the Signora upon the death of her daughter."

More gasps. Signora Contini, however, regarded Holmes, her lovely dark eyes glistening wet with tears.

"How did you know?" she said.

So it was true.

"Come now, Signora," he replied. "You can't do the same trick over and over and expect no one to figure what is going on." He turned to the assembled company. "I regret to inform you that you have all been fooled tonight, fooled by two very clever people. Excuse me, Madame. I think you are left-handed."

Signora Contini nodded, puzzled, whereupon Holmes caught hold of her right arm and, loosening the cuff, pulled something from the sleeve. A balloon. He held it up. Flattened and shrivelled, it was yet recognisable as the same ghastly face that had loomed over us.

"You see," he said to Eliza Pyne. "You aren't likely to be at risk from this deflated fellow."

An indignant, nay angry, rumble spread through the company. The Signora shrank back in her chair.

"Fear not, Signora," Holmes smiled at her. "I shan't ask you to reveal what other devices are concealed beneath that flowing garment of yours."

"I won't believe it," said old Mrs. Herbert. "All those things flying about. The piano. The clock. That couldn't be faked."

"Sleight of hand," Holmes replied. "And an elaborate system of wires and small explosives. I have already found certain suggestive traces beside the Signora's chair. It's quite simple, you know. Any magician worth his salt could explain it better than I, and even reproduce the effects. I imagine the Signora and her assistant were granted free access to the parlour before the event."

"Oh yes," Mrs. Herbert agreed. "In fact, Mrs. McDuffin was rather put out." She looked across at the Signora. "How could you, Alma? I trusted you! And all my lovely ornaments – smashed!" She pressed a lacy handkerchief to her face.

"Your stupid ornaments! Is that all you care about? A few trashy trinkets." The Signora leapt to her feet in a sudden Latin fury. "What about my daughter! It was you, wasn't it! You killed my daughter! You envious old woman! Grace Herbert!"

"I – " Mrs. Herbert fell back in her chair, amazed. "Alma, whatever are you saying?"

"It must be either you or the Doctor here. Only one of you two could have done it."

Now everyone turned to me with hostile eyes, even Mrs. Herbert. I felt most uncomfortable

Holmes stepped forward.

"I can answer for my friend and colleague, Dr. Watson," he said. "He is entirely blameless. As for Mrs. Herbert," he regarded that lady for a few moments, "I'm convinced that she too had nothing to do with it."

"Then who, Mr. Private Detective?" the stout gentleman demanded. "If you're so clever, you tell us. Who committed this impossible crime?"

Holmes smiled charmingly at him, and shook a finger at him. "Improbable, not impossible," he said. "If you will kindly hold your horses, sir, I am about to explain." He sat himself on a convenient chair, leaned forward, and built the fingers of his two hands into a steeple. "First of all, we have to ask ourselves what motive could there be for such a killing. Young Annette or... What was her real name? Guilia?"

"Guilietta," said the Signora, with emotion. "My lovely girl. *Bellissima ragazza.*"

"Hmm," Eliza Pyne grumbled, "so even the name is fake!"

"What had Giulietta done to deserve her fate?" Holmes continued, ignoring the interruption. "Yes, she had taken part in some dubious trickery, but surely that was no good reason. So maybe the question should be not what had she done, but who she is."

"And how did you find that out, might I ask?" Lestrade was clearly put out that he wasn't privy to Holmes's reasoning.

"After seeing the article in the Italian newspaper, I simply did some further investigations, and soon discovered that the Signora was blessed with a daughter, now aged about sixteen."

The lady nodded.

"We are famous in Italy," she said.

Infamous more like, I thought.

"I can see," the stout gentleman remarked, "how, on discovering the fraud, someone might have borne a grudge. Of course I can't speak for anyone else, but I personally was prepared to make a sizable donation for the privilege of attending a séance held by the renowned Signora Contini." A murmur of agreement spread through the company, while the speaker glared at the lady. "Yes, indeed, I think we were all prepared to pay over the odds.

Now, I don't say that, even in the heat of the moment, finding himself – or herself – duped in the way Mr. Holmes has explained, someone would have been angry enough to commit murder, but even if they were, surely she – " He pointed at Signora Contini. " – would be the proper victim."

"You are correct," Holmes said. "But isn't she a victim, too? The Signora has lost perhaps the only person in this world who means anything to her. Isn't that right, Miss Beynon?"

That lady, taken aback at being suddenly addressed, mumbled, "Yes, I suppose so."

"How long have you been in the Signora's employ?" he continued.

"Oh, just a few weeks. Since she arrived in England."

I was surprised, having thought the association far more established than that.

"And before?"

"Before that what?"

"What did you do? Worked in a pharmacy, perhaps. Alongside your husband?"

Her eyes were wide. She didn't contradict him. The rest of us waited, all agog.

Holmes continued. "Have you always believed in spiritualism, Madam?"

"No!" The reply burst out perhaps a little more forcefully than Miss Beynon intended.

"Mothers," said Holmes. "What they will not do for their children. Isn't that right?"

The room was hushed in expectation. No one could imagine what was coming next.

"You too have a daughter, I believe. Or rather, you *had* a daughter."

In Afghanistan, I once saw a snake hypnotise a pika. The little creature stood frozen in its tracks until the snake pounced and swallowed it whole. That was a little like what I was witnessing here. Miss Beynon too was staring, immobilised, at Holmes.

"My daughter..." she murmured at last.

"What was her name?" He spoke gently.

"Lilian."

"And tell us, please, how did Lilian die?"

Violet Beynon rose up, suddenly full of fire. "How did she die? She killed herself." She glared at us all. "She killed herself after attending a séance." She turned on Signora Contini, who shrank back further into her chair. "Remember the last time you were in England? You claimed to have made contact with Lilian's betrothed, Frank, who had been killed fighting in South Africa." Miss Beynon laughed, a chilling sound. "Frank 'told' Lilian that he was in a beautiful garden where he would await her until they could be reunited for all eternity. It's part of Alma's regular patter, you know."

"Designed to bring comfort, Violet," the Signora murmured. "No harm meant at all. The opposite."

"Yes, but you see – Lilian *believed* it. She believed that if she killed herself, she would be reunited with her beloved and spend eternity with him in a paradise garden. So she came home and took poison."

"Oh, my God, Violet! I am so sorry."

"The Signora took away your daughter," Holmes asked, still gently, "so you decided that you would take away hers. Isn't that right?"

Miss Beynon fingered her crucifix. "An eye for an eye. A tooth for a tooth. A daughter for a daughter. Let her suffer as I have suffered. I bided my time." She looked triumphantly at the Signora. "Using my maiden name, Alma, I persuaded you to employ me. But I don't think you even remembered poor Lilian."

The company looked at Miss Beynon aghast. She actually seemed proud of what she had done.

"The question still remains, how she pulled it off." Lestrade said. "You haven't told us that, Mr. Holmes."

"Oh, that's the simplest of all, Inspector. The girl had already applied the bloody handprints to give the appearance that her mother's claims were true. After the girl pretended to collapse, Miss Beynon hurried round as planned, apparently to see what was the matter with her. What did you do?" He turned back to the assistant. "Prick her with a rapid-acting poison? I saw a tiny mark on her neck."

Miss Beynon said nothing.

"Or maybe you gave her a draught of something before the séance? You remarked on how cold she was, Watson." He turned back to the woman. "No matter. The autopsy will tell us what we need to know."

It was over. The spring storm had passed and we were back in Baker Street enjoying a warming cup of Mrs. Hudson's excellent Smoking Bishop.

"How did you uncover all that so quickly, Holmes?" I asked.

"Having nothing better to do, I amused myself with some basic research into the Signora and her entourage. Of course, I had no idea then that it would end in tragedy."

"But Miss Beynon seemed a sound woman, devoted to her employer. I should never have suspected her. In unmasking her, you yourself looked to possess some psychic powers."

"Nothing of the sort. I reasoned that since both you and Mrs. Herbert could be ruled out as murderers – along, of course, with the vengeful ghost – there was only one other person with an opportunity to kill the girl and that was Violet Beynon. I then simply employed the basic trick of the quack medium's trade. You deduce one small thing and then get the subject to tell you the rest, without them realising they are doing it."

"But what small thing did you deduce?"

"I spotted the faint mark of a wedding ring on the finger of her left hand. That sounded an alarm at once. Why would Violet Beynon wish to pass herself off as unmarried? Most women of her years like to be thought of as wives or at least as widows, some spinsters even wearing their mother's wedding band to give that impression. Clearly then she wished to pass herself off as something that she was not."

"But how did you know about her daughter?"

"I take it you didn't notice the brooch pinned to her blouse?"

"I only saw the crucifix."

"Well, of course that was another clue to Miss Beynon's creed, since the Christian Church abhors meddling with the paranormal the way mediums do. You must have noticed the vigorous way in which she dismissed spiritualism." I nodded. "But back to the brooch – a mourning brooch. It contained a curl of blonde hair, cut from the tresses of a child or young woman. A daughter, I surmised, quite recently deceased. Miss Beynon told us the rest herself."

"I am still amazed that you happened to turn up at Steeple Street at all, Holmes."

"Oh, I had one of those feelings, Watson, of which you think me incapable. A feeling, based of course on my researches, that something was up. In fact, I visited earlier in the day and had a most interesting chat with the inestimable Mrs. McDuffin. As a result of what she told me, I was determined not to miss the fun. As you so nearly did."

"I?"

"Thank goodness for the old tramp who set you to rights. By the way, Watson, here's your sovereign. Absurdly generous, I might say."

I sat, open-mouthed, while he tossed the coin back to me.

Dr. Watson's Dilemma

The following troubling narrative should, I think, make clear why I, a doctor bound by the Hippocratic Oath, have delayed decades in recording it, the events here described relating to the earliest years of my association with Sherlock Holmes, when we were first residing together in Baker Street. It was early January, a miserable damp and foggy month. Christmas, a season I love but which my associate abhors, had passed, hardly remarked at Baker Street, despite Mrs. Hudson's best efforts at festivity.

"Goodwill to all men, indeed," Holmes would blast. "Look around you, Watson. Truthfully, how much real goodwill do you see? Sentimental twaddle. I blame Mr. Charles Dickens for this mess."

He was hardly less enthusiastic about celebrating his birthday which followed hard on the heels of Yuletide, on 6 January. The first couple of years I spent with Holmes, I made the mistake of purchasing a gift for him, only to have it dismissed out of hand.

"You keep this scarf, Watson," he would say, "for I shall never wear it. I cannot abide a checkered pattern."

Or, "Do you not consider, Watson, that if I had need of a leather-bound notebook embossed with my name, I could have purchased it myself?"

Needless to say, he never reciprocated with a gift for me on my birthday which falls in the altogether pleasanter month of August, and thus it was that I had decided not to buy him anything on this occasion. It was to my considerable surprise, therefore, that over the New Year, as we were finishing our supper, he gave a great stretch and said, "I have been thinking, Watson, of what gift you might buy for me this year. Rather than the dreary little surprises that it is your wont to offer, how much better if I tell you exactly what I should like to have."

"Well now – " I started to reply, but he held up his hand.

"Please do not tell me I am too late, that the wretched thing has already been purchased," he said, a smile tempering his harsh words.

I shook my head.

"Then I should like very much for you to go to Charing Court, one of those paved alleyways between the Charing Cross Road and St. Martin's Lane, where you can find all manner of fascinating book and print shops."

"Yes," I replied, "I know the place."

"Good. Well about halfway along you will find a dingy-enough establishment with, in the window, some ancient maps. I am particularly interested in the one featuring Asia Minor with its illustrations of the preposterously exotic humans imagined to inhabit those wild places."

An inscrutable expression on his face, he then reached for his pipe and stuffed it from the Persian slipper with the abominable weed it pleased him to smoke.

As it happened, I had business in the West End district on the following morning, and, that accomplished, made my way on foot to Charing Court. The day was cold, dank, and dismal, with a chill that penetrated to the very bones, a stink of smoke infecting the air and turning it yellow. My spirits thus being already low, worse was to come. The shop in question turned out to be a dark hole of a place hardly warmer inside than out, with a door bell that clanged like a veritable knell of doom. Nor did my mood lift, when, on requesting the Asia Minor map displayed in the cobwebbed window, I was informed that the price was six guineas, much more than I had intended to spend, especially for something so stained and torn at the edges. The grey-bearded elderly owner, as cobwebby as his establishment, saw that I hesitated.

"It is a beautiful map, your honour. An antique. Eight-hundred years old, it is. One of a kind. You won't get anything like it anywhere else."

As it happened, my business in town had resulted in an unexpected bonus payment, so that I had coins a-plenty rattling in my pocket.

"Will you take five guineas?" I heard myself say, having judged from the man's face that he would be ready to bargain."

"Oh sir, your honour," he replied. "You want to rob a poor bookseller of his profits..." He paused. "Well, let's say, five-and-a-half guineas."

He held out a hand for me to shake.

Holmes is, after all, a very good friend, I thought, relenting, and I grasped the man's horny claw.

"Since I know what it is you have bought me," Holmes said, on my return to Baker Street, observing what I was holding, "you might as well give it to me at once."

This being three days before the anniversary in question, I was somewhat bemused. However, I duly handed the thing over and wished him many happy returns, receiving only a perfunctory nod and no thanks as he eagerly pulled the map from its tube. He spread it out on the table and pored over it.

"So how was old Balthazar?" he asked me.

"Who?"

"The bookseller. How did you find him?"

"Easily enough," I said, deliberately pretending to misunderstand, for I was annoyed with him. "Given your most precise directions."

He looked up at me. "No, what were your impressions of the man? How did he look?"

"Not very prepossessing," I replied. I had not realised I should be required to make a report and thus had not paid the man any particular attention.

"No more than that? You disappoint me, Watson."

"Old. A grey-beard."

"Yes . . . and?"

I closed my eyes to think. "A foreigner, though he speaks good English. Wearing a long robe and a kind of turban. An Arab, perhaps. A Jew."

"An Arab," Holmes said. "I should say so."

"You have met him yourself then?" I asked. So why then did you need to hear it from me, I wondered? It was all most provoking.

"No, I have never met the gentleman," Holmes replied. "Though I have heard of him, and, moreover, in more precise detail than you have been able to give me."

"I didn't take to him," was all I replied to that remark.

"Let us hope, anyway, he didn't charge you overmuch," he said after a while, studying the map. "A guinea or two would be a reasonable price, I think."

I wasn't about to reveal what I had paid – it was a gift, after all – but my dismay must have shown on my face, for Holmes exclaimed, "More! Much more! Oh, Watson, Watson. He saw you coming."

After a few moments, he continued. "And what of his esteemed companions, Mr. Kaspar and Mr. Melchior. Were they in attendance too?"

"I saw no one else, "I replied. "Only Balthazar." Whereupon Holmes raised quizzical eyes to mine, and I grinned. "Of course, the three wise men. Apologies, Holmes. I am very slow today."

"Not at all, dear friend. I have been teasing you. But come. There isn't a moment to be lost." He rolled up the map again, and replaced it in its tube.

"Where are we going?" I asked.

"Back to Balthazar, Watson. I'm afraid he has sold you a fake."

206

As we approached the alley, dark as a tunnel in the fading afternoon light before the gas lamps were lit, Holmes seized my arm.

"Now I'm going to surprise you, Watson, but whatever I say, keep a straight face and back me up if necessary."

My suspicions were growing by the moment that I had been used, and not for the first time, in one of Holmes's investigations. Why the man felt he could not fully confide in me was beyond my comprehension. However, I was becoming intrigued enough with the present case not to turn on my heel and abandon him, despite a little voice telling me I should do just that, to serve him as a lesson.

We entered the dusty shop to the clang of the doomful bell, Holmes stumbling somewhat and having to cling to my arm. At first it seemed as if the place were empty. Then, from the shadows, the old man emerged – again, to my mind, looking as if the cobwebs everywhere in evidence were clinging to him too.

Holmes raised his head and sniffed appreciatively. "Ah, the musty scent of old books."

"Good day again, honoured sir," Balthazar said to me. "Have you come to buy another of my fine maps?"

"Not at all," Holmes cried out angrily. "We have come to demand my friend's money back. You have sold him a modern forgery."

The old man shook his head vigorously.

"Certainly not, honoured sir! The map is genuine. One-thousand years old."

"You told me eight-hundred," I said.

Holmes removed it from its roll.

"I doubt it is one-thousand hours old," he said. "Where do you make them, old man? In the back of the shop? Is it coffee you use to stain it to look so ancient?"

"No, sir. I assure you. My reputation as an honest man is well known. Ask anyone. If it is a fake, as you say, then I too have been fooled, although…"

To my horror, at that moment, Holmes clutched at his breast and staggered, falling against the counter.

"Sacker!" he gasped. "My elixir…"

It took me a moment to realise that he was addressing me. Had he gone mad? Was he having a stroke? A man not yet thirty!

"My elixir, if you please." His voice was barely above a murmur. "In my breast pocket."

I reached in under his jacket and drew out a little vial of I knew not what. Uncorking it, I put it to his lips and he drank of it, seeming to find therein some assuagement.

"Thank you, dear friend," he muttered. "Thank you. Then he turned to Balthazar, who had been hovering anxiously.

"Is there somewhere I could sit down," he asked, "until the worst has passed?"

"Come back here, honoured sir," the old man replied, drawing aside a ragged curtain. "Rest for as long as you need."

Given the sharp way in which Holmes had previously addressed him, Balthazar's behaviour now showed, I judged, an unexpectedly worthy degree of compassion.

The room we were in was small and windowless, furnished with a table and three spindly chairs into one of which Holmes fell as with great relief. Bookshelves, filled with dusty tomes surmounted by rolls of ancient looking manuscripts, lined the walls of this gloomy space. A map lay spread out on the table, apparently of an age with the one I had so foolishly purchased. An antique or another fake?

The old man's eyes lit up as he smoothed his hand over the map.

"The North Atlantic, honoured sirs, as imagined by the old cartographers. See what monsters they thought to be lurking there."

It was hard to make them out but gradually I discerned grotesque forms emerging from the waves, threatening tiny ships with certain destruction.

"What fancies they had!" Balthazar remarked. "No sirs, it would be beyond my powers to make copies the likes of these."

He poured a cup of water from a jug and offered it to Holmes.

"I am sorry if we offended you," the latter said, accepting the drink. "Only I was sure, you know, the map was forged. It is this damned condition of mine. It gives me brain fever."

"You are badly afflicted then, honoured sir?" Balthazar asked.

"Sacker could tell you," Holmes replied looking at me. I was about to speak, not quite sure what to say, when Holmes went on. "It will prove fatal in the end, an end I confess that I crave, for the pain and suffering are sometimes beyond belief."

"Yes indeed," I said at last. "My friend's suffering is indescribable." True enough, I thought, for I had no idea what he was talking about.

"We are quick to put common beasts out of their misery," Holmes continued, "but when it comes to human beings whose awareness of pain is so much more acute, those of us suffering unutterable torments must endure until nature takes its course. It isn't right. And yet – and yet I fear the final coup. I tell you frankly, my friend, I would end myself this minute, if I had the courage to do it."

After this astonishing speech, Balthazar sat looking at Holmes for a while, then said, "Honoured sir, fate has led you to me."

"Indeed. And how is that?"

"For the moment, I should prefer not to say." He glanced at me. "However, if you would care to return tomorrow, alone, at this same hour, I shall be happy to enlighten you."

Holmes leaned across the table and grasped the man's hand.

"Can you help me then? Do you have some elixir stronger than the one I have to take away the pain?"

"I can most certainly assist you – but tomorrow, honoured sir, if you can wait that long."

"Every instant will drag for me until that moment," Holmes said rising, staggering again so that I was obliged to support him.

"In the meantime," Balthazar remarked, "I shall be glad to return the five guineas your friend here spent on the map."

"Five-and-a-half," burst out of me.

The old man regarded me with lidded eyes. "Five-and-a-half. Just so."

"Not at all," Holmes replied. "I was mistaken. I shall treasure the map for as long as – " His voice broke a little. " – for as long as I live."

"Till tomorrow then, honoured sir," the old man said. "By what name shall I know you?"

"You can call me Sherrinford," said Holmes. "Henry Sherrinford."

We left the shop to the accompaniment of the clanging knell of doom.

It wasn't until we were well away from Charing Court that Holmes no longer leaned on me but regained his normal sprightly step.

"That went rather well," he said cheerfully.

"I hope you will explain to me now what it was all about."

"My apologies, dear fellow. Yes, indeed. I shall be glad to tell all as soon as we get back to Baker Street."

"I am surprised you decided to keep the fake map," I said, chafing at the thought of my wasted five-and-a-half guineas.

"Good heavens, Watson. It's no forgery. Do you doubt I could recognise the genuine article? The map is exceedingly old and worth as much if not more than what you paid for it."

"But… but…" It was all quite beyond me.

"A ploy, don't you know, to get me an introduction to the old gentleman. By the way, Watson. Remind me what it was that the original Balthazar brought as a gift to the child in the manger."

I paused for thought. "Hmm... Gold, frankincense and myrrh. But which..."

"Myrrh, that's the thing. Myrrh, a reminder of mortality, used to anoint the bodies of the dead." He nodded as if it was all now quite clear to him. As for me, the foggy miasma rising about us was hardly thicker than the fog of incomprehension in my head.

Holmes could really be the most aggravating of men. It wasn't until we were warm and comfortable in front of a good fire, with glasses of Mrs. Hudson's fine Smoking Bishop in our hands, that he started to explain.

"You recall no doubt the circumstances relating to the death of Mr. Alfred Parkinson."

I nodded. The sorry accident that had caused the demise of that well-known merchant had filled the newspapers for a brief time some weeks before. It seemed that Mr. Parkinson had been heading on foot to his club when he had become disoriented in the fog and had stumbled into a ditch, drowning in just a few inches of water. As well as a glowing obituary of the merchant, I recalled that *The Times* had taken the opportunity to print a cautionary tale regarding elderly gentlemen who might (reading between the carefully worded lines), have over-indulged in spirituous liquors, thus rendering them incapable of clear thought and subject to unfortunate accidents.

"I have been approached," Holmes explained, "by Mr. Parkinson's nephew, a Mr. William Darnley, who suspects dark doings with regard to his uncle's death. Acting as one of the executors, Darnley recently received a bill from something called The Proxy Club, of which Mr. Parkinson was apparently a member. It seems the Club was looking to be paid what seemed an excessively high membership fee, the strange element being that payment was only to be made after the member's death."

"*After* the death! How very extraordinary."

"Yes, indeed. In fact, it was quite by chance that the nephew uncovered this detail. In the normal course, had Mr. Parkinson not retained the original contract – which I understand was hidden away in a secret compartment of his desk – the sum would have shown as a simple fee owing, which the executors would have paid among all other such pending debts." Holmes made a steeple of his hands and tapped the forefingers against his lips before continuing. "The other factor, of which Darnley informed me, was that in latter years his uncle was suffering from a painful wasting disease."

Holmes leaned back and looked at me.

"I see," I said.

"Do you? Do you, Watson? Tell me exactly what you see."

"Well..." Of course, he had thrown me off kilter again. I had not a notion in my head.

"I have, as you may surmise, been looking into this same Proxy Club," Holmes went on, ignoring my confusion. "With some difficulty, I might add. It isn't listed among the regular clubs of the country. A lucky chance meeting with Inspector Lestrade recently – you recall of course, the Barlow case, in which I was instrumental in returning a fine Stradivarius to its owners – revealed to me that Lestrade wasn't unaware of the existence of this club, having noted it, without realising its significance, as having among its members such dignitaries as Maria Angelotti, the opera singer, Herr Gartner, the German cultural attaché, and Benjamin Mortlake, the portrait painter."

"All dead!" I exclaimed.

"Precisely. And all suffering from incurable diseases."

"Good heavens, Holmes. What evil lurks here?"

He sipped his Smoking Bishop, smacking his lips. "There is after all one good thing to be said for the present season: It encourages Mrs. Hudson to brew up this most delectable and cheering beverage."

I refused to be distracted. "This Proxy Club is somehow linked to Balthazar, is it?"

"At last, Watson, light dawns in your benighted brain." He smiled, again to mitigate the stab of his words. "A complex trail, which I won't bother you with, has indeed led me to those unlikely premises at Charing Court. Today I essayed an experiment, and must thank you for playing your own part in it most admirably..."

Had I? All unbeknownst, anyway. However, I nodded acceptance of this unwonted compliment.

"You think the bookseller is behind these deaths, then?"

"From my investigations, it seems most likely."

"And yet he seems so kindly! Good Lord, Holmes, what a cunning villain to be able to dissemble so well."

"Indeed, as you say: A cunning villain..." Holmes nodded. "However, to be sure, I shall return tomorrow, as he requested, and beard the old greybeard in his lair."

"Is that safe?"

"Until this poor suffering individual signs a contract with him, yes, I am sure it is."

On the following day, I was most unwilling for Holmes to venture forth alone. However, he reminded me of Balthazar's stipulation.

"I don't think he will reveal himself fully if you accompany me."

"Can I not at least bring you to the shop? Ill as you are." I sniffed. "After all, you can hardly reach it safely alone. What if you were to collapse in the street?"

He regarded me quizzically. "My word, Watson, you are becoming as devious as I. An ungainsayable argument. Yes, by all means, bring me, limping and staggering, to the shop and then, if required, make yourself scarce until the time comes to remove me again."

I noticed that his skin was turned grey and that his eyes seemed shot with blood. Was he truly ailing?

"You are looking askance at me, Watson. I haven't over-done the cosmetics, I hope."

Understand that in those days I was still unused to the degree to which Holmes could change his appearance in the twinkling of an eye.

Once again at the appointed hour, what light there was already fading, we made our way to the dingy little shop in Charing Court, Holmes becoming ever more reliant on my support the nearer we approached.

"Who knows who might be keeping a look-out," he whispered to me.

The old man frowned as we entered.

"Alone, I said, Mr. Sherrinford."

"I cannot manage by myself for any distance," Holmes replied. "And Sacker here is entirely in my confidence."

"Not possible, honoured sir," Balthazar replied firmly. "There must only be the two of us."

"So be it," Holmes replied with a sigh. "I suppose you can occupy yourself elsewhere, my friend, for – " He looked at the other. " – a half-hour?"

Balthazar nodded.

I was loth to leave, but Holmes nodded reassuringly. However, just as I was on my way out, a little girl entered. She was thin, with tangled dark curls and a grubby face, wearing a ragged dress and shawl, hardly sufficient for the chill of the day. At least she was not barefoot as were so many of her ilk, even if the boots she was wearing were several sizes too big for her.

"Ah, Sal," said Balthazar kindly. "Have you come for your basket?"

"Yes, if you please, Uncle," the girl replied, watching us warily.

"Wait just a moment," the old man said, disappearing into the room at the back of the shop.

"Are you sure?" I started to say softly to Holmes. "I'd much rather stay."

Sal's bright eyes passed from one of us to the other.

Holmes just shook his head as Balthazar returned, carrying a large basket, its contents covered with a cloth.

"How is little Tommy?" he asked the girl.

"Not so good, Uncle. A bit better, mebbe."

"I hope so. I've put in some linctus. It should help him. Now will you be able to manage by yourself?"

Sal lifted the basket. It was evidently almost too much for the little mite, but she nodded.

"Why don't I carry it for you?" I said. "I have time on my hands, after all."

The girl looked reluctant to yield her treasure until the old man said, "Thank the kind gentleman, Sal." While to me, he added, "It isn't too far. The Devil's Acre."

I shuddered. Despite efforts to clear that particular district in recent times, it was notorious as a dangerous slum. Still, I had offered and could not now very well demur, so I lifted the heavy basket and accompanied Sal from the shop.

The girl kept a close watch on me as if suspecting that at any moment I might make off with whatever was in the basket. Together we dodged the traffic to reach Trafalgar Square, Sal more adept than I at circumventing the rushing hansom cabs and carriages, even with the handicap of the too big boots. She waited for me by one of the great bronze lions, a mocking expression on her face.

"That's a scary beast," I said, attempting to engage her in chat.

"It isn't real," she replied dismissively, tossing her curls.

215

This wasn't at all promising and I resigned myself to a silent trek, down Whitehall with its imposing buildings and palaces, past the gothic glory that is Westminster Abbey, such a contrast to the place whither we were bound. Indeed, all too soon we found ourselves in the warren of slum streets known as the Devil's Acre. I had visited here several times before in the course of my medical duties, on each occasion ever more horrified at the conditions these poor people had to endure. Tumbling down tenements with broken or no windows, tiles fallen from roofs, leaving interiors open to rain, hail, and snow, the wretched inhabitants crammed to overflowing in mildewed rooms, unspeakable filth running in the streets between, fat rats glimpsed in all corners. Still today it makes me angry that the authorities have failed so dismally to improve the lot of this portion of the population, some self-righteous individuals even justifying their inactivity by claiming, erroneously, that it is their own immorality that has reduced the poor to this level.

Meanwhile, Sal had stopped at a door patched up with odd planks of wood. She stretched out her hand for the basket.

"This is us," she said. "Upstairs."

"Let me bring it for you," I replied. For it was indeed very heavy.

She shrugged and led the way up a gloomy stairwell, the treads treacherous from rot.

The room occupied by her family was in no way luxurious, but at least it was clean. Clearly some effort had been made to render it homely with pictures from almanacs pinned to the walls and a bunch of those flowering weeds that grow so freely on waste ground set in a jam jar, but it was very cold, a miserable fire struggling in the grate. Two little mites played on a thin rug on the wooden floor. A thin and harassed looking woman stared at us in astonishment as we entered.

"Who's this then, Sal?" she asked

216

"Don't know, mammy," came the reply. "He *would* carry the basket for me."

The woman's eyes lit up at the sight of that receptacle.

"Oh, you got it. God bless the old man," she said. "And you too, sir," she addressed me, "if you have anything to do with it."

I quickly disabused her of any association with Balthazar.

"He may not be a Christian by religion," the woman went on, examining the contents of the basket which seemed to me comprised of meats and cheeses and other comestibles, combined with items of woollen clothing, even a woven blanket, "but he's more of a Christian than many who call themselves that."

She picked out a bottle that was lying on top, "What's this?"

"Something for Tommy, Uncle said," Sal replied.

I became aware of a bed in the corner covered, as I had thought at first, with a heap of rags. But they shifted from time to time, and now a small wan face emerged from under the sheets. A paroxysm of coughing ensued.

"Here Tommy, love," his mother said. "Here's something to make you better."

I stepped forward.

"May I see it, Madam?" I asked. "I happen to be a doctor."

Perhaps she was astonished to be addressed so politely, but she handed me the bottle readily enough. I opened it and sniffed at the linctus provided by Balthazar. If the man was indeed a murderer, I was disinclined to let the boy partake of anything he provided. However, it smelt sweetly of elecampane and I judged it harmless enough, and indeed, even perhaps efficacious.

"Would you like me to examine the little fellow?" I asked, giving the woman back the bottle.

She stared at me for a moment.

"I can't pay you, sir," she said finally.

"No. I wouldn't look to be paid," I replied. "Just to see if there is anything I can do for him."

217

"Well, God bless you too, then, sir."

Poor Tommy had a racking cough and a fever that caused his body to go into frequent convulsions. Recovery from what was clearly a bad chest infection would not be helped by the fact that he was clearly undernourished. In my opinion, which I expressed to his mother, Tommy should be in hospital. She looked horrified.

"Oh no, sir. Not the hospital. When people go in them places they never come out again."

I was taken aback at the force of her words.

"Not at all, my dear woman. They help the sick get better."

"Not my mother nor my father neither. Never seen them again after, except they be cold and dead."

She was not to be convinced and Tommy clung to her in terror at the very suggestion. I therefore relinquished the idea, and instead gave instructions as to his further care, writing out what medicines he should be given, and handing her a couple of sovereigns to cover the cost and more.

"Plenty of beef tea, too," I said, "for all of you."

Mrs. Mullins, for that had proved to be the poor woman's name, was overcome, tears streaming down her worn face as she grasped at my hand. I think she would have kissed it, had I not gently withdrawn it.

"What of your husband?" I asked, since I had discerned signs of a man's presence in the shape of a cocked hat and a waterproof coat. "Is he a working man?" A seafarer I was thinking.

Mrs. Mullins lowered her eyes, silent.

"Working, is it!" exclaimed Sal, with a cynicism way beyond her years. "Oh yes, Mister. Working hard lifting mugs of ale in the Pig'n'Whistle."

"Sal!" said her mother, blushing with shame.

"Well, it's true and you know it, Mammy."

I was careful not to express a judgement and just remarked, "Be sure, then, to keep those sovereigns for the purposes I told you of.

In fact, Sal, why don't you come with me now to buy that medicine for Tommy?"

Thus it was that I was tardy enough returning to Charing Court where I found Balthazar and Holmes sitting together in that same poky back room. There was a tension in the air. Balthazar looked to be almost pleading with Holmes, who, I noticed, was no longer acting the invalid.

"It must stop right now," Holmes was saying, "or I shall be forced to take further action."

"But honoured sir – consider the unnecessary suffering."

"Mr. Alfred Parkinson – " Holmes began.

Balthazar interrupted him. "I have already tried to explain that the case of Mr. Alfred Parkinson was a terrible mistake. No one expected the old gentleman to attempt to walk out to his club on such a terrible foggy evening. When I left him, he was as comfortable as he could be, with his glass of brandy to hand – "

"His poisoned glass," Holmes said.

Balthazar lifted his shoulders, making that open-palmed gesture of submission with his hands that I recalled as characteristic of persons encountered on my travels in Asia.

What was going on here? Had Parkinson been poisoned? In error?

"Ah, Watson," Holmes exclaimed. (So I was no longer to be – what was it? – *Sacker* any more then.) "Mr. Balthazar here has been explaining to me the mysterious workings of the Proxy Club."

"You tricked me, honoured sir," Balthazar said reproachfully, shaking his hoary locks. "I took you on in good faith."

"A necessary deceit, I'm afraid."

"Can anyone tell me what you are talking about?" I said.

There was a pause. Then Balthazar spoke in low tones.

"It began with my wife," he said. "Mariam. A wonderful woman. The light of my life." The depth of his emotion could be read on the man's face. "But she fell sick – so very sick that nothing

219

could be done to ease the pain. I saw this strong woman turn to a skeleton. And yet she didn't die." He wiped a tear from his face.

"Go on," I said gently. I had seen many cases like it in the course of my work, a cruel fate indeed.

"Mariam begged me to help her pass," he said. "At first I was shocked – *horrified* at her request. She confessed that she had wished to end it many times but could not bring herself to take that final step. I tried to convince her that it was a terrible sin, but as you said yourself, honoured sir, on that first visit, she asked me in reply how is it that we don't hesitate to put beasts out of their misery, but refuse that mercy to our fellow humans. Allah would understand, she said, hanging on to my hand." He shook his old head. "That night Mariam's suffering was unspeakable. For hours on end she screamed out in agony. I could not bear it." He wrung his hands. "Honoured sirs, I have some knowledge of herbal remedies, and so, like the Ancient Greeks, prepared a concoction of opium and hemlock that would cause her to die quickly and without pain. Her last words to me were a blessing and a promise to meet me one day again in Paradise."

He fell silent. We too were lost for words.

"I then swore to myself, honoured sirs," he said, "to assist similarly any poor suffering soul who wished it, and the Proxy Club was born."

"Death by proxy," I muttered grimly.

"Precisely," he replied. "An acquaintance of mine is a medical man – like yourself honoured sir," he said, bowing to me. When I looked surprised that he knew of me, he added, "Oh, I have heard many times of the esteemed Dr. Watson, associate of Mr. Sherlock Holmes here."

I inclined my head, though rather suspecting that he flattered me more than I deserved.

He continued to explain. "This acquaintance, whose name I shall never reveal, will indicate to me from time to time anyone he thinks might benefit from membership of the club, any suffering soul who dares not take that final step or who has scruples regarding suicide."

"A doctor sends you people to kill!" I exclaimed, deeply shocked. "But that is against all our principles. Our calling, as medical men, is to preserve life, not to take it. Good Lord, man, has your friend not sworn to the Hippocratic Oath?"

"Have you never administered a medicine to a dying patient that eases the pain but speeds the end?" Balthazar asked me. "It is a question of humanity, honoured sir."

We gazed at each other. Truly, the man had answers for everything.

"Putting ethical questions aside for a moment." Holmes interrupted the silence, "how exactly does it work, Balthazar – this club of yours? You told me earlier that the subject of your dubious ministrations knows not the day nor the hour when their end will come."

"Not exactly true, honoured sir. Some wish to know it and that obviously makes it easier for me. Others prefer not, for whatever reason. In addition, as I indicated, I like to wait a while after they have signed the contract in case they change their minds. Few do, I might add. In that case, since payment to the club only occurs after the... er... *passing*, no funds are sought and the contract is torn up."

"Yet many of your clients are rich and pay well for your services. At least, I assume so," Holmes remarked with disdain, "given what you suggested I should pay,"

"I charge what I think each person can afford, which sometimes is nothing at all," the other replied with some dignity. "Look at me, honoured sir. Am I a rich man? No, I live off what I earn from this little shop, which isn't very much. All the money from the Club goes to help the living – people like little Sal who was here earlier. You will have seen how that poor family lives, Doctor," he said, bowing again to me. "But there are so many, so many in the same predicament. What I can provide is a mere drop in a great ocean."

Again we fell silent. For me, while I could not in any way condone the source of the man's philanthropy, yet I was beginning to understand why he acted as he did, misguided though he was. As for Holmes, he stood up abruptly.

"Give me your word, Mr. Balthazar," he said, "that the Proxy Club will cease its operations as of today, and no more will be said on the subject."

"But Holmes," I interjected, "surely the police must be informed."

"Mr. Balthazar?" he said again, ignoring me.

"I cannot make such a promise," the old man said. "So many depend on me. Do what you must, honoured sir, as will I."

"Come, then, Watson." Holmes swept from the room, I following out of the shop, that awful bell clanging behind us.

"Straight to Scotland Yard, I suppose," I said.

He did not answer me, and I was most surprised when he turned, not to Whitehall, but homeward, to Baker Street.

All the way through the foul fog of the streets, he kept silent, his head down as if deep in thought. Finally, he muttered, "If there are any more 'mistakes', like in the case of old Parkinson, I shall surely inform Lestrade. Otherwise – "

"Otherwise?" I stopped short. "Holmes, I cannot believe it of you. Are you really intending to let Balthazar continue with his murderous ways?"

He turned towards me then. I was shocked at the agonised expression on his face.

"I have never told you this, Watson, but someone very close to me suffered the way the old man described the sufferings of his wife. That person had no means of liberation, and lived on in agony until at long last succumbing to the disease. It was terrible to witness. Terrible."

"I understand," I started to say. "But as a doctor – "

Holmes laid a hand on my arm.

"Hush," he said. "Hush."

My friend did not bid me stay quiet about what we had discovered: He left it to me to decide, which in some ways was worse. How I struggled with my conscience. It was not right. It could not be right. And yet, and yet... Many a night turned to dawn before my exhausted brain succumbed to a disturbed sleep. In the end, Holmes not reporting any crime and even letting Mr. Parkinson's nephew understand that there was nothing untoward about his uncle's demise, I kept silent too, though whenever I heard of a sudden and unexpected death I could not but wonder if we had made a morally justifiable choice.

It is only now when both Holmes and I are old and approaching that same portal with its ominously clanging bell, that I have felt able to reveal all. Balthazar is long gone, his shop sold, the Proxy Club, as far as I know, no longer in existence.

As far as I know.

The Adventure of the Deathstalker

Early on a dull morning in mid October, Holmes and I were just about to tuck into the usual substantial breakfast, as provided by the inestimable Mrs. Hudson, when that lady herself reappeared clutching the morning mail. For once there was nothing for Holmes, and only the most recent copy of *The Lancet* for me, along with a letter addressed in a hand I failed to recognise.

"Well, well," I remarked, having perused it. "Here's a surprise – an invitation from an old colleague of mine, Major Blunt, to visit him the weekend after next. Good Lord, I don't think I have seen Blunt since Afghanistan! Or maybe at that reunion – ? Let me think…"

"Pass the butter dish, Watson, would you. It is in imminent danger from your elbow."

I slid it across to him, adding, "He extends the invitation to you, Holmes."

My friend laughed.

"Now why would I wish to travel all the way to Wales at this dreary time of year?"

"How the devil did you – ? Oh, I suppose your eagle eye spotted the postmark." I consulted the envelope. "St. Asaph."

I recognised his methods.

"Elementary," he agreed, nodding. "St. Asaph in the county of Flintshire – the second smallest city in Great Britain, with a cathedral and little else. Not a place I have ever felt inclined to visit."

"All the same, listen to what Major Blunt has to say before you dismiss the offer completely."

"Well?" He formed a steeple with his fingers and gave me a quizzical look.

"Since his retirement, he has apparently taken up a rather strange hobby – namely…" I paused, "collecting scorpions."

I sensed a subtle change in Holmes, a slight stiffening in his demeanour, a new alertness.

"He has, he says," I continued, "recently acquired a rather interesting specimen, an *Omdurman*."

"Has he indeed?" Holmes said, now truly engaged. "The little devil also known as the *Deathstalker*."

"Ah, you have heard of it."

"Do you not recall my paper on arachnids? No? Ah well, wasted on the desert air as usual, with you, Watson."

"*I* may not have read it, but Major Blunt no doubt has, and that is why, recognising a fellow enthusiast, nay a specialist, he has invited you in particular down to stay."

Holmes chopped the top off his boiled egg with a degree of smug satisfaction.

"In that case, please inform your friend that I should be delighted to accept his generous offer."

Ten days later, however, it was a highly disgruntled Holmes I found unpacking his bags when I joined him in his bedroom, having just arrived at Major Blunt's establishment in Wales.

"I had not realised, Watson," he stated in accusatory tones, as though it were my fault, "that we should land ourselves into the middle of a veritable house party. I had assumed that we were invited for a quiet stay with someone who shared my zoological interests. Instead, I find myself in Bedlam."

To tell the truth, I had been taken aback myself, first at the grandeur of the Major's mansion – thanks, as it turned out, to an inheritance from Mrs. Blunt's father, who had made his money in soap – and then at the sheer number of people presently in occupation. Hoards, it seemed, of noisy young folk in particular who had the run of the place, the daughters of the house and their friends. In addition, our host proved no longer to be the trim young man of my memory. He had quite gone to flesh, with the hair that had once graced his head now descended to his chin in the abundance of a reddish beard. Furthermore, John Blunt, rather than living up to his name, displayed the vague geniality of one devoted to an obsession, to whom the practical concerns of daily life were mere distractions, and he seemed quite oblivious of the present hullaballoo. In vain, I looked for the disciplined soldier he had once been, and then had to ask myself if he had ever truly been that soldier. Had he not always chased butterflies, so to speak, even on the battlefield?

That he was delighted to see us, there could be no question. No sooner had we stepped through the door than he would have carried us off then and there to view his collection, had his wife not demurred.

"The gentlemen will surely wish to go to their rooms and rest, John, after their long journey." She turned to us with a warm smile. "Don't let John bully you. Tea will be served in the drawing room, when you are quite ready for it"

Angharad Blunt was a Welsh woman in her forties, plain of countenance, it must be said, and possessed, in particular, of an unfortunately long nose, but with an amiable manner that offset these deficiencies.

"Speaking for myself, Mrs. Blunt," I replied, "I should greatly appreciate a cup of tea now, if that is at all possible. There was little enough in the way of refreshments on the train, and the coach trip from Rhyl has left me quite parched."

Rather to my surprise, Holmes nodded in agreement, since he is usually indifferent to such bodily needs as liquid refreshment.

"Well then, gentlemen, this way. Jenkins can arrange for your bags to be taken to your rooms."

226

Jenkins turned out to be the butler, very properly clad in black, and sporting spotless white gloves, a long, thin lugubrious individual of considerable age, with a Welsh accent so pronounced that, at first, I thought him to be speaking that unfamiliar Celtic language itself. (In my account, I have rendered his speech into the Queen's English for the convenience of my readers.) He had come with the house, as Major Blunt told me later, a devoted old retainer.

Mrs. Blunt led the way into a large and comfortably furnished parlour, at which point a tiny but noisy dog rushed over to us and fastened its teeth onto Holmes's leg. He kicked it away with such force that the creature let out a loud squeak of protest.

"Oh, my poor Emperor Tzu! What has the nasty man done to you? Come to mamma, my poppet!" These words boomed from a lady of advanced years and considerable girth, seated on a chaise longue. She presented a formidable sight, decked out in a huge dress of bright turquoise silk in a style harking back many decades, her wide crinoline skirt bedecked with so many frills and flounces that she called to my frivolous mind the vision of an elderly Thetis rising from the sea. Her hair, surely coloured in some way to achieve that unnatural look of tarnished brass, was similarly old-fashioned in style, parted in the middle, with ringlets of curls cascading down each side of her craggy face. A many-stranded necklace of pearls hung around the double chins of her neck, along with a lorgnette.

She glared at us, clutching the dog to her bosom.

"The thing bit me," Holmes said, in a cold voice.

"The *thing*! The *thing*!" Now she was become a veritable Lady Bracknell.

"Oh dear, Mr. Holmes," said Mrs. Blunt. "I hope you aren't badly hurt."

"I don't suppose I will die of it, unless the dog is rabid."

"The Emperor Tzu himself might have died of that kick, sir," the lady said angrily. "Poor little darling!"

She cuddled the pampered creature, letting it lick her face. Holmes, beside me, scowled in disgust.

All in all, not an auspicious start to our visit, and Mrs. Blunt tried her best to calm tempers down.

"Well, well" she said. "Neither party badly hurt, so not too much harm done. Gentlemen, may I introduce Lady Manning, a relation of my husband's. Lady Manning – Dr. Watson and Mr. Sherlock Holmes."

I am afraid mention of my friend's name made no impression at all on the lady. However, she raised her lorgnette to her eyes and looked upon me with interest.

"A doctor!" she said. "Well, now – "

Before she could launch into a list of her ailments, the which intention I discerned, from bitter experience, in her eager expression, Mrs. Blunt hastily added, "Dr. Watson served with John in the East, you know."

"Come and sit next to me, Doctor," Lady Manning said, patting the narrow area of the chaise longue that she herself did not occupy.

It was an order rather than a request and, although I was reluctant, given the proximity of the wretched dog's sharp little teeth, courtesy overcame my misgivings and I sat myself beside her.

The antipathy The Emperor Tzu had shown towards Holmes was not, I am relieved to say, displayed towards me. I was encouraged by Lady Manning to pet him, which I did, and in return he licked my hand and wagged a fluffy tail.

"He likes you, Doctor!" she said, her smile revealing long yellow teeth, stained and notched – could it be? – by clay pipe smoking. Surely not? I had observed such signs before among people living in the slums of the East End of London, yet I could hardly think it of a woman of the upper class.

I couldn't puzzle the mystery for long, since at that point a maid arrived with the tea, followed by Major Blunt, two big, ruddy-cheeked girls of about fourteen or fifteen hanging off either side of him. These were introduced to us as Blodwen and Gwen.

"Our daughters," the Major announced proudly, while the two maidens collapsed in giggles.

More girls, the friends, tumbled in after, and descended on the plates of sandwiches and buns with a ferocity that left little or nothing for Holmes and myself. Even The Emperor consumed more than I did, her Ladyship feeding rich titbits into his ever-open muzzle. No matter, for at least we could enjoy cup after cup of strong and reviving tea, which was all I really wanted.

The house party, as it turned out, was being held to celebrate a Celtic festival marking the end of summer.

"I was quite cross with John for inviting you this particular weekend, since I am sure you weren't expecting such mayhem," Mrs. Blunt said, smiling indulgently at her husband. "He can be so thoughtless, sometimes."

"Not at all," I felt I had to reply, since Holmes was scowling the more. "It will be most interesting to experience your Welsh customs."

"Welsh poppycock!" exclaimed Lady Manning. "A pagan excuse for all sorts of goings-on. The Emperor and I shall play no part in it, as I am sure, Dr. Wilson, you will not, when you see the nature of things. No, indeed, Angharad." She turned to Mrs. Blunt. "Try as you might, you shall not persuade me."

Judging from the expression on the latter's face, she had no intention of so doing. It was all rather discomfiting, and I could not help but wonder into what exactly we had landed ourselves.

Holmes and I soon made our excuses and departed to our rooms, conducted thither by the same maidservant, Polly, who had served the tea.

"What is this festival exactly?" I asked her as we climbed the stairs.

"'Tis *Nos Calan Gaeaf*, of course," she replied in a tone which suggested that surely everyone knew of it. "When the speerits go wandering and the *Yr Hwch Ddu Gwta* comes a-looking for souls to eat."

I nodded, but wasn't much the wiser.

"Three whole days of this!" exclaimed Holmes, once Polly had departed. "Good Heavens, Watson, how will I bear it?"

"Remember the Deathstalker," I said. "And the rest of Major Blunt's collection, which I am sure will divert you."

"Ah yes. I suppose I can hide away with those predatory arachnids. They will no doubt prove better company than that below. And who, the deuce, is Lady Manning?"

I confessed that I had no better knowledge than himself. Major Blunt and I had never been close enough to exchange personal histories.

"It is you he wanted to see," I added.

"Clearly, although apparently no one else in this backwater has heard of me."

The Major was lurking in the hall when we descended the stairs a while later, agog to carry us off instantly to what he called his menagerie. This proved to be a stone-built outhouse in the garden, with a stove constantly fired up to keep the heat high enough for his tropical pets. The walls were lined with terrariums, some containing sand, some stones and peaty soil. Holmes stared into them appreciatively.

"Ah," he said, "*Pandimus imperator, Heterometrus*. Yes, I have seen these specimens before. But can these be..." Peering into another case. "Yes, indeed. A pair of the genus *Androctonus*?"

"Ha! Trust an expert like yourself to know all the Latin names." Major Blunt rubbed his hands together in pleasure. "Big fellows, aren't they?"

I gazed at the horrid looking things and wondered that anyone could feel enthusiasm for them.

"See the slender *pedipalps*, Watson?" Holmes went on. "And the distinctive thick tail."

"The *pedipalps*?"

"The *pincers*," explained Major Blunt. "As for its rear end, that's why in English those particular chappies are dubbed 'Fattails'. Get a sting from them and you'll soon know about it!" He laughed merrily, though I failed to appreciate the humour.

Holmes had already moved on.

"Now where is this famous *Leiurus quinquestriatus* of yours?" he asked.

"Over here," the Major replied, moving to another sand-lined case. "Here she is. All by herself, for I'd be afraid of her eating her friends and relations otherwise. As well as her husband," he added. "Beware the female of the species, gentlemen. Much more aggressive, don't you know." He gave a little grin. "Naughty of me, perhaps, but I call this one 'Lady Manning'."

The scorpion in question, yellow with a striped back, seemed to be staring back at us balefully, as if longing to grab us with its *pedipalps* and sink the sting in its curled tail into our flesh. Holmes, however, was enchanted. I trusted that this would make up for the other disappointments of the trip.

"Exactly how poisonous is it?" I asked.

"Not as deadly to humans as her Ladyship's nickname suggests," Blunt replied. "Unless you are old or sick or very young. Her prey is usually insects or small mammals, like mice. However, I'd strongly advise against getting bitten by Lady Manning. Very painful, what, Holmes?"

"So I understand."

"Who is Lady Manning exactly?" I asked, while my friend continued to study the Deathstalker, and it him. "The real one, not the scorpion."

Major Blunt looked doleful.

"That's a very good question, Watson," he replied.

"You must know, surely."

"She's some distant relation of mine, fallen on hard times. That is to say, her late husband blew the lot..." He lowered his voice for some reason. "Gambling dens, vice, that sort of thing. She only found out after he died. Nothing left of her fortune."

"Good Heavens! The poor woman."

"Poor us, rather. She landed on us for a short stay – seven months ago. Not a penny to her name, but the way she carries on – well, you'd think she was Lady of the Manor. She's a great trial to us, never mind the expense. Eats like a horse. And drinks..."

I thought him rather indiscreet, talking in that way to us whom, in truth, he hardly knew. However, I felt I had to ask why he did not simply send her on her way.

"That's what Angharad says. But Aunt Hermione is a frail old woman. I just haven't the heart."

She hadn't looked at all frail to me.

"She must surely have other relations she could go to."

"They won't take her."

There seemed no more to be said on the subject. Holmes called Major Blunt over to another of his collection, and they embarked on an intense discussion which held no interest for me. I excused myself then and took myself out into the garden, rejoicing in the fresh autumn air after the stifling atmosphere within the menagerie.

That part of North Wales is pleasant, rolling hills without the grandeur of the mountains of Snowdonia further west. In fact, a gentleman I found out strolling, like myself, was able to inform me that the city of St. Asaph – it still felt strange to me to give such a grandiose designation to such a tiny place – lay in the Vale of Clwyd on the River Elwy, and that, if I was interested in historic remains, I should certainly visit both the cathedral and the ruined castle in the nearby town of Rhuddlan.

This Mr. Broderick Williams, as he introduced himself, was a distinguished-looking, sleekly clean-shaven man in his early fifties.

232

He proved to be half-brother to Angharad on the maternal side. I should soon have guessed a relationship, for he possessed the same long nose that she did, giving him, together with his leanness, something of the appearance of a greyhound.

"You are here for the festival?" I asked.

"For my sins," he replied with a smile, "being father to a young lady who wouldn't miss the party for the world. My wiser wife has stayed home with our two boys, judging them to be too young for the excitement. That is her excuse, at least."

"Please tell me more of what to expect," I said. "My friend and I had no idea we would be attending such an event."

"No?" He sounded surprised. *Why are you here, then?* was quite clearly the question in his mind.

"Major Blunt invited myself and Mr. Holmes down from London to view his collection of scorpions."

The other laughed. "Oh dear. You poor things. John is a renowned bore on the subject."

"For my part, I should be happy never to see a scorpion again, but my friend is quite fascinated. He has written on the subject, do you see, and was especially keen to see the Deathstalker."

Mr. Williams shot me an astonished glance.

"The what?"

"It seems to be a rare-enough specimen and highly poisonous."

"Indeed. Well, good luck to them both. I have to say I prefer more harmless pets. Dogs for instance – Lady Manning's over-indulged little tyke excepted." He shook his head in repugnance. "But you wished me to tell you about the festival of *Nos Calan Gaeaf*."

I nodded.

"It is full of superstition, as you might expect. A night when spirits walk abroad. For your own good, Doctor, tomorrow evening please avoid churchyards, stiles, and crossroads."

"Why?"

233

"Because that's where the spirits gather, of course."

"So it is really just a Welsh name for Hallowe'en."

"Well, of course the origins are the same, but there are specific traditions and beliefs associated with *Calan Gaeaf* that you won't find in that festival. For instance, on the eve, a bonfire is lit and only the women and children dance round it. Everyone writes their name upon a stone and throws it into the fire. Then, when the blaze dies down, we all run home as fast as we can."

"It sounds very energetic," I said. "Especially for the ladies."

"If you were to linger by the dying fire," Mr. Williams informed me in ominous tones, "your very soul would be in danger of being devoured by *Yr Hwch Ddu Gwta*."

"I heard that nonsense before from the maid. What does it mean?"

"It is an evil spirit – a black sow without a tail. Even worse if it is accompanied by *Y Ladi Wen*, the headless white lady."

"I shall endeavour to avoid the pair of them at all costs. So is that the end of it, then?"

"By no means. The following morning, the stones in the fire are checked. If your own stone is clean, your name burned off, then that signifies good luck. However, woe to you if your stone is missing. You will be sure to die a short time afterwards."

On that grim note – although, as Mr. Williams said, there was much more to the festival – by then, we had completed a circuit of the grounds, and since it was getting late, bade each other a cordial farewell for the present and went our separate ways to dress for dinner.

This repast, although good and plentiful, was marred by the domineering presence of Lady Manning: Her demands, her complaints, her loudness, her sheer greed. I was made sit beside her, as the new favourite. Holmes, for his part, facing me across the table, cast reproachful looks my way, and winced every time the woman opened her mouth to speak, which was almost constantly. Our only respite, in truth, was when she opened that same orifice to insert food within it, and even then she didn't always keep quiet while masticating. Her chief grievances were directed at our hostess who, it seemed, could do nothing right. Mrs. Blunt's dress (too youthful for a matron), her hair (not frizzed enough, her Ladyship touching her own bright locks with satisfaction), her demeanour (so sulky) all came in for comment over the bone-marrow toast.

"Sometimes, indeed," she said self-pityingly, "I think you don't want me here, any of you."

Angharad Blunt cast her eyes down, while the Major protested, "Not at all, Aunt Hermione."

"For if that were the case – you know, if I was no longer welcome – well, there is always the workhouse for the likes of a poor abandoned widow."

Here Lady Manning lifted a lacy kerchief to dab at an eye which to me looked to be quite dry.

"Goodness, Aunt, we would never turn you out! Would we, my dear?"

Angharad, head still down, shook her head.

"All the same," the Major continued, "you might – you… might, well, er – "

"What might I, pray?"

The Major quailed under the gimlet gaze, the hardened tones.

"Excuse me, Madam." The butler had noiselessly approached her Ladyship from behind, making her start. "Would your doggie like the bones?"

"Bones, Jenks!" she screeched. "Do you want to kill the poor innocent creature? Cause him to choke to death? Well, I suppose you do, at that. I know how much you hate him." She turned to me. "The sensitive little thing can tell, you see, who are his enemies, Dr. Wilson. That is why sometimes he has to defend himself against those who wish him harm." She glared across at Holmes. "He cannot abide Jenks."

The butler, expressionless, was meanwhile removing the plate from in front of her, the bones sucked clean.

"Give them to the yard dogs, Jenkins," said Mrs. Blunt, adding pointedly. "*They* will enjoy the treat."

"Yes, by all means throw them to those barbarians," Lady Manning said, as though giving her permission. "The Emperor Tzu has a delicate palate, Dr. Wilson." (I had given up correcting her regarding my name.) "My poppet would appreciate some marrow, if there is any remaining."

She had saved none of her own, but now looked at my plate accusingly, as if I might have thought to leave something for her pet. As Jenkins left the room with the bones, she remarked, "Can you believe it, Dr. Wilson, that horrid man is the reason my dear sweet innocent pup is forbidden to sit at table with me? Jenks has refused point blank to serve if The Emperor be present, on the pretext that he has been nipped a couple of times." She turned to Mrs. Blunt. "I am astonished, Angharad, how you let yourself be bullied by a mere underling. I am sure, Dr. Wilson," she addressed me again, "you would never countenance your staff making so free."

Thoughts of the excellent Mrs. Hudson brought a smile to my lips. "I am afraid I could hardly claim to have staff. We live very modestly, you know."

"You wife surely has help."

"My wife – " But I wasn't about to discuss my dear late Mary with this woman, nor to explain my current living arrangements. In any case, Lady Manning had moved on to another subject.

"I suppose I should, in all honesty, Angharad," quoth she, and even I could hear how she mangled the pronunciation of the mellifluous Welsh name, "bequeath *you* my pearls." Here she toyed with her necklace. "They are all I have to leave, since Reginald abandoned me to my sorry fate." Another recourse to the lace handkerchief. "However, I fear that you wouldn't appreciate them as you should, and so…" Now she lifted the lorgnette that lay, with the pearls, across her vast bosom, and studied Gwen and Blodwen at the far end of the table, "I have decided that one of your girls shall inherit these priceless gems. Which of them, I haven't yet chosen. Whoever shall prove herself the more deserving." After which speech, and leaving the girls gaping at her, and the friends giggling, she dropped her lorgnette and focussed her attention on the dish just placed in front of her. This proved to be *cawl*, a traditional Welsh soup, substantial in nature, which, though her Ladyship pronounced it to be unsatisfactory – "It is overly salted as usual, Angharad." – she consumed to the last drop.

If every meal was to be like this, it must prove quite an ordeal. Of course, Holmes and I were here for the weekend only, but the Major and his poor wife had to put up with her Ladyship, day in and day out. I wondered that they could.

This sentiment was echoed by Williams, when the ladies had withdrawn, allowing us men to partake in the traditional way of port or brandy and cigars.

"Really, John," he said to our host. "I cannot understand how you let that dreadful woman bully my sister so. It makes me rage."

Major Blunt looked sheepish.

"I know," he replied, "and I have tried. But you see, the poor woman has come down so far in the world. She is used to a much more splendid way of life than we can supply. In any case, she behaves much better without an audience, when we are alone with her."

Holmes, who had remained largely silent during the meal and subsequently, leaned back in his chair, and drew on his cigar before speaking.

"I rather doubt that," he said.

"No, no. I can assure you. She can even be almost quiet sometimes."

"I didn't mean that," Holmes replied. "I meant that I doubt she was used to a much more splendid way of life, as you put it."

"Oh yes. She has told us all about it."

Holmes put on the superior expression that I recognised so well of one who knows better.

"I grant perhaps many decades ago, that might possibly have been the case, but her dress is outmoded and shabby – the silk quite rotten in fact. And as for those renowned pearls, I am convinced they are paste."

"My dear fellow," I said. "Surely – "

"Before dinner, I took advantage of some moments of calm to visit your library," he informed Major Blunt. "I was fairly sure no loud young person would break in on me there. However, what I did find was a *Burke's Peerage*, alongside a volume of *Burke's Landed Gentry*."

"Did you, indeed?" replied the Major. "Well bless my soul, I had no idea we owned such things. We inherited the library, and in fact, the house itself, do you see, from Angharad's father. And I am afraid I'm not much of a reader – Unless, of course, it be works like your own most excellent paper on scorpions, Mr. Holmes."

"Well," my friend replied, brushing aside the compliment, "had you investigated, you would have found no mention of Reginald Manning in either volume."

"You mean," said Williams eagerly, the greyhound sniffing the hare, "she isn't who she says she is? She has been pulling the wool over our eyes all this time?"

"As to that," Holmes continued. "I have no means of knowing. Perhaps she fell prey to a scoundrel who led her to believe he was of noble birth."

"Or perhaps there never was a Reginald at all!" Williams was chasing the hare now. "Perhaps she isn't even related to you, John."

"I am sure she is," the Major replied, though quite evidently the new intelligence had shaken him. "She arrived with excellent credentials, you know, as some sort of a cousin of my late mother. Used to play with her as a child. Best friends. Knew all about her."

"The cook's daughter, perhaps." Williams sank his teeth into the hare with vast satisfaction. "I have always thought that though she has pretensions to class, she displays low habits."

"Like the pipe smoking," Holmes said, pre-empting me as usual. "And the rum drinking. Her breath stinks of pineapple."

That I hadn't particularly noticed, or at least had thought her Ladyship was wearing a rather stale and pungent perfume.

"Well, well." The poor Major was quite distressed. "Yes, indeed, she likes her pipe, but told us it was a habit she developed on the Continent. As for the pineapple rum – she says it settles her stomach"

Both Holmes and Williams snorted in derision.

We were all agreed, however, that nothing should mar the forthcoming festivities. Afterwards, it would be up to the Major and his wife to decide whether or not to challenge the lady in question regarding her identity.

The following day was *Nos Calan Caeaf*, that on which the spirits were said to walk. Holmes and I, feeling somewhat superfluous amid the bustle of preparations, headed out with Broderick Williams to walk the few miles to Rhuddlan to view the castle there, a handsome, though ruined pile dating from the Thirteenth Century. In truth, Holmes was soon bored by the history of the place, as recounted in considerable detail by Williams, and took himself off to sit upon a piece of tumbled masonry, while we two explored further. Since I fear my readers might well share the indifference of my friend, I shall not burden them with repeating the history of the place, which, if they are interested, can be found by consulting a *Baedeker* or an encyclopaedia.

Having fully admired the ruins and the pleasing prospect of the river than ran beside it, we took refreshments in the adjacent Castle Inn before heading back to St. Asaph.

There we found the construction of the bonfire almost completed. It rose high over a patch of rough ground away from the well-kept lawn, the young ladies flitting like butterflies around it and quite getting in the way of the workers. On spotting us, a decidedly pretty maiden of thirteen or thereabouts rushed up to Williams.

"Oh, Papa," she said. "I cannot wait for night to fall! Gwen says that if I make my room dark and then look in the mirror, I might see the face of my future husband, but if I see a skull I shall die within the year. Imagine! Oh, Heavens, I cannot bear it!"

"I think, my dear Sophy," he replied, caressing her curls, "that if you look in a mirror in the dark, you are likely to see nothing at all."

"Well, in that case, Gwen says I must throw the peel of an apple over my shoulder, and how it falls will form the initials of my future husband."

She flew off as quickly as she had arrived, having been summoned in peremptory fashion by the self-same Gwen. Williams smiled at us and shook his head.

"Girls and their fancies," he said.

"She is quite charming," I remarked.

Luckily, I thought, Sophy hadn't inherited the long Williams nose, her own snubby one sitting in perfect harmony with the rest of her face.

What to do next? Holmes had been dragged away willingly by Major Blunt back to the menagerie. Williams and I betook ourselves to the nearby Cathedral of St. Asaph, a saint of whom I knew nothing until enlightened at some length by my companion. We spent an hour or more exploring that Gothic construction and surrounding graveyard, Williams reassuring me that it was quite safe, even given the day that we were in it, to linger there *before* sunset, though – with a wink – to be sure to avoid it once darkness fell.

"You don't really believe the superstitions, do you?" I asked.

"Not a jot," he replied, "although I should rather prefer to be safe than sorry. Now, come and look at this most interesting inscription, Watson."

He proved rather more intrigued by the gravestones than I, but finally, his commentary on the subject faltering, we addressed more personal matters. I discovered, hardly to my surprise, that he was a school teacher with a particular specialisation in history.

"So what exactly does your friend do?" he asked me, as we made our way out through the lychgate.

"Do?" I asked, somewhat bewildered.

"Well, I assume from his interest in scorpions and the fact that he has written a paper on the subject, that he is either a learned arachnologist, or at least an entomologist."

"Good Heavens!" I exclaimed, astounded. "That is just one of his many hobbies. Really, Williams, have you never heard of Sherlock Holmes?"

He shook his head. Not heard of the greatest detective of our time! What a backwater we found ourselves in! I soon corrected his ignorance.

"A policeman?" said he. "I should never have guessed it."

"Not a policeman, Williams. A private detective."

"I see." He became thoughtful, and we spent the rest of the walk back in silence.

Upon entering the house, I was immediately waylaid by Polly, who said that Lady Manning particularly wished to speak to me. I received the news with, I am afraid, extremely muted enthusiasm, but again felt that courtesy required me to attend the lady. I found her, as before, on the chaise longue, in the self-same turquoise dress, The Emperor scampering at her feet and showing great delight at my presence, wagging his tail furiously and licking the hand I stretched out to pet him. His mistress looked on approvingly. There was a cloyingly sweet smell in the place that, now I had been apprised of the lady's habits, I recognised to be that of pineapple rum.

"You wished to talk to me, your Ladyship," I said.

Of course, it concerned her health. She was soon describing, in vivid and disconcertingly grisly detail, various symptoms, the which, I rather felt, could be put down simply to a daily overindulgence in rich foods, combined with a total lack of exercise. However, opining to myself that Lady Manning would hardly appreciate such a forthright diagnosis, and knowing how sufferers often prefer to treat themselves with medication rather than change the way they live, I suggested she might try papaya tablets, which should aid her digestion, and certainly do her no harm.

"It has proved efficacious in a number of my patients," I told her.

She nodded graciously, as I wrote her a prescription, then frowned.

"But you know, I am sure that my affliction is partly the fault of the Blunts. The way they vary mealtimes, you know. Regular ingestion is so important, is it not? No wonder I suffer, given the inconsistency of arrangements in this establishment. It wouldn't be borne for a moment, Dr. Wilson, if I had the running of the place."

Her chief grievance, as it emerged, was that on this same night she would be required to wait for her supper until after the festivities.

"My stomach will hardly support the delay," she said. "I am sure that if you speak to them as a doctor, you can convince them that I must not wait, and that dinner must be at the usual hour."

I hardly thought that the timetable of events would be changed on a whim of hers, but suggested a compromise.

"Perhaps dinner could be brought to you earlier, your Ladyship."

"You mean that I should eat by myself, alone?" In her displeasure at the suggestion, she was turned to Lady Bracknell again. "Why should I be discommoded for their sport? Why should I be dismissed from their table? A personage of my breeding treated like a poor relation!" (Which is what she was, of course.) "It is too cruel, Doctor. But I know their game. They want to drive me away."

In vain I tried to sooth her, even though, again, it was naught but the truth.

"No, no. You cannot understand what I suffer here. How constantly *she* plots to get rid of me." She struck a tragic note. "I shall be in the workhouse before another year is out. There, or in the grave, you mark my words, Doctor. And it will be all *her* fault. That soap-maker's daughter! Blunt, you see, is quite under her thumb. Shameful in a man, but the hussy winds him round her little finger!" Lady Manning was working herself to a frenzy of self-pity, The Emperor leaping up and down betimes in excitement, and contributing to the general commotion with his yelps.

"Perhaps," I said, "I can ask Jenkins, or," in response to her dark look, "Polly to bring you a little snack – to fill the gap, so to speak before you join us all later for supper."

"Dr. Wilson," she said, instantly calm, "you have saved my life."

She could, of course, quietly have requested the same from Polly earlier, but I understood her. She had to be the centre of attention, and resented it greatly when she was not.

Now she begged me to stay with her, patting the space remaining on the chaise longue with a fat, beringed hand, and – Good Lord! – a flirtatious fluttering of her eyelashes.

"For I am sure," said she, "an educated man like yourself has no interest in such silly superstitious antics, the like of which will be indulged in tonight. Let you stay here and enjoy some civilised conversation with me."

Courtesy to an elderly lady was all very well, but I was not prepared to forgo the festivities – especially given the alternative she offered – and, as politely as possible, informed her that, on the contrary, I was most interested in observing local customs.

"As you please," she replied coldly.

243

At that moment, Gwen burst into the room, a rock in her hand.

"Good Heavens, girl, whatever have you there?" Lady Manning exclaimed. "Have you been sent to stone me to death?"

"Not at all, Aunt Hermione. Everyone is writing their names on rocks to throw into the fire. We thought you might like to do so as well."

"I? Have I not made it perfectly clear that I wish to take no part in these tomfooleries?"

"But it's for good luck!"

The girl looked at me. Her expression wasn't quite pleasant, sly in fact, and I wondered what she was up to. Then she smiled at her aunt, holding out the rock.

"Should I, Doctor?" Lady Manning appealed to me. "What do you think?"

I was about to make a non-committal reply when Gwen forestalled me.

"Dr. Watson will, I am sure, be wanting to put his name on a rock, too," She pulled another out of her pocket.

I laughed. "Well, I can always do with some good luck." I took the proffered rock and signed it.

"As you know," Lady Manning remarked, "The Emperor and I will not be attending the bonfire, but perhaps you, Doctor, would be so kind as to do the necessary on my behalf."

I bowed assent, and thereupon she took the other rock and inscribed her name upon it.

"Only for you, Gwen," she said, fingering her pearls. "You're a good girl, aren't you?"

"I hope so, Auntie." Gwen smiled winningly.

"Give your Auntie a kiss then."

The girl did so and then turned away, an expression on her face I can only describe as triumphant. What exactly was she up to?

"But how," I asked, "if the names are burned off in the fire, will you be able to tell whose is whose?"

"That's easy," the girl replied. "We count up the ones with no names on them."

It sounded random to me, but after all, it was just a silly childish game, wasn't it?

Having asked Polly to bring a sandwich and glass of milk to her Ladyship, I dressed myself in my overcoat and muffler and made for the garden where the rest of the party was already gathered. Rather to my surprise, Holmes had also deigned to attend the bonfire, although he resisted attempts to throw a stone bearing his name into it.

"I make my own luck," he said dismissively as the rest of us merrily cast our stones into the flames, Lady Manning's among them.

Holmes and I then stood for a short while, observing the flickering fire and the people dancing around it, but my companion had soon had enough of what seemed to me a rather charming spectacle, claiming that he had no intention of catching a chill on this autumn night.

"That's surely unlikely," I replied. "For my part, I am almost too hot."

"Will you not accompany me then?" he asked.

"I will follow shortly," I replied, and with a shrug he started back to the house.

Call me fanciful, but the sight of the girls and women dancing, silhouettes against the fierce blaze, or, as they reached the far side, their Maenad faces illuminated across it, aroused in me a sense of the primitive forces that lie beneath our veneer of civilisation. Over how many centuries had this same ritual been performed, what pagan gods to appease? It was both a disturbing and pleasurable notion, and when the fire finally died down, I ran back to the house with the others, quite as though believing I was being chased by a horde of evil spirits.

Alas, all good humour was dispelled by the row that ensued over supper. In her enforced solitude, alone but for the company of Emperor Tzu and – eschewing the milk – a bottle of pineapple rum, Lady Manning had clearly been brooding over what she considered her unjust treatment at the hands of a soap maker's daughter and her lily-livered spouse. Without reporting further the language employed (and that of a fishwife might have been rather less expressive), I can reveal that the result was Angharad Blunt leaving the table in tears, the Major staring at the tablecloth in distress, Williams seething, the girls exchanging glances and suppressing giggles, Jenkins looking daggers, and Lady Manning sitting back in her chair, exulting at the chaos she had caused.

We finished the meal in silence. Her Ladyship, to everyone's relief, then expressed her intention of retiring early – the company, as she remarked, having turned so dull. Polly and Jenkins had to support her as she banked, rather like a great galleon about to keel over, while The Emperor, who had somehow escaped from confinement, snapped and growled at Holmes. Then he chased the procession up the stairs, likely to cause disaster by making a beeline for Jenkins's ankles.

"She is an absolute monster," quoth Williams a few moments later, over the port. "John, I demand that you get rid of the woman forthwith for the sake of your wife's sanity."

"Yes, yes, yes – although you know, I am sure she didn't mean all the things she said." The Major looked appealingly at us. "So unpleasant, don't you know. Drink taken…"

"It's no excuse," his brother-in-law continued. "Pay for her to go away if you must. Put her on a slow boat to China, or something or the sort."

"Yes, yes," the Major repeated. "Certainly."

"You say yes, and yet do nothing!" The other struck the table with his fist. "It has gone on long enough, Blunt! The woman must be got rid of!"

While Williams sat seething and shaking his head in exasperation, I advised the Major to go to his wife. "She must need comforting," I said.

Blunt looked at me astounded then, as if the idea hadn't occurred to him before. Then he gathered himself together, and replied, "Yes, yes," again. And was gone.

Holmes, so uncommunicative that I was sure he still bore a grudge against me for landing him in this madhouse, excused himself soon after, but Broderick Williams and I remained talking until well after midnight. While trying to calm him down, I'm afraid that, in the process, the two of us consumed the greater part of a bottle of brandy before we finally retired.

After that, I slept heavily, although at a certain point was roused by what might have been the persistent ringing of a bell, followed soon after by the clamour of a barking dog.

"That d----d Emperor Tzu!" I thought to myself, burying my head in my pillow to drown out the racket, which in any case soon stopped.

I was late going down to breakfast, but in that respect was not alone. Lady Manning had failed yet to make an appearance – no doubt, as I reckoned, nursing a head as sore as my own. The others of the household, Holmes included, were already helping themselves from chafing dishes set on the mahogany sideboards to a huge spread of porridge, sausages, eggs, hams, venison pies, and all manner of other tasty comestibles. My poor stomach, however, could only face a round of buttered toast and blackberry jam – made, as I was told, by Angharad Blunt herself.

I complimented that lady.

"A regular taste of the countryside," I said.

She smiled wanly, her plain face made even more so by the evidence of hours of weeping, her long nose quite red.

"You must take a pot of it home with you," she said.

I rather suspected she hoped our departure was imminent, so that she might soon be excused from the duties of a hostess. For his part, Holmes, doubtless would concur enthusiastically with the notion of an early exit.

At that moment, Gwen, Blodwen, Sophy, and the other girls burst in excitedly, bearing some heavy items in their aprons.

"There's a stone missing," Blodwen cried out.

"Really, girls, it isn't the thing, you know, to come in shouting like that," Mrs. Blunt chided them. "Whatever will our guests think of you?"

"It's *hers!*" Gwen said, ignoring her mother. "We looked and looked, but hers isn't there."

"Whose?" asked the Major.

"*Hers!* The Queen Wasp."

"Do you mean your aunt, Gwen? That's no way to talk."

"What do you think, Doctor," the girl asked me. "You took her rock. Can you see it here?"

Despite Mrs. Blunt's protests, the girls spread their sooty collection on the floor for me to inspect. The names written upon them were burnt off but I had particularly remarked on the rock passed to Lady Manning by Gwen, which was of a distinctively irregular shape. Certainly, none of those in front of me resembled it. As I examined them, shaking my head, the girls around me giggled.

"You are right. It doesn't seem to be there," I said.

"Hooray!" cried Gwen. "She'll be dead soon, then, like she's always saying she will be."

"And you'll get the pearls, Gwen," said Blodwen, good-humouredly.

Her sister made a face.

The girls were instantly soundly rebuked, with Gwen in particular sent off to clean her mouth out with soap before being allowed any breakfast. Their parting giggles, however, didn't indicate any remorse.

"Well," said Major Blunt, after they had skipped off, "I wonder where is Aunt Hermione? It's late even for her."

He sent Polly to find out if Lady Manning would like breakfast sent up to her.

Did I have a presentiment then that something terrible had happened? I cannot say for certain, although I am sure Holmes did, for he sat alert, listening.

The scream was not long in coming, and with a bound he was out the door and up the stairs, closely followed by Broderick Williams and the Major. I went after, first advising Angharad to stay where she was.

Polly stood shivering outside Lady Manning's bedroom, the door closed.

She muttered, "Oh, do take care, sirs!" as we entered.

I shall never forget the horrific sight that greeted us: A mountain of soiled white on the bedroom floor, that soon revealed itself to be Lady Manning in a voluminous night dress, her eyes wide and staring, her fists clutched tight across her belly, her big dead face distorted by terror. At first, I thought that, in her final agonies, she must have torn out her hair, for it lay on the carpet beside her. Then I realised it was a wig, and that, under it, she had been almost completely bald. However, now her head was crowned with a new hideous embellishment, as over it crawled a yellow scorpion, the Deathstalker itself, waving *pedipalps* in our direction as if warning us, *This is mine! Stay away!*

Stunned into silence and immobility as initially we were, it was Major Blunt, displaying at last the soldierly qualities of his rank, who grabbed a dry glass from the bedside table and placed it over the creature, sliding a card underneath, thereby trapping it inside.

"I'll return her to her terrarium," he said grimly. And left to do so.

Meanwhile, Holmes was crouching down, examining the body, and then the floor around it.

249

"What a frightful accident," exclaimed Williams.

Holmes raised his head.

"Hardly." he replied. "Someone else must have brought the scorpion here, for I doubt very much that Lady Manning fetched it or that it found its way here by itself."

"A deliberate act!" Williams exclaimed. "My God! Who would do such a terrible thing?"

You might, I thought to myself, remembering his rage of the night before, and how the brandy could have fired him up further to a drastic and irrevocable action. And had I myself not told him how poisonous the thing was?

"Have a look at the body, Watson," Holmes said, "and tell me what you think?"

I knelt down and gently examined what I could see, mindful that the police would no doubt prefer that little was disturbed.

"There's a redness and swelling on her neck," I told him. "And a puncture mark, I think, though it is difficult to tell."

"Exactly what I found myself."

"So it was indeed the scorpion that killed her," Williams said.

"Strange, all the same," Holmes remarked. "Scorpion stings are seldom fatal."

"But the Major told us," I reminded him, "that it could happen in the case of an elderly or sick person. If Lady Manning's heart happened to be weak…"

"I don't like 'if's', Watson. But you're perhaps right."

He looked thoughtful.

"But where is The Emperor?" I suddenly realised the little dog was nowhere to be seen. Or heard.

A further search – I am sorry to say, even though the creature had been difficult to like – found him where he had crawled under the bed to die. Presumably, I remarked, another victim of the scorpion.

"Not possible," Holmes said. "The stinger would have to grow back, and that couldn't have happened instantly."

"Good Lord! Then perhaps there are other scorpions here!"

We looked around ourselves anxiously. Unfortunately, the intricate pattern on the carpet provided the perfect camouflage for the darker species, and none could be easily discerned. The Major, returning as we searched, announced gravely that yes indeed several others of his collection were missing.

"We should secure this room," he said. "The last thing we need is for the whole house to be overrun. I shall return properly protected and look for the runaways."

"We must inform the police," I said.

"The police?"

"Well, it's murder, isn't it?"

"Oh! I suppose." A blankness passed over his face. "Of course, you know," he said, "whoever did it might well not have intended to kill her. Only to give her a nasty jolt."

He suspects who it is, I thought. And he does not like it.

"Of course," Holmes said, "the police must be informed. However, in the meantime, if you will permit it, I should like to interview certain people, Major, starting with yourself."

"Me!" He looked aghast.

"Only regarding who might have had access to the menagerie."

"Oh!" His relief was evident. "That's easy. Anyone."

"You mean the place isn't locked."

"No. At least, yes – " (Holmes made an exasperated gesture.) " – in that the door is locked, but that everyone knows where the key is kept. It hangs in the kitchen."

"And was the door locked just now when you went back?"

"Er… no."

"So who, in this household, would know how to handle the scorpions without getting stung?"

"Everyone again, I'm afraid. You see, with such dangerous creatures around, I felt it necessary to give a demonstration."

"Would that include Williams here?"

"I say, Holmes – !" The schoolteacher reared up. "What the devil are you suggesting?"

"I am suggesting nothing. I am asking merely in order to eliminate."

"Well, I cannot be eliminated, because John showed me what to do, along with everyone else, including Sophy. I hope you don't intend to cast suspicion on her as well."

Holmes smiled. "We'll see," he said, which hardly calmed the man down.

"This is preposterous!" he raged. "Some fool of an amateur detective meddling in something too big for him. Call the police, John, and send this charlatan packing."

Now I was angry on Holmes's account.

"You should know that Holmes is constantly called in by Scotland Yard when a case baffles them," I declared. "And he always solves it!"

"I have noticed before that you have a very short fuse, Williams," Holmes said calmly. "You really must try and control your temper."

I thought the man might have struck him then, but – luckily for him, Holmes being adept in the martial art of baritsu – Major Blunt intervened.

"Now, now, gentlemen, a woman lies before us dead. Some decorum, if you please. Mr. Holmes, you are welcome to question anyone here, but only if they are willing to talk to you."

"What do you think, Holmes?" I asked as we walked away. "Was it the brother-in-law? Last night he made threats, you know."

"Well, it could be. On the other hand, it might not."

How frustrating he was!

"The Major," Holmes continued, "suspects his wife."

"Good Heavens, surely not!"

"Could you not tell from his demeanour? His words? He thinks his wife released the scorpions to frighten Lady Manning, not to kill her. To frighten her to such an extent that she would leave of her own volition."

"Do you believe that?"

"I should first like to talk to some others. Ah, here they are."

We had entered the parlour where Angharad sat sewing, her daughters, cousin and friends huddled together on the chaise longue, no longer ebullient, but silent and shocked, their eyes red from crying. Had they then loved their aunt after all?

"Gwen and Blodwen." Holmes went up to the girls, talking in gentle tones. "I wonder could I have a little chat with you."

He looked at Angharad for permission. She nodded, somewhat surprised, and the girls most reluctantly got up. Sophy, too.

"We can go to the library," he said.

"Well, girls," he continued, once we had established ourselves in that cosy little room, "what have you to tell me?"

"Nothing." That was Gwen, ever the spokeswoman.

"Now, that isn't quite true, is it?"

He looked at them keenly, but not unkindly. Time passed. The girls fidgeted. Finally, Blodwen blurted out, "We didn't mean it!" For which outburst she was given a sharp nudge by her sister.

"I'm sure you didn't," Holmes continued in the same calm tone. "Just a silly prank that went wrong, wasn't it?"

I was aghast. These little girls killed their aunt! And her dog!

"We just thought they would give her a sting." This was Sophy. Also involved, then.

"She deserved it. She's always so horrid to Mama," said Gwen, adding defiantly. "I'm not sorry she's dead."

"Hmm, I see. But what do you think the police will say to that?"

Now they looked wide-eyed at him. Blodwen and Sophy burst into tears. Gwen, however, was of stronger stuff.

"I don't care!"

"Even when you go to prison?"

Now even Gwen looked chastened.

"However," Holmes said, ringing the bell, "there may be more to it, after all."

The ensuing silence was broken only by the occasional sob.

"We didn't know the dog would die, either," said Sophy.

Gwen sniffed. She clearly cared nothing for The Emperor.

The door opened, and the butler came in, looking questioningly from Holmes and myself to the girls.

"Ah, Jenkins," Holmes said. "The police will be coming soon to arrest these girls for killing Lady Manning. What do you have to say to that?"

The man's mouth hung open.

"The girls!" he finally spluttered. "Miss Gwen and Miss Blodwen, is it?"

"And Miss Sophy. You see, they have just confessed to taking scorpions to her Ladyship's bedroom, intending to give her a fright. Instead of which, she died."

"No, that isn't right," the butler said. "No, sir."

"I agree. That isn't quite how it happened, is it, Jenkins?"

The man continued to stare at him.

"Let me tell you what I think transpired." Holmes sat back, his fingers making the customary steeple. "Lady Manning discovers the scorpions in her bed. One stings her on the neck. In a panic, she rings the bell. You respond. Meanwhile, and before you arrive, she has got up to go to the door for help. However, the agonising pain of the poison overcomes her and she sinks to the floor. You enter and find her there."

We were riveted, the girls staring wide-eyed at Holmes.

"And that," he continued, "is when you kill her. You simply hold her down, your gloved hand over her nose and mouth, until she runs out of breath."

Jenkins looked at Holmes as though he were clairvoyant. Then he broke down, the words bursting out of him.

"I didn't see the scorpions. I just saw her lying there, sir – nasty drunken old woman – and it came over me, she might die like that. I reckoned you'd all think she had a heart attack. Natural causes, you know." He looked across at the girls. "I would have said, sir. I wouldn't have let the little girls suffer for what I did."

"I know that," Holmes replied, still in that calm voice. "You are devoted to the family, and especially to Mrs. Blunt, aren't you, Jenkins."

"I've been with Miss Angharad since she was a baby," the man said. "I hated what that woman was doing to her, sir. The life she made her lead. I saw it more than most. More even than the Major."

"How ever did you know it was the girls who let loose the scorpions?" I asked Holmes later, after the police had taken Jenkins away.

"Once I learned there was more than one of the arachnids in the bedroom, it was a simple deduction. No single person could easily transport so many. And those girls both knew how to handle the scorpions, and quite evidently were up to some mischief. I imagine it was they who removed Lady Manning's stone from the bonfire and disposed of it. To give her yet another fright."

"Very well, but how did you guess that it was the butler who killed her?"

"How did I *guess*, Watson? Really!.. I was reading late and heard the bell, and then the dog barking. Of course, at the time I had no idea what had transpired, but remember thinking to myself, it would only bark like that at a perceived enemy, which meant either

Jenkins or myself, and knowing it wasn't me, reckoned it had to be Jenkins going to see what her Ladyship wanted."

"Then you knew all along that he did it."

"Not quite. I had to make sure it wasn't the sting after all that killed her. Luckily, Jenkins confessed."

"And the girls? What will happen to them now?"

Holmes leant back in his chair.

"They have assuredly learned their lesson, which is enough for the present. No need to complicate the issue further. But I shall impress on Major Blunt that he must keep the menagerie locked from now on and the key safely about his person."

"So it was a case of the dog that barked in the night," I said. "And the butler that did it."

"Precisely."

We left shortly afterwards to return to Baker Street (and civilisation, according to Holmes), on good terms with everyone, including even Williams, who had quite come round to the advantages of a discreet private detective. As for Lady Manning's pearls, she left no will, despite her threats, and so they went to the Major, as her closest relation. (He was. She hadn't lied after all). When he had them valued, to everyone's surprise and delight, they turned out to be genuine and worth a pretty penny to boot. Which just goes to show that even Sherlock Holmes isn't always right.

ACKNOWLEDGEMENTS

Thanks as ever to my wonderful publisher, Steve Emecz and his team. Special thanks to David Marcum, exemplary editor of the MX Anthologies of New Sherlock Holmes Short Stories, for his encouragement as well as his encyclopaedic knowledge of the canon that saves me from falling into embarrassing errors.

Thanks to my readers, Ann O'Kelly, Phyl Herbert for their penetrating comments, and to Pete Morriss for his ability to identify anachronisms.

Thanks to my family, Karl, Jenny and Leo and their partners and children, for keeping me grounded.

Susan Knight has written four Mrs Hudson books: *Mrs Hudson Investigates,* a collection of short stories (2019) and the novels *Mrs Hudson goes to Ireland* (2020), *Mrs Hudson goes to Paris* (2022) and *Death in the Garden of England* (2023), all under the imprint of MX publishing. In addition, she is the author of three other novels and two short story collections, as well as a non-fiction book of interviews with immigrant women living in Ireland. She lives in Dublin.

Milton Keynes UK
Ingram Content Group UK Ltd.
UKHW020614131023
430517UK00012B/263